**Adventure House**
**Presents**

# FAR EAST ADVENTURE STORIES

**April 1931**

This reprint edition is a facsimile edition. Variations in print and quality are mostly attributable to the rough woodpulp original this reprint edition is based on.

ISBN: 1-59798-561-9
ISBN-13: 978-1-59798-561-1



Published by Adventure House
914 Laredo Road
Silver Spring, Md 20901
www.adventurehouse.com
gunnison@adventurehouse.com
First Published: March 2016

# WIN FAME and FORTUNE in RADIO!

Don't spend your life slaving away in some dull, hopeless job! Don't be satisfied to work for a mere $20 or $30 a week. Let me show you how to make REAL MONEY in RADIO—THE FASTEST-GROWING, BIGGEST MONEY-MAKING GAME ON EARTH.

## THOUSANDS OF JOBS ARE OPEN

**Paying $60, $70 and on up to $200 a Week**

Jobs as Designer, Inspector and Tester, paying $3,000 to $10,000 a year—as Radio Salesman and in Service and Installation Work, at $45 to $100 a week—as Operator or Manager of a Broadcasting Station, at $1,800 to $5,000 a year—as Wireless Operator on a Ship or Airplane, as a Talking Picture or Sound Expert—THOUSANDS of JOBS Paying $60, $70 and on up to $200 a WEEK!

# Learn Without Lessons *in* 10 Weeks

You learn ALL branches of Radio at Coyne—in 10 short, pleasant weeks—NOT BY CORRESPONDENCE, but by actual work on actual Radio, Television and Sound equipment. We don't waste time on useless theory. We give you just the practical training you'll need in 10 weeks' time.

## No Books - No Lessons

***All Practical Work at Coyne***

Coyne is NOT a Correspondence School. We don't teach you from books or lessons. We train you on the greatest outlay of Radio, Television and Sound equipment in any school—on scores of modern Radio Receivers, huge Broadcasting equipment, the very latest Television apparatus, Talking Picture and Sound Reproduction equipment, Code practice equipment, etc. You don't need advanced education or previous experience. We give you—right here in the Coyne Shops all the actual practice and experience you'll need.

## TELEVISION

**Is Now here!**

And Television is already here! Soon there'll be a demand for THOUSANDS of TELEVISION EXPERTS! The man who learns Television NOW can make a FORTUNE in this great new field. Get in on the ground-floor of this amazing new Radio development! Learn Television at COYNE on the very latest, newest Television equipment.

## TALKING PICTURES

***A Great Field***

Talking Pictures and Public Address Systems offer thousands of golden opportunities to the Trained Radio man. Here is a great new field of Radio that has just started to grow! Prepare NOW for these marvelous opportunities! Learn Radio Sound work at Coyne, on actual Talking Picture and Sound Reproduction equipment.

## COYNE

**Is 32 Years Old**

Don't worry about a job! Coyne Training settles the job question for life. You get Free Employment Help as long as you live. And if you need part-time work while at school to help pay expenses we'll gladly help you get it. Coyne is 32 years old! Coyne Training is tested—proven beyond all doubt. You can find out everything absolutely free. Just Mail Coupon for My Big Free Book.

H. C. Lewis, Pres. **Radio Division** Founded 1899

**Coyne Electrical School**

500 S. Paulina St. Dept. 41-5E Chicago, Ill.

H. C. LEWIS, President
**Radio Division, Coyne Electrical School**
500 S. Paulina St., Dept. 41-5E, Chicago, Ill.

Send me your Big Free Radio Book and all details of your Special Introductory Offer. This does not obligate me in any way.

*Name*............................

*Address*............................

*City*.............*State*........

1000 HOTEL POSITIONS OPEN!
BE A HOTEL MANAGER
Hotels, clubs, apartment hotels everywhere are calling for managers, etc. Splendid salaries, fine living, luxurious surroundings for you!
HOTELS, restaurants, clubs, apartment hotels, hospitals, institutions, camps, schools and colleges everywhere need trained men. Over 70,000 positions as Manager, Assistant Manager, Steward, Room Clerk, Sports Director, Auditor, and scores of other executive positions paying $2,500 to $10,000 a year, open annually in hotels of the United States. Nearly one billion dollars' worth of NEW HOTELS, APARTMENT HOTELS, CLUBS and INSTITUTIONS being built this year will need over 100,000 trained men and women. Hotels start you at salaries up to $2,500 a year. Fine living, luxurious surroundings. C. G. Webb, Jr., says: "Have taken the position of executive secretary and house manager. Your instruction is helping me wonderfully."
Previous Experience Unnecessary
You can have one of these fascinating, big-pay positions. Our Personal Coaching Plan, which adapts the training to your own personal needs and requirements, trains you for a well-paid position, right at home in your spare time. Age no obstacle. Lewis Training qualified William J. Kennedy, 62, for a position at double his previous salary. A good grade-school education is all you need.
We Put Our Students in Touch With Positions
We train you and put you in touch with big opportunities. National Employment Bureau FREE of extra charge. All of your training individually directed by hotel experts under the personal supervision of Clifford Lewis, who has been appointed Managing Consultant by over 300 hotels throughout the United States. Our students employed by leading hotels everywhere. Send today for Free Book, "Your Big Opportunity," explaining our Money-Back Agreement, and showing how we can train you for one of these splendid positions.
LEWIS HOTEL TRAINING SCHOOLS
Room DB-3101 CLIFFORD LEWIS, President WASHINGTON, D. C.
The Original and Only School of Its Kind in the World
Proof!
Our files contain hundreds of letters like these, which prove that the hotel industry is the field of big opportunity today.
WARREN F. CROCKER: "I am to start my duties as Steward. I wish to thank you for your cooperation and I am sure I will prove that Lewis Students are all you recommend them to be."
JAMES F. DORROH: "I have secured the position of Auditor you so kindly notified me of."
EARN $2,500 TO $10,000 A YEAR
Your Big Opportunity
Lewis Hotel Training Schools,
Room DB-3101, Washington, D. C.
Send me the Free Book, "YOUR BIG OPPORTUNITY," without obligation, and details of your Personal Coaching Plan.
Name
Address
City State
OPPORTUNITY COUPON

Play the Hawaiian Guitar like the Hawaiians!

SONG REQUIREMENTS of TALKING PICTURES
BOOK SENT FREE

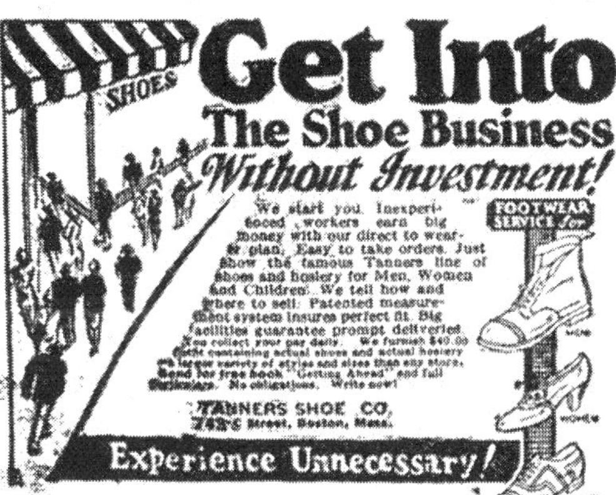
SHOES
Get Into The Shoe Business Without Investment!
We start you. Inexperienced workers earn big money with our direct to wearer plan. Easy to take orders. Just show the famous Tanners line of shoes and hosiery for Men, Women and Children. We tell how and where to sell. Patented measurement system insures perfect fit. Big facilities guarantee prompt deliveries.
FOOTWEAR SERVICE
TANNERS SHOE CO.
Boston, Mass.
Experience Unnecessary!

## ...until you've sent for our FREE *demonstration lesson*

TIME and again you've wanted to learn to play your favorite instrument; you've longed to get your share of the popularity and personal pleasure that every good musician enjoys —to know the thrill that comes with being able to entertain *musically*.

Yet, so far, you've been "scared" to start.

Why? Is it because you're under the impression that learning music necessitates long years of uninteresting study—lesson after lesson crammed with dry-as-dust theory and endless practicing? Has somebody told you that you need *special* talent to become a musician?

Then you're in for the surprise of your life. For, now, thanks to the famous U. S. School of Music, the reading and playing of music has been made so downright simple that you don't have to know one note from another to begin.

### Easy As Can Be

The lessons come to you by mail. They consist of complete printed instructions, diagrams and all the music you need. Compulsory practice? No. You study only when you feel like it. Personal teacher? No. If you make a mistake you correct it *yourself* and continue. Monotonous scales and harsh-sounding finger exercises? Never. From the very first lesson on you are playing real tunes by note. It's as easy as A-B-C. For before you strike a note, you are told how a thing is done. Then a picture shows you how. Then you do it yourself and hear it. Little theory. Plenty of accomplishment.

A few short months pass quickly by. Almost before you realize it, you are playing selections that fit your mood —you are entertaining others with wonderful classical compositions . . . lighter airs and ballads of haunting beauty . . . dance music that thrills with the fascination of jazz. No wonder that this remarkable method has been vouched for by over 600,000 people from all parts of the world.

Bear in mind no matter which instrument you select—the cost of learning in each case will average the same—just a few cents a day!

**Pick Your Instrument**

| | |
|---|---|
| Piano | Violin |
| Organ | Clarinet |
| Ukulele | Flute |
| Cornet | Saxophone |
| Trombone | Harp |
| Piccolo | Mandolin |
| Guitar | 'Cello |

Hawaiian Steel Guitar
Sight Singing
Piano Accordion
Italian and German Accordion
Voice and Speech Culture
Harmony and Composition
Drums and Traps
Automatic Finger Control
Banjo (Plectrum, 5-String or Tenor)
Juniors' Piano Course

### Get Proof Free!

Don't let a lot of false impressions and silly bugaboos delay your start toward musical good times. If you really want to learn to play—if social popularity and increased income appeal to you—then reserve your decision until we send you a Free Demonstration Lesson and a copy of our free illustrated book which describes in detail the famous U. S. School print-and-picture method. Then it's entirely up to you. You're the judge and jury. No obligation involved, of course.

When writing, kindly mention your favorite instrument. Forget that old-fashioned idea that you need talent to learn music and fill in and mail the coupon now. Instruments supplied when needed, cash or credit. U. S. School of Music, 863 Brunswick Bldg., New York City.

---

**U. S. SCHOOL OF MUSIC**
**863 Brunswick Building, New York City**

Please send me your free book, "Music Lessons in Your Own Home," with introduction by Dr. Frank Crane, Free Demonstration Lesson and particulars of your easy payment plan. I am interested in the following course:

.......................................Have You Instrument?.......

Name ........................................

Address ........................................

City ..............................State........

# *"Jim!" she exclaimed..*

## *So then I told Marge how the Hawaiian Guitar had made my ambitions all come true*

# *"why didn't you tell me that before?"*

I WAS just a plain discouraged "wash-out." No talent, no friends. No "social presence," no worthwhile prospects at my job; no hard, solid cash salted away at the bank.

And then what could a girl see in me? No matter how much I thought about girls—the way I felt about Marge, for example—I couldn't **do** anything about it.

One night I tried reading a magazine. I began spinning the pages past my thumb.

**And THEN it Happened!**

Somehow one page flashed out from the rest. "Learn the Hawaiian Guitar at Home," it read. And it urged me to send for a Free Book. That was three months ago.

Now let me tell you about the other night.

I asked Marge if I could call. She told me to come over after supper. Excited? I'll say I was!

Marge came out in a few minutes. I couldn't restrain myself any longer.

"Marge!" I cried, "I've got a surprise for you!" I reached down and lifted up my Guitar. Even in the semi-darkness I could see Marge's eyes grow big.

I played to her. Dreamy "Aloha"; throbbing "Carolina Moon"; all the blues of "Moanin' Low"—and two others. When I stopped, Marge didn't say a word for a full minute.

Then she exclaimed excitedly, "Jim! Why didn't you tell me before?"

I swallowed hard. "Because—" I began, "because, Marge—well, I guess there wasn't so very much to tell—before.'

"But **now**," I rushed on—"I'm started for the biggest things that ever were opened up to me! Listen, Marge! I've done it at home, without a teacher, by a wonderful new method.

"I took a trip over to Bridgeton one night and played my Guitar at the 'Y.' They went wild, Marge! Paid me **ten dollars** for it.

"Since then I've played at two dances there, too, and **Johnny Farrell says I start with his orchestra the first of the month. Think of it! It will mean doubling my salary.**"

Marge was quiet again. Then looking at me with level eyes, she said—"Jim, you've **found yourself**. I didn't know it was in you. I'm so happy."

* * * * *

You can be the popular master of this thrillingly beautiful instrument—in 1 to 3 short months. Without one bit of previous musical knowledge or experience, you can begin playing **actual tunes** right from the **very start.**

Here at last is the unlimited Opportunity for making friends. Here is the chance above all others to make $15 to $25 **a week and up**, for part-time or full-time playing.

Get the FACTS **now. With** the very first lesson of **this** time-tested Course you **re**ceive a full-size, sweet-toned, genuine Hawaiian Guitar; picks, bar, tuner, etc. **And we** give you Phonograph Records which demonstrate every lesson in the Course—55 in all.

The coupon below **brings your** copy of "The Hawaiian Way to Popularity and **Big** Pay." We want you to read it, that's all—then make your own decision. Do as Jim did—get that coupon into the mailbox **tonight.**

**A. F. BLOCH, President**
**Hawaiian Studios 218-031 of**
**New York Academy of Music**
**100 Fifth Avenue NEW YORK**

*This* **FREE Book** *will open your eyes* **Send for it**

**Clip and Mail NOW!**

**A. F. BLOCH, President**
**Hawaiian Studios 218-031 of**
**New York Academy of Music,**
**100 Fifth Avenue, New York City.**

Yes—without obligation I want to read "The Hawaiian Way to Popularity and Big Pay." Rush my copy.

Name ........................................

Address ........................................

City ........................... State ............

FOR THE COMING ISSUES OF

## FAR EAST ADVENTURE STORIES

We Are Lining Up For Your Delight

**Two-Fisted Stories**

by the following

**Two-Fisted Authors**

H. Bedford-Jones
Ernest Haycox
Hugh B. Cave
Jack D'Arcy
Albert Richard Wetjens
Malcolm Wheeler Nicholson
Arthur J. Burks
Ormond E. Case

---

**WATCH FOR THEM**
**MAY ISSUE**
**on Sale APRIL 10th**

Action Adventure East of Suez

# FAR EAST Adventure Stories

VOLUME TWO APRIL, 1931 NUMBER 4

## CONTENTS

COVER by Lyman Anderson



Manuscripts for FAR EAST Adventure Stories should be submitted to Fiction Publishers, Inc., 25 West 43rd St., New York City.

PRINTED BY WILLIAM GREEN, A CORPORATION, NEW YORK, U. S. A.

MAP OF THE WORLD
Showing
Location of Stories in this Issue
NORTH AMERICA
ATLANTIC OCEAN
Gold of Ishmael
Lope da Gamma
PACIFIC OCEAN
SOUTH AMERICA
ANTARCTIC OCEAN

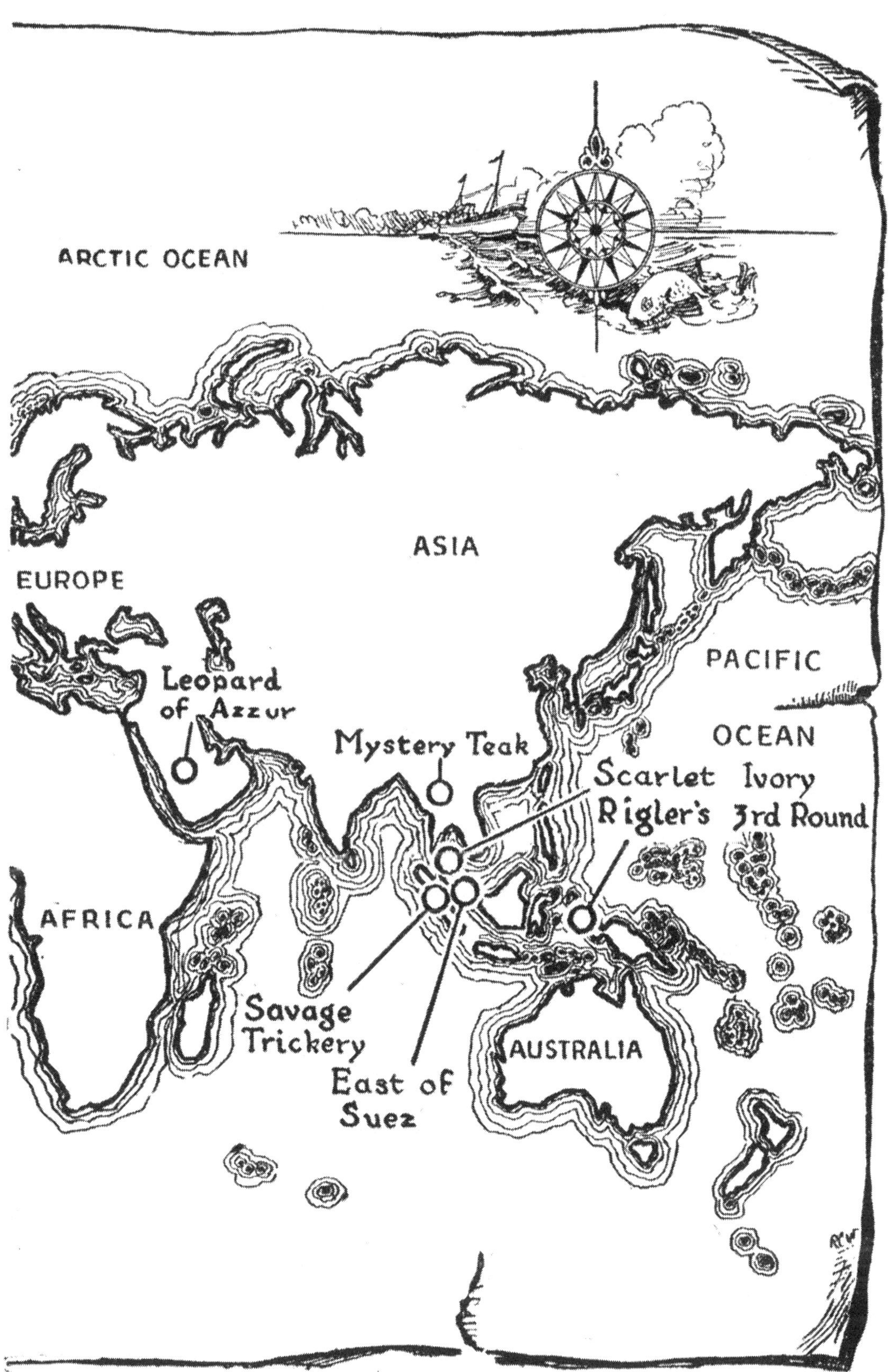
ARCTIC OCEAN
ASIA
EUROPE
PACIFIC
OCEAN
Leopard
of Azzur
Mystery Teak
Scarlet
Rigler's
Ivory
3rd Round
AFRICA
Savage
Trickery
East of
Suez
AUSTRALIA

# EAST OF

Where Hell Is

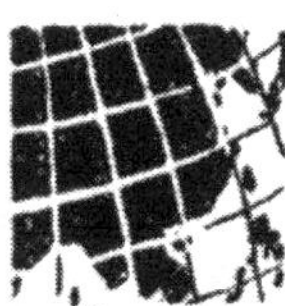

SINGAPORE . . . melting pot of the races . . . hot, crowded, stinking. Singapore, where every man's hell is to his own choosing.

The noonday gun in Fort Canning boomed its sullen challenge of the hour. Captain Drummond, his long frame slouched low in the sea-stained rattan chair, shadowless beneath the protecting canopy of the *Lucy B's* brass-railed stern, glanced up from his tall glass of cold tea and rum and nodded ever so slightly to the half naked Javanese who squatted sleepily against the wheelhouse.

The giant native scrambled to his feet, his great naked shoulders glistening like bronze in the creepers of sunlight forced between the awning lashings. Moving in an ape-like crouch to avoid the stanchion braces of the canopy overhead he hurried to the captain's side.

*"Saja Tuan,"* his husky voice whispered, as the fingers of his left hand touched his temple, first to the captain and then to the burnt-faced, puffing individual poured into the chair opposite him.

*"Saja, minta dua koppie,"* the captain spoke, in Mayalan.

*"Baai, Tuan,"* the Javanese answered, as he whirled and hurried forward.

# SINGAPORE

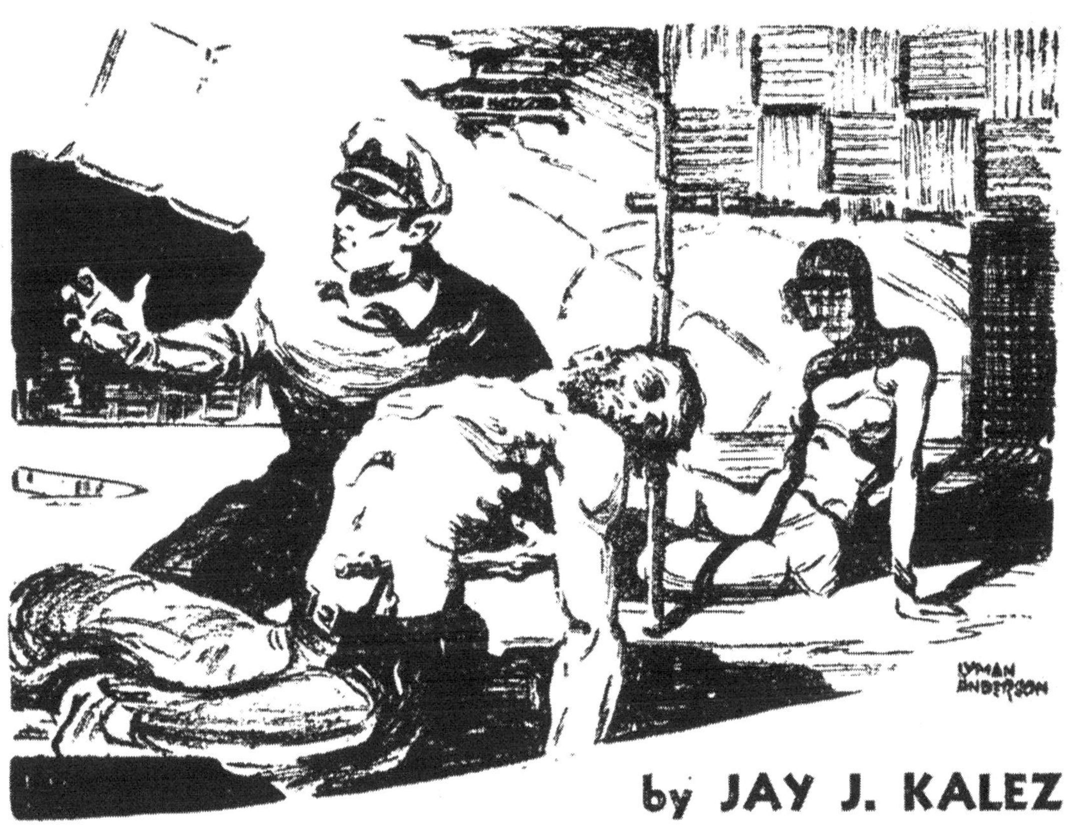


by JAY J. KALEZ

## Every Man's To His Own Choosing

Captain Drummond turned back to the man opposite him. "You may as well have tiffin aboard, Mr. Von Dorn," he spoke. "A little coffee at least, then we can put ashore. The police commissioner is not likely to be in his office until after two."

Von Dorn nodded willingly. Suddenly his brow wrinkled in a frowning effort. "Captain," he began, half apologetic, "I don't just know about seeking further police aid. Enough that they've located this man Tretner for us without asking too many questions. Do you think it best that under—under the circumstances we should confide in them further?"

The captain's thin lips cracked into a smile. "The Dutch East Borneo Company mistrusts even the British police?" he ventured, chidingly.

Von Dorn answered the smile with a clumsy wink. "You understand, Captain," he offered quickly, "there is always the matter of independent pride in our ability as a company. Why do we employ you, furnish you with this craft and . . . and . . . ?" Von Dorn's hand swept in a meaning wave about the *Lucy B's* stern.

The captain's throaty chuckle cut the gesture. "I understand perfectly, sir," he offered to soothe Von Dorn's visible embarrassment. "What concerns the Dutch East Borneo Company concerns Dutch Borneo. The government is not always as considerate of financial sacrifices in affairs such as this, as it might be. You prefer to settle your own interior difficulties, perhaps with less stern and less costly a hand than the government might insist upon should the matter reach the British Colonial office and be forwarded to the attention of the Dutch officials at Bandjermasin."

Von Dorn nodded in admittance. Boundaries are vague in the Jungle interior. Native unrest recognises them not at all. What concerned the Dutch Borneo concessions concerned the British as well. The policy of the British Colonial office was to nip native unrest in the bud and crush it with a hand that made no recognition of financial loss in its press for respect and authority. Von Dorn's apprehension was easily comprehensible. His company reasoned in pounds profit, not patriotic pennance. It was for purposes such as this they kept and bore the expense of the auxiliary sloop, *Lucy B*, and its capable envoy, Captain Drummond.

"Let's get back to facts, Mr. Von Dorn," the captain suddenly switched, as thought of the task ahead wiped his lean features with a stern hand. "Just what connection do your *residents* place between this young chemist, Tretner, and the unrest among the upper river Dyak tribes?"

"Nothing but the conincident of time, Captain," Von Dorn hurried to answer. "As district manager of our rubber concessions in the Bandjermasin district, I, of course, have access to all resident manager reports. This young chemist, Tretner . . . by the way, he's an American like yourself . . . was employed in the coagulate plant above Poeroek Tajoe for over a year. Later we moved him to one of the *Kampong* stations further up the river. There are several independent concessions operating under contract in that district and we wished to stop the practice of the tappers watering the *latex,* by having a chemist on the grounds. The natives were becoming quite apt at watering the rubber tree sap and cutting the specific gravity. Of course, as the coagulate plant purchases by measure, the process was becoming expensive to us.

"Tretner was at the upriver *Kampong* for about six months before the . . . the . . . well, we've discussed that, Captain. You know what opium and native *arrack* do to a white man in these damn tropics. It got Tretner fast.

"I learned of it all only after the *resident* had notified me of Tretner's leaving and the authorities having cancelled his passport at Bandjermasin. It was at this same time that the *resident* made mention of the uneasiness among the natives and of the disappearance of Kio-mo-uau, the Dyak *dayong* or medicine man of the district. The *resident* insinuated no connection in the disappearance of Kio-mo-uau and the hurried departure of Tretner, but there is a curious angle to the affair.

"It is only the natives about the company's concessions that are causing trouble. The private concessions operated by a Portuguese named Pedro Pringo are still able to continue work. In fact Pringo's plantation is practically supplying the entire output of the coagulation plant at the upper river station. The home office is even considering Pringo's offer to lease the entire company holdings of the upper district."

"And this Portuguese, Pringo—"

the captain spoke, in a questioning tone,"—he is under suspicion of inciting the trouble?"

"No, no," Von Dorn hastened to assert. "Of course, Pringo is raking in a rich profit by the trouble and should he secure the operating lease to the upper concession, would even add to that. But we have no suspicion of Pringo. His immunity to the trouble lies in his blood relationship to the Dyak tribes. His blood runs to a quarter native, I believe, and his wife is a daughter of the Dyak chief at Hamangan.

"The connection is, Captain, that only since Tretner left the company station have the natives gone out of bounds in fanatic religious ceremonies. Every native *dayong* on the concession is offering sacrifices to the jungle spirits and, worst of all, it is only the forbidden of these religious rites that seem to appease them."

"*Purri-purri*, eh?" the captain interrupted, mentioning that curious mixture of native sorcery and plain murder as practiced by the native medicine men. "They're drumming up their devil god myths again?"

"Worse," Von Dorn answered. "It's *tauva'u* this time. *Tauva'u*, with the crocodile fixed as the reptile in which the spirit of Kio-mouau has taken up body. You know the extremities to which the *dayongs* will carry this form of ancestral worship once they have whipped the natives into a fanatic frenzy with their crude magic. Our *resident* reports rumors of the worst."

THE CAPTAIN'S lips pressed hard. "Human sacrifice, eh?" he barely muttered again, as his eyes seemed to dull in memory of what his jungle years were capable of recollecting.

Von Dorn's head was slowly nodding. "*Gnomes*," he finally said. "Children they have captured from the jungle Punan tribes in night raids away from the river. So far only rumors, to be sure, but who knows when they may reach the ears of the government officials or . . . or where it may all end. You know native psychology better than I. One thing certain, the concession's output is suffering. What native will work with the festival drums booming day and night and the *dayongs* chanting their rites at every bend in the river? My personal belief is that this man Tretner holds some secret as to the underlying cause. Why should a missing medicine man from one tribe work the entire district into such a pitch?"

The captain did not answer. From for'd appeared the giant Javanese, herding before him a shriveled, barefoot Chinese bearing a tray of curried rice and coffee. The Javanese himself served the captain. Von Dorn watched, amused.

"Your *jonges* seems most attentive, Captain," he finally offered, grinning widely as every second the big native's eyes searched the captain's features as if in fear of missing some wink of a signalling command.

"Not *jonges*, Von Dorn; first mate," the captain corrected. "Six-six seems to think, however, that serving me is a part of his first mate duties. He's a valuable man, Von Dorn. Speaks English, a dozen native dialects and, besides that, he's a sailor. Right, Six-six?"

"*Baai Tuan*," the Javanese, called Six-six, answered, holding to his native dialect, his wide grin, however, appreciative of the captain's words.

A moment the captain appraised the native's physique. Then, suddenly snapping a few brief commands that sent Six-six hurrying for'd, he turned back to his conversation with Von Dorn.

Throughout tiffin the district resident manager chatted on of the situation at hand and of his own precarious position should the Dutch government decide to step in and correct the impending hazard with its usual drastic method. The captain listened, mostly in silence.

AN HOUR later a sampan set the trio . . . Von Dorn, the captain and Six-six . . . ashore upon the worn stone steps of Johnson's Landing. Six-six, his naked waist now covered with a torn white jacket, followed a few respective paces behind the captain as the latter walked toward the upper street with Von Dorn.

"You'll haul anchor with the tide?" Von Dorn asked as they walked.

"Sundown at the latest," the captain answered.

For several paces Von Dorn moved in silence. Suddenly his fingers snapped as if in a remembered thought. "By the way, Captain," he spoke, "the district inspector is here in Singapore and is returning to Poeroek Tajoe at once. We wish him back on the concession as soon as possible. If you could give him passage, he would save at least a week."

"Gladly," the captain answered. "Have him put aboard as soon as possible. There's an extra cabin aboard."

"Fine," Von Dorn exclaimed. "I'll get in touch with him immediately. His name is Mantos, don't believe you know him. I'll give him a letter of introduction to you, however. Mantos may be able to tell you more of the trouble. He left Poeroek Tajoe only a few weeks ago."

Making his adieu to the district resident manager at the street corner, the captain stepped into a rickshaw and ordered the barefoot chinese on his way. The rickshaw moved as by a miracle through the tub-to-hub jumble of traffic, Six-six trotting watchfully at its side. The captain directed a course down the water front.

A rapid passage through the rows of chanting Kling traders and wailing money changers soon swung the rickshaw up a narrow thoroughfare running at an agle from the water front. Dismissing the rickshaw at a corner, the captain inquired a moment of the native policeman lazily directing traffic, and, turning into a narrower, alley-like street, began working his way along, observing the entrance markings to each building. Behind him still trailed the Javanese, Six-six.

Suddenly the captain halted. Across the street loomed a sun faded sign that branded the establishment beneath it as the "STEP-AND-A-HALF." A dust covered window display of bottles and tall rum jugs announced its wares. The address, given by the police as the man Tretner's most frequented haunt, looked none too inviting.

THE CAPTAIN crossed the street and moving cautiously through the screened doors, entered. A Chinese boy in dirty whites scrambled forward to lead him past the long bar that fenced one side of the room, to an array of small tables opposite. From the street door, Six-six watched until the captain was seated and served, then dropped into a squat with back braced against the building wall, head cocked to one side so that one ear was constantly alert to the jabber of voices from within.

At his tiny table the captain stared about. The place was a dive, catering to those of any race or breed. A jumble of water front riff-raff crowded the bar while a double table's length away a crescent shaped counter was more closely lined with an array of jabbering Chinese and a few sweat-streaked whites.

Pulling a thin leather folder from his pocket, the captain studied the photo within what had once been the Dutch passport of Flex Tretner. Memorizing the picture's features, he began scanning the white men about for one that might be possible of identification. Slowly his eyes passed along the bar line across the room and to the half circle about the waist-high counter.

From the slow, chanting count of the Chinese tender behind the counter and pendulum-like swing of his arm to the click of dried beans, he recognized the game of fan-tan in progress.

It was as he studied the faces here that a sudden commotion seemed to break loose at the far end of the barroom. A man in soiled white duck struggled to free himself from the tangling grasps of a scantily clad dancing girl who seemed fighting to hold him from leaving the curtained retreat at the end of the barroom. The captain instantly recognized the man. It was the young chemist he sought, Flex Tretner.

Von Dorn had tempered his remarks on the wages of opium upon a white man in the tropics. The dull, ashen skin of Tretner's features hung in loose puffs beneath his eyes and about the corners of his sagging lips. His sandy hair was matted and disheveled while his soiled, wrinkled whites seemed to hang from his spent frame like gathered sailcloth.

A sudden fling of his outstretched arms and Tretner sent the dancing girl, who clung to his neck, flying across the room. With scraping footsteps he advanced toward the bar, paused halfway and then, as his eyes caught the circle about the fan-tan game, his features seemed to contort into a spasm of misery. He dragged himself toward the game counter.

Captain Drummond was on the point of rising when, from the corner of his eye, he caught the quick move of a tall, swarthy-skinned individual who seemed to appear from nowhere and with a snatch of his arm jerked back the blazing-eyed girl who was then in the act of again charging forward.

Dividing his attention, Drummond allowed Tretner to pass a few feet from his table and shoulder his way to the fan-tan counter. A moment the action of the man and the girl at the end of the room held him. The man seemed to be whispering a few brief words of instructions as his one hand twisted the girl's wrist cruelly. The tight, drawn lips of the girl bespoke fear and respect for the words hissed at her despite the flinch of pain that traced itself across her face with every shake of her gripped arm.

A moment and the girl was released, but in place of rushing across the room toward Tretner as had seemingly been her original intention, she now sauntered carelessly up to the bar.

DRUMMOND turned back to the fan-tan game. Over the heads of the crowd he suddenly caught a slow, deliberate nod of the game tender toward the end of the room as if in response to some signal. The captain turned quickly about, barely in time to see the man who had a moment before released the girl, swing his eyes back toward the bar. A flash of understanding swept over Drummond. Some signal had been passed toward the fan-tan table. A signal that seemed to forewarn of something unsuspected about to happen. It occurred before the captain could rise from his chair and make his way to the game counter.

From the fan-tan counter came a sudden smothered oath. An instant the half circle about milled close in and then as each individual scattered like the pot of dried beans that crashed to the counfer, one man staggered into the clear with hands clasped tight against his abdomen. From above his gripped thumbs appeared the hilt of a knife. The man was Tretner.

Drummond did not rise. The staggering Tretner swayed weakly past his chair and slumped to the barroom floor not a dozen feet away. Before he had even touched prone, the wild-eyed dancer at the bar had hurled herself across the room and with howls of terrorized grief, was striving to cover the lips of the fallen man with kisses. As she did so, her one hand slipped down and crawled beneath Tretner's torn jacket.

Drummond's eyes followed every move. With the push of the dancing girl's hand beneath Tretner's coat, he understood the maneuver. The girl was attempting to frisk her victim. Frisk him before the wondering eyes of the bar crowd as, with her body, she shielded her efforts under a sham of grief.

Drummond slipped from his chair. As he did so, he caught the weak attempt of Tretner to push clear of the girl who pinned him down. One hand pulled from his midde, dived to his belt pocket and drew forth clinched tight. Quickly the girl's hand covered his blood stained one.

Drummond stooped and with a quick jerk pulled the girl bodily to her feet to send her sprawling across the room. Instantly a wild curse bellowed from a hidden voice amongst the circling crowd. A voice that quickly identified itself as belonging to the tall, swarthy-skinned individual the captain had a minute before followed in his course to the bar. The man now hurled himself forward. In his hand glittered the sheen of naked steel. Drummond straightened to meet the attack.

THE MOVE was unnecessary. As the drawnback hand of the attacker made to lunge at the captain in a downward thrust of his knife, a tentacle arm of white lashed out, gripped with a claw of black and with no more effort than the sweep of a cargo boom, sent the attacker sailing through the air to crash against the bar rail. Hands held chest high, the towering form of Six-six pushed between the captain and the awed crowd.

Drummond moved fast. A grasp of the knife hilt protruding from Tretner's middle, and he pulled the bloody blade free. As quickly he gathered the moaning form into his arms and with Six-six covering his retreat, backed across the room and through the entrance. Luckily a rickshaw was moving down the alley-like street. A hail, and the captain shoved his groaning victim into the rickshaw seat. The blast of a police whistle from the opposite end of the alley warned him that the sound of the rumpus had reached the ears of the native policeman at the corner. A command to the Chinese in the rickshaw's shafts, and with Six-six still covering the retreat, the rickshaw rattled down the street, Drummond shouting the direction across Cavannough Bridge to the government first aid station in Coleman Street.

AT THE first aid surgery, the surgeon in charge shook his head doubtfully as he turned to Drummond. "Not much chance," he muttered in a low voice. "He's bleeding too bad internally."

Though the surgeon's words were scarcely audible to the captain's ears, the man lying on the surgery table seemed to catch their meaning. "I can't die; I can't die," came his moaning gasps. "God, I mustn't die."

The captain stepped to the side of the operating table as the surgery nurse hurried in preparation for the task ahead. The wounded man turned his head. "You're . . . you're the man who saved me?" Tretner's lips spoke as his eyes raised up and caught the captain's. "You . . . you brought me here?"

The captain nodded slowly. His own eyes appraised the glassy film in the other's. The death rattle was already in Tretner's throat as he attempted to speak. He struggled to reach up and grasp Drummond's hand.

"If . . . if . . . I should . . . " Tretner's lips mumbled, as the warning of his own weakness seemed to spear the certainty ahead. "If I should die, my . . . my . . . sister, she mustn't know. Mustn't know anything. Just . . . just bring her back here and see that she returns home. Don't . . . don't let her leave Poeroek Tajoe. Warn her . . . stop her some way. Don't . . . don't let her go to Pringo."

Drummond's lips tightened as he caught the dying man's words. Poeroek Tajoe . . . Pedro Pringo . . . his sister . . . Von Dorn had mentioned no sister of Tretner's nor fear of Pedro Pringo in his absolution of the Portuguese plantation operator. Tretner was struggling in a plea for help.

"Your sister has been here? She has left for Borneo and Poeroek Tajoe?" the captain questioned quickly, as he bent toward the dying man's lips and allowed his one hand to grasp the groping clenched fist that seemed seeking his own in a paw for courage and strength.

"Yes . . . yes," Tretner fought to answer. "I learned it to-day . . . I had no chance to warn her . . . she thinks me still at the upriver *kampong* . . . I . . . I never wrote her different. My mail was forwarded from there. I wrote her through Pringo. He forwarded my letters so . . . so she didn't even know I was here . . . here in Singapore."

A contortion of pain gripped Tretner silent. His one hand attempted to raise. His lips opened and trembled to speak as his eyes rolled weakly. Then slowly the clenched fist, gripped in the captain's hand, opened, spread and pressed something cold and hard into Drummond's palm. The captain felt but dared not drop his eyes from the quivering lips attempting to speak on.

"Take . . . take this to her. God, get it to her some way. It's all that will ever save her if she goes to Pringo. All that will save her if Pringo ever . . . ever . . . ever . . . "

The lips quivered in a tremble. A rasping choke, and the fingers in the captain's palm slipped free to drop lifelessly in a dangle over the operating table's side. The attending surgeon passing the table, paused, glanced a moment, then tossed the rubber gloves in his hands back into the instrument case. Tretner was dead.

A MOMENT the captain stood still. A police sergeant had appeared in the doorway. The captain understood his presence. For himself it meant nothing but identification and a verbal explanation. The cold hard object in his hand seemed to breathe a protest against being a part of that explanation. Half turning his back toward the surgery door, Drummond opened his hand and glanced down. His lips barely pressed back an exclamation of surprise. In his palm rested a flat cut ruby the size of a guinea. A glittering, fiery red ruby, smooth and polished. The captain's hand closed and raised to his jacket pocket. As his empty fingers withdrew, he advanced to meet the police sergeant.

Three hours later Drummond was still within the police commissioner's office, examining the record of a passport issued the week previous to one Kay Tretner, granting her the privilege of embarking for Bandjermasin, Dutch Borneo. With it lay a summarized police report covering the known facts surrounding the affair at the Step-and-a-Half. Masking his true desire for information behind his incidental presence in the dive, Drummond succeeded in gaining what added knowledge he wished without making known to the police commissioner his true mission as linked with the Dutch Borneo Company. Neither did he make mention of the ruby Tretner had passed to him with his dying gasp.

To the police the whole affair held the appearance of merely another of the fatal brawls common in the dives of Singapore's water front district. Tretner, for lack of funds or to be near a supply of the drug that had gripped him, lived in the cheap quarters above the dive. He had been intimate with the dancing girl. The girl claimed so, at least. Tretner had a sudden need for money and sought to raise it by gambling what funds he had. The dancing girl attempted to keep him away from the game. Tretner gambled, tried to cheat or grab some other player's stake and in the brawl, was fatally stabbed. The game tender could offer no clue as to the assailant. Every known person in the establishment could vouch for his position at the moment. The knife was impossible of identification. It was just another case. There was no mention of the ruby Tretner had held in his closed fist which the girl had attempted to open nor of the swarthy-skinned individual who had confronted her and talked with her a moment before. No mention of even a knowledge of such a jewel existing.

Drummond had no intention of pressing the investigation as offered from the assigned officer's report. To contradict the facts as presented would have meant the opening of his true knowledge of the affair to questioning. At present such jeopardy seemed unnecessary.

Thanking the police commissioner for his courtesy, he bowed himself from the office. At the street, Six-six still awaited him, squatted upon the curb. Drummond boarded a rickshaw and directed the way back to Johnson's Landing. At the rickshaw's wheel trotted Six-six, a worried smolder in his eyes as he watched the set features of his captain's face.

Reaching the landing, Drummond stepped into a sampan and directed the course back to his craft. As the sampan darted across the water, he lost himself in meditation. His mind flashed back to the events of an hour before. Regardless of the police report, the dancing girl had known of the ruby Tretner had.

Known of it and attempted to gain it while the man she claimed as a lover lay dying upon the barroom floor. The man that had forced her back in her first rush must have known of it as well. The girl had seemed to be acting under his commands.

Instinctively Drummond's hand raised to his jacket pocket. He felt of the hard, round stone within. Then cautiously his fingers groped and pulled it into his palm. His eyes blazed anew as he gazed down. It was a gem, priceless, flawless. A gem fit for a rajah's crown.

As the sampan rubbed the *Lucy B's* side, he snapped to himself. Pushing the ruby back into his jacket pocket, he grabbed the Jacob's-ladder dangling from the rail and climbed the craft's side. His feet touching the shaded deck of the *Lucy B's* stern, he straightened in surprise. Before him stood the tall, swarthy-skinned individual of the Step-and-a-half, one hand concealed deep in his coat pocket.

"WELL," the captain spoke curtly, his eyes holding to the pocketed hand, "what do you want aboard here?"

The man before him seemed to swallow hard as his narrowed eyes slowly widened into an unbelievable stare. "You . . . you are Captain Drummond?" he finally spoke, a faint Spanish accent to his faltering words. "You . . . you . . ."

The man smothered his words with a wild shake of his head as his empty hand pulled itself from his pocket. "Captain, Captain," he began chanting, "I have been a fool . . . fool. How can I ask your pardon, a thousand of them? Here . . . here, perhaps this will explain. Captain, I swear it, until this moment I did not know you to be the man in the employ of my own company. Here, Mr. Von Dorn's instructions were to present this to you. Perhaps it will explain."

The man extended an envelope bearing the Dutch East Borneo stamp. A faint suspicion of the man's true identity flashed across Drummond even as he opened the envelope and pulled the letter clear. This man must be the company resident inspector, Mantos, Von Dorn had requested passage for. But if so, what explanation was there to his action back at the Step-and-a-Half a few hours previous?

Drummond did not have to ask for an explanation. Even as he read the letter, Mantos was babbling out an apologetic flow of words as an alibi to his action.

"The young man Tretner, he was my friend, my dear friend," Mantos was explaining. "We lived together at Poeroek Tajoe. To me he was as a brother. To-day I went to him, pleaded with him to grasp himself anew and come back with me. Begged him to give up his filthy existence and start over again. Senor . . . Senor Captain, when he was lying there on the floor and you pulled that woman from him, I did not know who you might be. I swear it, Captain. I placed you for a lover of the wench who held such a grip on him. I thought you even were the man who had struck him down with a knife. Captain, you must understand. There is no other way to explain. I was seeking only to avenge my friend."

The captain glanced up from the letter. His mind had gathered in the plausibility of Mantos' words as he read the letter of introduction from Von Dorn, identifying Mantos as the district resident inspector he desired passage for. Undoubtdly Mantos had not been aware of his identity. The very expression of the man as he climbed over the *Lucy B's* rail was proof enough of that. His suspecting of the captain as the man who had knifed Tretner or as the sweetheart of the dancer was possible. However, in Drummond's brain still flashed clear the remembrance of that silent signal to the Chinese game tender and the actions of the man when he had pulled the girl back in her first pursuit of Tretner toward the fan-tan game. But he had no intention of accusing. Even that might be possible of an explanation.

"Tell me, Captain," Mantos was speaking again, his Spanish accent almost predominating as he rattled off his words, "the police, they have discovered nothing? They have caught no one?"

Drummond shook his head. "Not even a suspicion," he answered. "You . . . you knew Tretner was dead?"

"Yes, Captain," Mantos spoke. "I followed you to the first aid station. I viewed his body. They told me that you had just left with the police sergeant. Then I knew I must have been wrong in my quick suspicion but . . . but . . ." Mantos turned his palm out in a gesturing plea of hopelessness. "You understand," he went on, "surely you understand my actions now. You do not hold them against me?"

Drummond smiled a forced smile. "I believe I understand," he offered, his voice even. "Perhaps it is best that we recognize it all as a mistake and forget it. Tell me, Mantos, your luggage is aboard?"

"Yes, Captain. I came aboard an hour ago," Mantos hurried in reply. "From the first aid station I went at once to Senor Von Dorn to report the affair. He . . . he had asked me considerable of Tretner on my first arrival in Singapore. He gave me my letter of introduction to you and I hurried aboard. I am ready any time, Captain."

"Very good," Drummond snapped, as he turned about to confront Six-six, standing a pace behind him. A few quick commands and Six-six was scrambling for'd, not without, however, a few backward glances down the deck to where the captain pointed the way below to Mantos as he himself went to the wheelhouse. Minutes later the *Lucy B* had headed her prow toward the sea.

IT WAS at dinner that night before Drummond again had a chance to talk with Mantos. Riding a smooth sea under full sail, the *Lucy B* pushed herself out to sea. Mantos and the captain, seated in the tiny cabin aft, were about to enjoy their after dinner cigar. Mantos approached his topic cautiously.

"Flex . . . young Tretner," he began, between puffs. "You . . . ah . . . you were with him when he died?"

The captain nodded absently

"He . . . ah . . . he was conscious? He spoke before he died?"

Again Drummond nodded as from behind a cloud of exhaled smoke he watched the curious pinch of Mantos' eyes.

"Some dying request, perhaps?" Mantos pried.

"Yes," the captain half grunted. "He has a sister and he didn't want her to know of his past as far as Singapore was concerned."

"Eh," Mantos muttered. "This sister, he said where she was?"

"Yes." The captain leaned forward. "He said she was at Poeroek Tajoe. You knew of her?"

Mantos' expression twitched. "Yes, yes," he answered hurriedly. "Flex had told me of her. He told me he had written for her to come to him."

The captain leaned back as he fathomed the lie. "Tretner seemed greatly worried should she go beyond Poeroek Tajoe," he went on. "Feared for her safety should she ever reach the plantations of Pedro Pringo."

Mantos seemed to start. "He told you why he feared?" his voice sounded, a cold tremble to the words.

"No, not why," Drummond answered. "Merely that he feared. You know this man Pringo?"

"Very well," Mantos replied. "A wonderful host. You will enjoy meeting him, I am sure."

"I believe I will," Drummond agreed. "Both him and Tretner's sister. From Bandjermasin I'll telegraph her to wait at Poeroek Tajoe for me."

Mantos seemed to start. "Tretner's dying wish was that you see his sister?" he inquired, a bit eager. "Some dying bequeath?"

The captain thought fast. It was the opening he had pried for. Perhaps Mantos could give some clue to the unfinished dying words of Tretner as he had pressed the ruby into his hand. Some slip of the tongue.

"Yes, a rather queer bequeath," the captain spoke, as his fingers fished into his jacket pocket. "An odd and quite a valuable one for a man in Tretner's position. Here isn't it a gem?"

Drummond pushed his hand toward Mantos and opened his palm before the *resident's* gaze. Then he watched the man's face. Mantos seemed to struggle to control a desire to grasp the glittering, fiery stone. His eyes seemed to dilate in eagerness.

"Yes, yes . . .beautiful," he babbled. "Remarkable. Of great value, undoubtedly. Too valuable to carry around so carelessly in one's pocket, Captain."

The captain met Mantos' meaning glance. As quickly Mantos turned away. His next words were in deliberate ignorance of the palm-held gem. The captain understood. Mantos sensed the trap. The captain slipped the ruby back into his jacket pocket and, excusing himself, went to the wheel for a checking of his course.

NOT ONCE during the ensuing three days at sea did Mantos again make mention of the gem. He avoided every pry of the captain as to its possible origin, value or history. Rather, he shielded himself in the necessary mealtime talk behind an offer of his late knowledge as to the status of affairs in the upper river *kampongs* beyond Poeroek Tajoe. From him the captain learned much.

Mantos had been at the upriver *kampong* at the time of Kio-mo-uau, the Dyak medicine man's disappearance. Kio-mo-uau had been the most influential *dayong* of the tribes. It was he with his magic that kept the bad spirits or *toh,* away from the tribes. He claimed a mythical blood-brotherhood to the crocodile and possessed the power of granting immunity to his tribe from their danger. When this immunity was encroached upon, as it often was, Kio-mo-uau had more magic whereby with priestly pomp and ceremony the offending reptile was trapped from the river and revenge disbursed to the hearts of the wailing relatives in a fantastic ceremony known to the natives as *Booayah tauva'u.*

It was lack of this ceremony since the disappearance of Kio-mo-uau that seemed to cause the unrest. Having no knowledge of the magic Kio-miouau practiced, the natives had reverted to ancient sacrificial forms in an effort to please the crocodile gods which this season seemed to be infesting the rivers in droves. However, it was only in the rivers about the concession that they appeared to have become such a menace.

Further up the river at the plantation of Pedro Pringo they had bothered little. Some secret omen about which the natives refused to talk seemed to account for this. The Dyaks of Pedro Pringo's region believed themselves blessed with some unknown power and refused to leave even beyond the plantation bounds.

"I believe you have an impossible task ahead, Captain," Mantos offered, on their third night out. "Not even the government can restrain the natives when it comes to this religious unrest. Mr. Von Dorn told me of Pedro Pringo's offer to lease for operation the entire concession. To me it looks like the only way out unless, of course, the concessions are closed for a few seasons and the government takes its usual methods. Pedro Pringo knows how to pacify them like no white man can ever hope to."

Drummond offered no comment to Mantos' declaration. He plainly stated his intention of proceeding directly up the river, past the last river fort, Poeroek Tajoe, to the concession *kampong* and see conditions for himself. Mantos, his destination being only to Poeroek Tajoe, offered no protest.

At dawn on the fourth day they entered the river and soon were off the Dutch Borneo town of Bandjermasin. Quickly gaining clearance to proceed on to Poeroek Tajoe, Drummond took a native pilot aboard and, forwarding a telegram to Tretner's sister in care of the controleur's residence at Poeroek Tajoe, moved out immediately.

The *Lucy B* did herself proud in following the urge for speed against the sluggish current. Drummond was at the wheel almost constantly and only at meals did he have a chance for a hurried word now and then with Mantos.

Four days in the river, and on the fifth the cliffs of Poeroek Tajoe loomed ahead. Anchoring at once, Drummond immediately sought an audience with the resident controleur of the district. The controleur greeted him cordially. Here again the captain heard a confirmation of the cause of the native unrest as given him by Mantos in their run from Singapore. However, the controleur was more emphatic. Unless the affair was settled within the next week, he stated, he would be forced to take the matter up with the military government. A river gunboat, the Voorwaarts, was already stationed in port. The unrest was spreading. Where a few weeks before the natives of the upper plantation operated by Pedro Pringo had been peaceful, they, too, were now working themselves into a frenzy. A frenzy that made it dangerous for a white man to even enter the jungle.

Realizing the seriousness of the controleur's words, Drummond made haste to inquire for the girl Kay Tretner and to find out if she had gone on to Pedro Pringo's. The controleur seemed both surprised and worried.

"Captain," he exclaimed, "your wire puzzled me. Surely you must be mistaken. No white woman has landed at Poeroek Tajoe in months, much less proceed up stream to the *kampongs*."

An instant the captain was blocked. To be sure he had not stopped at Bandjermasin long enough to make inquiry as to whether or not Tretner's sister had reported in to the Dutch authorities and gone on. The fact that her Colonial passport at Singapore had cleared her for Poeroek Tajoe made the journey up the river that far almost certain.

"The upper *kampongs* are not safe for a white man, much less a white woman," the controleur was speaking again. "Even Pedro Pringo is none too sure of himself. He came down from Boeroek a few days ago and has been tied up at the wharves ever since, waiting for the return of messengers he has sent on up the river to make sure of things before he starts on up home. Undoubtedly this woman you speak of is still at Bandjermasin."

From the controleur's positiveness Drummond was inclined to believe as much himself. Poeroek Tajoe was the jump-off point to the isolated jungle *kampongs.* It would have been impossible for a woman to land and proceed up-stream without the controleur's permission. The officials kept account of every craft moving up or down the river, even to such cases as the motor launch of Pedro Pringo.

In information of value, the controleur had little to offer. A few questions as to Pedro Pringo, and Drummond made known his intent of proceeding immediately on up the river as far as his craft was able to draw clearance.

He left the controleur's residence and hurried back to the *Lucy B.* Mantos, the Chinese *jonges* aboard informed him, had put his luggage ashore an hour before and departed for the company station. The captain hurried to his own cabin below.

DARKNESS WAS dropping from the sky with the speed of the tropics and as the captain entered his cabin he switched on the electric lights, operated from a storage battery for'd. A small electric fan placed before the cabin's open porthole immediately set up its song. Drummond stepped toward his desk, then stopped short. The top was open and strewn about were the contents of its many pigeon holes.

A quick inspection brought a curse from his lips. His cabin had been ransacked. Gone over from wall chests to strewn bedding. Angrily he stepped to the cabin door and bellowed for Six-six. As he touched the door handle, a curious metallic sing hissed past his ear and into the door before his face appeared, as by magic, a strange feathered dart.

Drummond dropped to his knees as his eyes caught the dart's quiver. On hands and knees he crawled across the cabin and, rising carefully to the open porthole, slammed its glass cover closed. In the same instant Six-six appeared breathlessly in the cabin door.

"Six-six, quick," the captain snapped. "Look! A *supit!* Some one let go at me with a poison dart from a blow gun. Quick, see who's on the wharf."

Drummond appraised the cabin as he reached into a wall chest for his automatic. Only the whirling air current of the tiny fan had saved him from the poison dart. It had barely missed his cheek. Some one had stood upon the wharf outside and with himself flooded in the cabin's light, made him a target through the open port as he reached for the door to summon Six-six.

One thing was positive. It had been no native who had rummaged his desk. None of the curious little trinkets that would have been irresistible to a native were missing. The search had been too thorough, as well. Not a corner of the room had been missed. A curious smile toyed at his lips as he raised his hand and touched the hard object within his jacket pocket. Perhaps the ruby he still carried upon his person might offer some solution as to the cause.

Shoving his automatic into his belt, he hurried on deck. Tropical darkness had already wrapped the wharf in black night. He moved forward to where the narrow gangplank led on to the wharf. As he did so, from somewhere within the black shadows of the river's bordering godowns came the noisy purr of an exhaust as it echoed through the night. The captain caught the hiss of a launch's prow against the current.

Leaping to the deck, he snapped on the switch control to his searchlight lashed to the rail. Instantly a stab of brightness cut the dark as the light's beam shot out across the river. Drummond gripped the controls and swept the light back and forth across the water in an effort to locate the moving launch from the sound of its pounding exhaust.

Suddenly the light sparkled upon the glittering reflection of tumbling water at a boat's prow. He lifted the beam ever so little. In that instant a muffled scream seemed to sound above the purr of the exhaust. A terrified scream and, in the frame of whiteness from the searchlight, the outline of two forms within the launch's cockpit. Two struggling forms, the one with a tangle of tossing hair that marked her plainly as a woman; the other . . . Drummond cursed as the launch swerved past the edge of a protruding wharf beyond. He could have sworn the other was that of the resident inspector Mantos.

Six-six's pattering feet sounded on the gangplank. The captain called. Six-six hurried forward. "See anyone?" Drummond shouted.

"*Saja Tuan,*" the Javanese hurried to speak. "See boat belong chug-chug. Two *Tuan* . . . one *Sinabada.* They go, hurry-up-quick."

Drummond's muscles stiffened. He had been right in his sight. Six-six had seen the same as he except for an added white man. Enough that he was now sure it was a woman who had been struggling in that cockpit as a hand clamped over her mouth to muffle her scream. A woman who must have been in the boat and not taken aboard from the dock down which Six-six had raced.

The words of the resident controleur flashed to Drummond's mind. Pedro Pringo had come down from Boeroek a day or two before and was still moored at the wharf. No white woman had landed at Poeroek Tajoe in months. The possibility leaped clear. Pringo's launch might have gone well beyond Boeroek. Might have picked up a passenger almost at Bandjermasin. That passenger might easily have been Tretner's sister. Pringo's launch, tied up to the wharves at Poeroek Tajoe, would never be subjected to search. The girl, knowing she would have trouble being granted permission to proceed on to the up-river *kampong,* might be a willing secret passenger. However, a moment before she had been anything but that.

THE CAPTAIN'S decision came quick. A few snapped commands to Six-six, and the mooring lines of the *Lucy B* were drawn clear. A minute, and the craft's auxiliaries were pounding in an urge up the river. At the helm the sleepy-eyed native pilot peered ahead as the captain swept his searchlight back and forth across the current.

Quickly they rounded a bend in the river and left the lights of Poeroek Tajoe behind. As the jungle's silence dropped about them, Drummond shut down his engines and for minutes listened in the stillness. From far ahead came the steady chug-chug of a motor's exhaust. They were on the right trail. The launch that had cleared the dock was pushing its way up the river ahead of them. Quickly Drummond again urged the *Lucy B* on her course.

Hours passed. Several times Drummond ordered his engines halted and listened. Evidently the handicapped for speed. The pound-pursued launch had the *Lucy B* ing exhaust had faded with the *Lucy B's* second halt. Still Drummond felt confident of his course. With his searchlight sweeping about, there was little chance of the craft being passed unless it crawled into the jungle thickness bordering each river bank. Positiveness of the identity of those in the launch made that unlikely.

It was near midnight when the captain, sighting a sudden straightening of the river's course, again ordered the engines silenced. As the night went quiet save for the hiss of the current against the *Lucy B's* prow, a dull, throbbing rumble drifted to his ears. A minute he listened. The soft pat of bare feet caused him to turn. Six-six was advancing toward his position in the bow. The eyes of the Javanese seemed to glisten white in the glowing reflection of the searchlight. The big native's lips rolled meaningly. "*Saja,*" came his whisper. "*Bagoose. Dayong* magic drum say, much trouble."

Drummond listened again. He recognized now the broken beats of rumbling jungle drums. Beats that, like the roll of far-off thunder, seemed to drift through the night in waves of sound, now low and solemn, now raising quickly to a wild, mad cadence as if shrieking the pent up tension behind them. The eyes of the Javanese Six-six grew wider in the searchlight's glow as the rolling drum beats held to their weird tempo.

"*Saja,*" suddenly spoke the native again, a note of awe in his voice, "better we go back. Them *toh drums.* They speak much bad. Bad for *tuan.*"

Drummond caught the native's arm. Six-six knew well the messages of drums, the jungle telegraph that sometimes even outdid in speed the magic wire of the white man's telegraph. Those drums were beating a message. A message to be caught up and relayed on to every river and jungle savage.

"Listen well, Six-six," Drummond whispered to the native at his side. "*Tuan* cannot turn back. He goes on. Read what the jungle drums say."

The silence of the night held about as both men harkened to the far-off rumble. To Drummond it was only a distant, meaningless booming, weird and captivating. To Six-six it seemed as a message of fear. His great eyes narrowed. His giant form grew tense. The hiss of the current past the *Lucy B's* side seemed to chant a melody to the rolling echo.

SUDDENLY THERE was a break in the far-off summons. A moment the night echoed in the silence. Then again they started. Six-six turned to the captain, his eyes leaping wide like saucers. His lips quivering as if in dread.

"*Dayong* make big magic," came his words. "Much magic to drive out *toh.* Drums say every man come. Much *tauva'u* to *mati dayong,* Kio-mo-uau."

Drummond scowled in the darkness. A feast of sacrifice to the dead medicine man Kio-mo-uau. Dead . . . until now Kio-mo-uau had been merely missing. Something new must have developed.

"Drums say Kio-mo-uau, *mati?*" he questioned. "Six-six is sure? They have found Kio-mo-uau's body?"

*"Baai tuan,"* Six-six answered. "They trap him *booayah,* find him Kio-mo-uau sign. Make big *tauva'u* feast now."

Drummond wondered. Kio-mo-uau had been missing for at least two months. What sign of identified death could authentically present itself after this length of time in the gruesome form Six-six mentioned?

Though the native Dyaks believed in the spirit of the crocodile, they also believed in revenge. If a relative is known to have been devoured by one of the reptiles, though the tribe will not set out to kill, they will set crude traps along the river shore at the supposed spot in the hope of catching the particular guilty crocodile. The trap is a monkey placed on a spit stick attached to a rattan line. The crocodile snapping the monkey carries the sharp pointed stick into its stomach and is trapped like a fish that has swallowed a hook. The crocodile is then pulled on to shore, disemboweled alive, and its stomach searched for some trace of identification to the missing relative's body. Evidently this is what had happened in the case of Kio-mo-uau.

It was possible. By some method unknown to native or white man, the crocodile is able to fasten the body of its victim to the river bottom and hold it there indefinitely, despite current and natural law of decomposition. Some body ornament or piece of official finery that could be identified as belonging to Kio-mo-uau may have been discovered in the stomach of the trapped crocodile and taken as positive proof of his death. Now would come the *tauva'u* ceremony to atone to the dead crocodile's spirit.

A worried frown flashed across Drummond's brow. The launch that had disappeared ahead . . . were they able to read the message of the drums? Could they translate their meaning and realize the danger they headed toward? The very tempo of the far-off drum beats vouched for the frantic frenzy into which the natives had worked themselves. It was a poor time for a white man to have his presence known.

Ordering Six-six to hold to his watch at the bow, Drummond hurried back to the wheelhouse. Starting again his engines, he snapped off the searchlight beam and bade the native pilot proceed as he might, without the light's aid. It was best that the *Lucy B's* presence be not known.

An hour later the *Lucy B* beamed a spot on the shore where the river swung into a wide bend as the jungle moved back to a low evenness. The captain marked his position. They were opposite the deserted *kampong* of the upriver concession. A few miles beyond were the river plantations of Pedro Pringo. Drummond held the *Lucy B* on her course.

Shortly, as the river again swung in its way, a sparkle of lights to one side the river bank loomed ahead. It was the river plantation quarters of Pedro Pringo. Drummond swung his craft into midstream as he worked his way past. He had no intention of landing boldly and making fast to Pringo's river wharves. For him, the thundering thump of the jungle drums beckoned with more importance. The heavy dampness of the midnight air now boomed leadenly with their pound. At half speed the *Lucy B* crept past the shore clearing and worked on up stream.

The jungle is too deceiving for any man to map by sound the exact location of drum beats, but as the river suddenly twisted ahead and seemed to close into a black alleyway, Drummond decided he had proceeded as far as he dared risk. Maneuvering the *Lucy B* close into shore, he succeeded in working her rigging into a tangle of the water edge growth and with the aid of a floating island of water hyacinths, camouflaged his craft so as to be invisible to any casual passing canoe that might venture by after daylight.

WITH THE silencing of the *Lucy B's* engines, the jungle drum beats rose to a thunderous roar. They were close, very close. The very water of the river seemed to carry the vibration.

Quickly Drummond summoned Six-six and ordered him to lower away the tiny dinghy dangling at the *Lucy B's* stern. Going below and arming himself with a rifle and a few extra rounds for the automatic at his hip, the captain made careful to muffle the oar locks of the launched dinghy as Six-six disappeared forward to re-appear in a minute with a long bladed *parang* at his wrist.

For once Drummond thanked his luck in having picked for a native pilot a Murut, one of a tribe not hampered by Dyak superstitions and beliefs. Instructing the pilot and his Chinese *jonges* to merely see that the *Lucy B* remained well concealed in her camouflage should they not return by daylight, he ordered Six-six on up the river. Pulling in long, silent strokes, the giant Javanese breasted the sluggish current.

Quickly they rounded the point ahead and, holding to midstream, followed the river's twisting course. The boom of the drums grew louder. Twisting to the river's winding, Drummond became conscious of a growing redness in the black skies ahead. Quickly he learned the cause.

Around a protruding finger of the jungle into the river and ahead of them, a dozen leaping fires appeared upon the shore. Black shadows danced in and out of them and above the rumble of the drums now sounded a weird jungle chant.

Drummond signalled Six-six to hug the opposite shore. A wide bend of the river had cut the bank here almost perpendicular. In the ghastly reflection of red light from the dancing fires, the captain sought its black shadows for protection. Silently they rowed on. Slowly the figures on the opposite shore took form. Leaping, waving forms dancing in and out of their fires and moving to the tempo of their haunting jungle chant.

They were now almost opposite the scene. Only the hundred or so feet of the river separated them from the wild picture on the opposite shore. Ahead, a barren point pushed out into the river like the apron of a stage, its bank a dozen feet high, its surface clear of jungle growth. Drummond feared to risk passing the point. Grasping a rattan tangle along the bank, he signaled Six-six to lay on his oars while he held the dinghy steady to the rattan mooring. The protruding stage of lifted land acted as a shield to the light across. He began studying the actions of the shoremassed natives.

Back and forth the savages danced, to the rumble of drums and tap of gamelan. Now and then would come a break in which a procession would march to the water's edge, pause as they howled in their chant, then cast something wiggling and squealing out into the river current. The quick thrash of water off shore shrieked its hazard. Shrieked, as well, the meaning of the pompous ceremony. The natives were offering sacrifice to the waiting crocodiles at the shore edge, of live dogs, pigs and fowl. A feast to the devil god. *Tauva'u* . . . sacrifices to the spirit of the crocodiles as the reptiles, seeming to scent the call, flocked in the thrashed water off shore.

Drummond's jaws set hard as he watched. Nothing had been exaggerated in the report of Von Dorn or the resident controleur at Poerock Tajoe. The savages were whipped to a mood receptive of any atrocity.

As he watched a sudden awed moan arose from the shore. An excited chatter that died in a mingle of terrified groans. Every dancer upon the shore across dropped prone and with wails and pleading cries faced the elevated stage of land within whose shadow rested the captain's boat.

An instant Drummond was puzzled. All eyes seemed to be turned to him. A moment he thought perhaps the dinghy had been sighted. Then as quickly the thought erased itself as from the river bank above him came a curious hissing sound, with now and then a belch of white light which flashed across the shore's blackness.

Drummond rose to his feet and made to peer above the bank alongside. The sound with its flashing beam came from his side of the river. It was toward this the savages on the opposite shore faced. Pulling the dinghy in closer, he made fast its painter to the rattan tangle and, stepping ashore crawled on his stomach to the raised ground above.

The sight that met his eyes froze him. There, squirming and twisting in a setting of inky blackness, showed plain the ghastly, glowing form of a giant crocodile, its eyes two piercing disks of fiery red, its mouth opening now and then to belch forth a tongue of red flame. From across the shore the moaning wail arose to a drone of the beating drums.

The spirit of the *tauva'u*. The captain was seeing it with his own eyes. Seeing a bit of jungle magic ghastly even to the blood of a white man. A bit of jungle sorcery, weird and terrifying.

Drummond felt a move behind him. Six-six had crawled to his side. Wide-eyed, he, too, stared at the haunting scene. He seemed to silently plea to the captain for an explanation.

"*Dayongs*, make big magic. White man magic," Drummond whispered. "We go see who belong. Maybe so bad magic."

The simple words "white man magic" seemed to satisfy the Javanese. He had seen greater white man magic than this in association with his master. If the captain said white man magic, there was nothing to fear. He followed as Drummond began crawling forward.

A DOZEN paces as they worked their way back into the jungle's growth fencing the river stage, and Drummond understood the queer phenomenon before them. With the fires of the shore across between them and the moving phantom, the deception leaped clear as an illusion from behind stage. The squirming form ahead was the hide of a crocodile covered with a coat of luminous paint and draped over a man. Against the jungle darkness across, it loomed lifelike and ghastly. The reflecting red disks of the eyes were undoubtedly merely red glass lenses catching up the firelight from across. The shot of flame from the form's mouth, a deception of red light from a flashlight. Against the firelight from across the river, Drummond caught even the sight of a white trouser leg lifted clear of the grass as the crocodile form moved about. It was no naked native making this jungle magic.

The phantom crocodile was now

beginning to work its way back from the river edge. Across, the moaning wails of the opposite shore still echoed in the night. Drummond made his plan. Quickly he crawled forward in a course to cut the retreat of the ghostly spirit at the jungle edge. Six-six followed at his heels.

Suddenly he felt a tramped path beneath his feet. The moving phantom was now but a few yards away, moving directly toward him. Drummond stepped back, pulling Six-six with him. A minute, and the glowing, ghastly shape passed, a bare leap away. The captain allowed its squirming form to bury itself in the jungle undergrowth, then hurled himself forward. Down into the underbrush tangle he went, his arms wrapped about the middle of the glowing shape as it suddenly attempted to raise erect.

A startled cry of surprised terror sounded from beneath the stiff mask of crocodile hide. Six-six, his cue taken from the captain's leap, grabbed beneath the form and now straightening erect, lifted aloft by his feet the trousered legs of a man half peeled from beneath the crocodile hide. Drummond's rifle pressed against the dangling head below as his voice hissed silence. Then with his own hand the captain peeled the victim free of the disguise. The teeth of the man tossed prone upon the ground, chattered in terror as his fear-stricken eyes caught the dim glare of the reflected firelight from across the river.

"Who are you? Quick! Quick! or out you go to feed them damn crocodiles." Drummond's fingers clutched his victim's throat.

The voice of the man below him seemed to choke for breath. "No! No! No, senor," came the gasp. "It is I . . . I, Pedro Pringo. Careful! *Por Dios,* careful, senor. You big government man . . . you know those devils across, they see us, we all die, *tauva'u.*"

The captain did not need the plea of his victim to realize the hazard of discovery. From across the river now came a riot of wild shouting and screaming. The jungle echoed with its chaos. The black figures prancing in and out of the leaping fires framed the meaning. Across, the jungle audience had been moved into a hysteric frenzy by sight of the moving jungle spirit that had loomed in its ghastly glow with blood-sparkling eyes and spit of flame from its tongue. Their minds had reverted back a thousand years in the tow of their ancestral superstition. Their weird chant echoed through the night.

Drummond pulled Pedro Pringo to his feet and, masked by the black shadows of the jungle curtain at his back, pushed his face close for a sight of the plantation owner.

"What's the meaning of this, Pringo?" his words bit, as his hand gripped into the Portuguese's shirt collar. "Why are you working this native magic in the face of these already crazed savages?"

"Quiet, senor; quiet," shivered the cringing Portuguese, as the sound of the captain's maddened voice, above the shrieks of the tumult across, carried loud in the jungle. "It is the only way. The only hope. Look, they make *tauva'u* now. *Tauva'u* to the spirit of Kio-mo-uau. No white man is safe in the jungle now. They know a *tuan* is responsigle for the loss of their *booayah* god spirit. They know a *tuan* has killed Kio-mo-uau."

"What *booayah* god?" Drummond shouted, as he shook the trembling Portuguese by the shoulder. "How do they know a *tuan* killed Kio-mo-uau?"

as, on the opposite shore, again sounded the pitiful squeal of live pigs as they were tossed into the river in sacrifice to the water-churning crocodiles beyond. "They know, senor. Only a *tuan* would rob the *booayah* of its spirit eyes. Only a *tuan* would dare lay a hand upon them. They know, senor, for to-day was found the green eye of the *booayah* wrapped in a magic bag carried always by Kio-mo-uau himself."

A MINUTE Drummond groped for words as he held the plantation owner, still struggling to bury himself deeper in the jungle. To the captain's mind leaped vague rumors of the *booayah* god as he had heard them from drifting natives' gossip. A giant crocodile carved from iron wood and mounted on a pedestal of stone somewhere in the jungle worship grounds along the river. A carved god that all the tribes worshiped in hope of protection from the river reptiles. Drummond knew nothing of the spirit eyes of which Pringo spoke so terrified. Some sacred charm attached to the carved image, he reasoned, as he pulled Pringo close to him. Some sacred omen that perhaps held the key to all this present demonstration.

"These spirit eyes, what are they? When were they stolen?" he barked, as he pulled Pringo about so that in the reflected glow from across the river he could see the man's contorted features.

"Senor, senor," the Portuguese only babbled, "you big government man, Pedro Pringo knows. Mantos tell him you come but Pedro Pringo is innocent. He has done nothing but seek to return to the natives what is their's. Pedro Pringo is innocent, senor. Innocent of all. He is not the guilty one."

"Innocent, eh?" Drummond growled, as his hand twisted tighter around Pringo's collar. "You look innocent, all right. Where is Mantos? Why did you run away from Poeroek Tajoe tonight? Why did you try to get me with a blow gun? Where's the girl that was in your launch when you skipped up the river? Answer me quick. Where is she? Where is your launch?"

"Senor, senor, Por Dios, Pedro Pringo does not try to lie," Pringo moaned. "My *jonges* warn me jungle drums say big *tauva'u* to-night. For months, senor, I have kept the men of my plantation at ease by this magic you saw me use to-night. They think it the spirit of Kio-mo-uau and are peaceful. This is their sacred worship grounds, senor, and they believe the spirit of Kio-mo-uau still here. To-night, though, they learn different. To-night they know Kio-mo-uau is dead and that the fire eye of the *booayah* has been stolen. They are mad for blood. *Tuan* blood, to offer as sacrifice to the *booayah* god."

A faint understanding flashed across Drummond with Pringo's words. This explained in part why the natives about Pringo's concession had not felt the unrest of the lower river tribes. Pringo, with his native knowledge of tribe worship and superstition, had stepped into the missing *dayong* Kio-mo-uau's place and played out the magic in his stead. The natives believed Kio-mouau's spirit still was with them. Believed it until to-day when the medicine man's magic bag which was always considered as a part of the dayong himself, had been discovered in the stomach of a trapped crocodile. The presence of but one spirit eye from the missing idol spelt plain to even the primitive native mind that the other had been stolen. The eye was too sacred for the hand of any but a white man to touch. The fear of its curse was too great for any native believer or unbeliever.

Drummond reasoned fast. Pringo's fear was genuine. He had undoubtedly told the truth. Their own position was a hazardous one. If they were truly upon the ground of the worshiping spot of the tribe, there was little danger of search as long as they remained unseen. Native superstition made the worship ground too sacred for an ordinary tribesman to tread. But if Pringo had sought its safety upon being warned by his *jonges,* what had become of Mantos and the girl, Tretner's sister? Drummond knew now it was they he had seen in that moment's flash of his searchlight back at Poeroek Tajoe.

"Your launch, where is it?" the captain snapped at Pringo, as the shrieks from the opposite shore seemed to never die. "Will the natives discover it by daylight?"

"No, senor, it is hidden well off the point," Pringo answered. "Mantos has seen to that. I left him while I made *dayong* magic."

"Left him?" Drummond repeated. "And the girl, where is she?"

Pringo seemed to hesitate as if fearing to answer.

THE TWIST of Drummond's collar grip choked the words from him. "She . . . she is safe," he sputtered. "She is in the launch with Mantos."

"Why did you bring her here?" the captain growled. "Why did you smuggle her past Poeroek Tajoe without reporting to the controller?"

"It was not me, senor," Pringo stammered back. It was Mantos. He brought her here in threat to her brother. He brought her here to force her brother to offer ransom."

"Ransom," Drummond exploded in disgust. "Young Tretner pay ransom?"

"*Si,* senor; ransom. Her brother has it. It is he that has the sacred stolen fire eye of the *booayah* god. A gem, senor . . . a jewel worth a fortune. It is he that broke all of Mantos' plans."

A sudden realization gripped the captain. The sacred fire eye of the *booayah.* A gem . . . a jewel worth a fortune. Young Tretner held it. It was the ransom demanded for his sister's safety. The dawn of an understanding flashed through Drummond's brain. He understood now the mass of queer circumstances surrounding the polished jewel resting this moment in his jacket pocket. Understood the trend of circumstances that had led to its possession. Understood Mantos and his plot.

Undoubtedly Mantos had been the power guilty of the attempt to gain for Pringo a lease to the entire concession. Undoubtedly it was he who had thought out the plan to create native unrest among the concession natives, yet still hold those of Pringo's concession at peace. Perhaps it was even he who had been responsible for the trouble at the coagulation plant, necessitating the presence of a chemist on the grounds. Tretner had perhaps been the underlying cause of it all.

An instant Drummond groped for a solution to the still untangled circumstances. Mantos might have easily created this unrest among the natives by destroying the *booayah* image and stealing its spirit eyes. But if the supposition that now toyed in his brain were true, how had young Tretner gained possession of the jewel? Could it be that Tretner had been hand in hand with Mantos and did the work? Could it be . . .

The captain stopped short. From the opposite river bank a sudden hushing silence had dampered the cries of the shrieking natives to an awed groan. A moaning stir in the silence seemed to reek the warning. Drummond whirled about to face the dancing fire glows upon the opposite bank. His breath caught in a queer hiss as his eyes stared at the single erect shadow moving with slow, faltering stride along the very edge of the river bank to the center of the stage-like worshiping grounds. A tossed-haired figure silhouetted against the firelight's glow. The figure of a woman.

"*Dios mio,* it is her. It is her," came the moaning whisper of Pringo as his eyes caught the captain's sight. "It is the girl."

Drummond barely heard the words. His own eyes had identified as well. The black shadow moving across the shore was that of a girl. From Pringo's own lips it was the girl he had left concealed in his launch with Mantos.

A sudden angry mumble rose from the opposite shore. Black shadows dashed about as voices screamed and outstretched arms pointed. The natives had sighted the girl. Sighted her and responding to the wild fever that had gripped them during the night, now gave vent to the rage that expressed itself in the sight of a human upon the jungle floor of their sacred worship grounds.

Realization gripped the captain. The girl was doomed. Her very presence was an act of desecration to the worship grounds. Already the herd upon the opposite bank screamed it. Already they were shoving their *proas* into the river and were rushing across the stream toward the guilty one.

For themselves there was still a chance. The natives in their frenzy would not search the island. Nor would they kill at once the intruder on their worship ground. The Dyak striving for the title of medicine man to fill the position of the now dead Kio-mo-uau would grasp this as too much of an opportunity for power to demand instant death. Death would come, but it would be one to the magic-maker's liking.

DRUMMOND'S blood pounded through his veins as he watched the native canoes slide through the water. On the shore the figure of the girl stood as if paralyzed in fear. Fear or, unrealizing the danger ahead, hope. A curse fell from the captain's lips as he whirled to Pringo.

"Quick! Your launch, where is it?" he barked at the Portuguese. "There is still a chance. We can ram right into them as they recross the river."

"Senor, senor . . . not now. Wait," the fellow pleaded. "First we hide until they go."

"Hide and let them put that girl through the torture their *dayong* will make up for her? Where's that launch? Quick, or by God . . ."

The Portuguese had caught the raise of Drummond's rifle. As quickly he began skirting along the screening edge of the jungle. The screams from across the river drowned the sound of their hurrying foot crashes. The shadows of the lashing proas across the river carried below the level of the raised bank. Boldly, caution cast aside, they rushed toward the river bank as they held to the worship grounds' framing curtain of jungle, Pringo leading, the captain with poised rifle behind him, Six-six bringing up the rear.

The natives were landing upon their side of the river bank now. Some fear of touching foot to the sacred worshiping ground seemed to hold them. The delay was enough for the rushing trio at the edge of the jungle to gain the drop of the bank. Then, with the screen of a moment's safety but a dozen paces away, a piercing scream from beyond sent them dropping flat to the jungle grass. The natives from the landed proas were streaming up the elevated bank.

Barely raising his head, Drummond watched. The crouching shadows of the approaching natives as they slowly circled the motionless girl showed plain. In the dawn's ghost of light the sudden piercing scream that sprung from the trapped girl's lips echoed through the jungle as the black circle closed in. A torturous minute. The captain's rifle raised and lay drawn to the toss of waved hair. Then the natives rushed their captive to the edge of the bank. Rushed, but did not disappear. Across the bank they howled their capture as they hearkened for the voice of their *dayong* for instructions.

In that instant the sudden chug of a coughing motor below the drop of the bank at the river's edge caught Drummond's ear. A flame of rage swept him. It must be Mantos. Mantos attempting to start Pringo's launch. He forgot caution. A squirm through the grass, and he slipped to the edge of the bank. Almost below him lay the launch. In the growing light he saw the crouched form of Mantos over the engine's flywheel. Already Mantos had pulled the launch clear of the rattan tangle at the bank's edge. The launch's beam was but a leap away.

Drummond dropped his rifle and crouched for a leap. Mantos suddenly glanced up from his task. His eyes were like burning coals as he sighted the captain's poised form. His teeth seemed to bare in a snarl as Drummond hurled himself forward in a leap that carried his clutching hands to the launch's cowling.

His fingers gripped as he made to draw himself into the cockpit. His eyes swung up, flashed the danger above but before he could even twist his body free, the engine crank in Mantos' hand swung down.

Blackness dropped about Drummond. By instinct his fingers still gripped the cowling as he fought the sweep of unconsciousness. He felt the grip of Mantos' hand at the throat of his jacket. Felt the push of Mantos' fingers against his jacket pocket. Felt and as his ears gathered Mantos' hissing curse, realized what was happening to himself. Mantos had gripped him and, holding him to the side of the boat, was fumbling at his jacket pocket where, aboard the *Lucy B*, Montos had once seen the captain stow the ruby given him by the dying Tretner.

Fighting back to consciousness, Drummond heard the chug of a racing engine as a mamoth hand grabbed his belt and pulled him on to the shore.

"He's leaving us marooned. He's pulling away," came the scream of Pringo's voice, as the captain, supported erect in the arm of Six-six, shook his head to clear his senses. "Look! Look! He's running for it alone."

Drummond snapped to himself. His hand grasped his jacket pocket. The ruby was gone. His unconscious groping senses had been right as to the feel of Mantos' fingers.

ABOVE THE road of the launch, now fighting for for speed as Mantos attempted to maneuver its bow about, came the shrieks from the opposite shore. The proas that had touched the worship ground and were now carrying the captured girl across, had not yet landed. Now they turned their craft down the stream. Down stream to where Mantos, suddenly erect in the cockpit of the launch, held his one hand above him. A round blaze of red brightness glittered between his fingers, hurled a taunting curse at the trapped men on shore. Hurled, but never repeated.

From Drummond's side came a singing swish. A deep grunt, and out across the space between the marooned trio and the swinging launch lurched a streak of brightness. Lurched with the speed of an arrow. A twisting blade of brightness that seemed to travel invisibly, leap through space and strike the standing Mantos with a force that hurled him backward over the cockpit and into the churning water. On shore, the lips of Six-six bared in a grin. The long blade parang was no longer in his hand.

Drummond barely stifled the cry upon his lips as he groped for his rifle. If Six-six's aim had not been sure, his own would be. The launch, her helm cramped over to make the swing within the river, now held to its circle. Its bow headed back toward shore. As her churned wake swept in a circle, the captain caught the sight of Mantos' battling fists as he fought for the surface. Six-six's blade had not been fatal. He was attempting to swim. His hands thrashed the water.

Then with a suddenness warned only by the click of snapping jaws, a green, slimy, gray head rose and lifted at Mantos' side. A great flat head, cut with a long bleeding gash where a propeller blade had slashed against it. The head of a crocodile, its tail whipping in a blind rage, its eyes flashing flame. A dull click of its jaws and the outstretched hand of Mantos disappeared. In the same instant the water about him thrashed wild. Now and then a sweeping tail arched through the air. Now and then an ugly head raised and glared. The hands of Mantos never again reached up.

Drummond shuddered as he stared. The crocodiles had Mantos. The leap of a proa around the point snapped him to his own position. On the shore opposite a black melee of naked savages raced to a point across from them. Proas were being slipped into the water at every point. The war cries of those ashore were already being drowned by the beat of battle drums.

Drummond appraised the impossibility of their giving hopeful battle even as he sighted the launch of Pringo suddenly push its circling nose into a rattan tangle of shore a dozen yards below. They might reach the launch, but what of the girl? Better death for all than leave her a captive with these savages.

A half dozen proas had rounded the point and now leaped toward them. The sheen of naked spear blades caught in the vaulting sun above the jungle crest. Drummond raised his rifle to his shoulder and drew down on the nearest naked form. Then, as he sighted across the water, a crimson-stained blot in the river current caught his eyes. A spreading blot suddenly rising. The great, slimy head of the crocodile with the wide propeller gash above its eyes.

A desperate hope flashed through Drummond's brain. A hope gruesome in its very thought. The crocodile, the same reptile that had disappeared with Mantos' clinched hand. There was a chance. A chance in a thousand, but a chance to grasp at.

The rifle in the captain's hand swung to the side. An instant it drew down on the mammoth gray-green head in its frame of crimson. Then as his finger pressed the trigger, the rifle roared its report across the river. Roared and echoed as off shore the great crocodile thrashed the water in its death agony.

Sound of the gun's report seemed to check the natives in their rush. An instant they stood undecided whether to take to the jungle in face of the white man's roaring magic or rush on. An instant they waited for some urge from the shore. Drummond seized the moment.

"Let he that is *dayong* of the tribe step forward," he bellowed across the river. "I bring a message to him from Big Government."

Again and again Drummond repeated his words, shouting with all the strength of his voice. His bold front, coupled with the rifle in his hand and the words "Big Government," seemed to check the natives for a moment in their madness. He repeated his cry, adding now a slur as to whether the great *daong*, with all his magic, feared the voice of a *tuan*.

SUDDENLY ACROSS the river bank a gayly decorated figure came forward. Drummond caught the move. As well he caught sight of the proas barely off the opposite shore in one of which was the girl captive. Barely whispering a command to Six-six to work Pringo's launch clear and toward them, he faced the native across.

"Big Government has heard the magic of the *dayong*," Drummond began. "Big Government has heard the plea. Big Government has said make *tauva'u* no more. White man magic is better. I make white man magic. Let you that are brave seek the *mati booayah* within the water and learn the power of white man magic. The Big Government make *tauva'u* with invisible hand. Let the *dayong* seek proof of *tuan's* words."

Drummond pointed out into the river to where the great dead crocodile now floated slowly down stream. An awed murmur drifted through the lined river bank on the opposite side. The captain's words had been understandable. He invited them to seek proof. Proof that the white man's magic was greater than the *dayong's* power of *tauva'u*. The *dayong* on the shore opposite dared not ignore the challenge.

Quickly a half dozen canoes skipped across the water toward the floating carcass of the crocodile. Soon they had it in tow and were making toward the shore where stood the *dayong*, a naked bladed *creese* in his hand. Drummond glanced down the shore. Six-six was tugging to bring Pringo's launch against the shore current as its still churning propeller pushed against him.

Across, the great crocodile was now being dragged on to shore. About the river bank a circle of canoes held against the stream, awaiting what comand might come from their medicine man. The *dayong* pushed the shore crowd roughly back as he cleared a stage about him. Then into the crocodile's gray belly he plunged his *creese*.

The hushed awe from across was the moment Drummond had been waiting for. A quick step and, signaling the crouched Pringo to follow, he leaped into the launch. The motor was still chugging as Mantos had left it. A quick boost and the captain landed in the cockpit. His hand grabbed the helm as he shouted to Six-six to push the bow out. Away from the bank swung the craft. Away and toward the opposite shore where, seated in a beached proa, loomed the hand-covered face of the girl.

The launch was darting ahead even before the natives ashore seemed to realize. A low mutter of astonishment had risen from the circling crowd about the *dayong* and the dead form of the crocodile. Now, as the launch darted across stream, a great cry went up from those upon shore. A chaos of wild commotion seemed to release itself as by signal. The speeding launch seemed ignored. Every native was running toward the closing circle about the *dayong*. Running and screaming as they waved their arms about. Even in the canoe where the girl was held a prisoner, the two guarding natives seemed to forget their charge and go dashing for shore with the rest. For an instant the girl was alone.

Drumomnd swung his craft in. Six-six stood poised at the bow. A second the launch scraped the shore. A leap to the proa, a grab of the terrified captive within, and Six-six was scrambling back aboard. The captain threw his lever into reverse.

Ashore a hundred voices were raising in a wild chant. Drummond barely heard as with one hand on the automatic at his belt, he maneuvered his craft's bow down the river. Then as he suddenly pulled his clutch into forward and threw his spark wide, he felt the grip of Pringo's hand upon his arm.

"Look! Look!" the Portuguese was muttering, as his eyes opened wide in an unbelievable stare. "It has been returned. It has come back. Look! The *dayong* holds the sacred eye of the *booayah* spirit in his hand!"

Ashore, the *dayong*, his blood dripping *creese* still in one hand, held above his head a round, flaming, red jewel which sparkled in the sunlight. At his feet lay the opened belly of the dead crocodile. The spirit of the crocodile had given up its omen. The sacred omen held in Mantos' hand as he went to his end amidst the snapping jaws of the river reptiles. The spirit fire eye of the *booayah* was back amid its worshippers.

AS THE *Lucy B* pushed her way down stream to the pound of her auxiliaries, a distant booming of jungle drums seemed to keep in rhythm with their pound. A pleasing rhythm as if the drums vibrated themselves in a message of joy. Above, the jungle sky hovered with its star-studded haze, seeming to echo the far-off rumble with a weird hollowness. Drummond glanced up from his chair at the stern. For'd, the eyes of Six-six sparkled in the darkness.

"Drums say *baai toh* come, *saja*," the giant Javanese spoke, as he arose and touched the fingers of his left hand first to the captain and then to the young girl seated upon a rattan chair at the captain's side. "Drums say *booayah* spirit come stay. No more *tauva'u*. Say every man come big *tuba feast*. Say white man magic belong better *tauva'u*."

Drummond only nodded.

"What does he mean?" the voice of the girl sounded, as she turned toward the captain. "What does he mean, *tauva'u?*"

"Just a form of native worship, Miss," he answered dryly. "A rather gruesome form. It merely means the natives are satisfied. The *tuba* feast and a week to sober up, and they'll all be ready for work again, I hope."

"But that man Pringo . . . at the dock when you left him, he was explaining something to you I didn't quite understand. Something about my brother and about this . . . this *tauva'u*."

"Pringo will do a lot more explaining when this report of mine reaches the government officials," Drummond added. "About your brother. You see, Miss, this dead medicine man Pringo was telling me about, Kio-mo-uau, he was a great friend of your brother's. Your brother used to give him little chemical tricks to work as magic, such as luminous paint that would glow at night and pieces of metallic sodium that would burn in water. Kio-mo-uau recognized your brother as knowing more magic than he and catered to him for the knowledge. For that reason your brother was given the privilege not even extended to a native chief, that of being allowed to visit the sacred worship grounds. That was one of the ways Kio-mo-aua took to show his appreciation for what magic your brother showed him."

"And this sacred jewel you spoke of to Pringo," the girl cut in quickly. "The ruby, he gave that too. Flex never . . . never . . ."

"Your brother is dead," Drummond said kindly. "Whatever may have been his faults, they have gone with him. However, he was no thief. Being on the grounds, he could not help but surmise Mantos' plan to gain for Pringo control of the concessions by native unrest so that he could profit with Pringo. Your brother was not in on that plan. We'll probably never know if Mantos murdered Kio-mo-uau and threw his body into the river or bribed one of the jungle tribesmen to do it for him. Enough that Kio-mo-uau was murdered and fed to the crocodiles. The ruby, your brother had that in his possession when he learned of Mantos' deed and that he intended to destroy the wooden image of the *booayah* in which it set."

The girl leaned forward anxiously. Drummond drew nervously on his cigar as he glanced for'd a moment to where the squatted Six-six sat grinning widely at the captain's uneasiness.

"You see, Miss," the captain went on, "Kio-mo-aua brought the ruby to your brother to make a bit of magic with it. Some kind of a simple rig up like a flashlight bulb behind it so as to make it sparkle at night. When Kio-mo-uau saw how the contraption worked, he returned for the other, the green eye, to have it made the same. It was on the return trip that he was murdered. Meanwhile, your brother had discovered the worth of the jewel and the crime Mantos had engineered, and fearing that he might be brought in for a part of the blame, he left the country.

IN HIS letters to you which he sent through Pringo so you would not know he had left his position and was in Singapore, he told all about the ruby and how he had gained possession of it. Of course those letters never reached you, no more than the letters you wrote reached him in their original form. Mantos forged the handwriting of both of you."

"Those . . . those are the letters you promised to let me read when we reach Poeroek Tajoe," the girl cut in. "Those are the letters Pringo gave you?"

"Yes, Miss," Drummond answered. "Pringo gave me the originals but I'll have to sort of hang on to them until the controleur at Poeroek Tajoe has satisfied himself. Then they're yours. You see, Pringo is really not so terribly guilty. He was more of a goat for Mantos. When he saw the natives were getting beyond even the power of his magic, he went after Mantos to have everything returned and the tribe pacified.

"Of course, no doubt Mantos really intended to get the jewel for its true worth. Pringo swallowed the plan to have you come here and then demand the ruby from your brother as ransom only because he wished to stop the native unrest. Mantos might have had other plans but Pringo was never in on them. Frankly, I believe Mantos intended doing away with Pringo once he saw his plan slipping, in the same manner that he did away with Kio-mo-aua. There is no doubt now, Miss. Mantos planned even your brother's murder. It'll be easily proven once we reach Singapore."

"Singapore," the girl repeated. "You are taking me there on your boat?"

"Why . . . why that depends, Miss," Drummond spoke, as he squirmed nervously. "I'll have to cable the home office for instructions first. The *Lucy B* is not exactly equipped for lady passengers. I'm afraid the journey would prove rather monotonous for you."

"The opposite, Captain, I'm sure," the girl replied, hurriedly. "I know I would enjoy listening to something of yourself. Something of your own life here in the South Seas. I'm sure you could tell me much of interest. Things that . . ."

Drummond barely nodded his head for'd. Against the wheelhouse bulkhead Six-six scrambled to his feet and hurried to his side.

"*Saja tuan,*" his voice whispered.

The girl glanced up wonderingly at the mumble of Malayan.

Drummond bowed apologetically. "Six-six says I'm needed at the wheel," he lied clumsily. "I'll see you in the morning. Good evening."

Then as he turned and faced the grinning Six-six he muttered, "*Trima kasih, jonges.* To which Six-six nodded understandingly. The captain was no hand with the ladies.

# RIGL ER'S THIRD ROUND

WHEN THE *Martin Jornsen* hove to in the treacherous harbor of Makassar, on the southern peninsular of the Celebes, the heathen gods in their respective heavens must have stared into each other's faces and frowned. After frowning, those same gods of the Celebes—Shiva, Buddha, Lao-Tze, Mohammed, and a hundred smaller deities—must have opened the big black book and scratched down the word *murder.*

There were reasons. Blood and knives run thick in the Celebes, even in the best of times. And the *Martin Jornsen,* being an unlovely tramp schooner of evil reputation, added a cut-throat crew of twenty half-breeds to the blood and knives already there.

In addition, the *Martin Jornsen*

by

**HUGH B. CAVE**

brought its Captain Kirk Waller; and Waller, too, had a reputation. The reputation was the result of two scarred fists, a hard revolver, six-feet-four of dirty carcass, and an ugly temper. Little wonder that the native gods muttered the word *murder!*

"There's two things," Waller said when he went ashore, "that I'm itchin' for. One's a damn good fight and the other's a stiff drink. What d'ye say, you lousy little wharf rat?"

The lousy little wharf rat said nothing. Old man Rigler was used to saying nothing, especially when Waller was within hearing. When a man has been kicked and rough-handled for two years, he learns to close his mouth.

Waller thrust the old man out of the way. It mattered little that old Arnold Rigler was second mate of the *Martin Jornsen.* Waller was captain.

But later, when Waller had lurched across the wharf and disappeared, Rigler shuffled across the deck of the schooner and leaned over the forecastle.

"Tommy!" he shouted.

The boy came up, like a monkey. Rigler's boy. A year ago the old man had found him in some filthy native hole, and brought him back to the ship. And now, leaning on the boy's arms, Rigler went ashore.

IT WAS fate that brought Rigler and the boy to a certain native saloon near the waterfront, half an hour later. The saloon was crowded, and stunk. Sinister faces were staring through the cigarette smoke. And Waller—drunk with bad whiskey—was leaning on the counter.

A glass, half filled, stood on the counter in front of the captain. He picked it up and held it with unsteady hands. He was grinning.

"So yer come after me, did yer—you pot-bellied bag o' bones! An' yer brought yer snivvelin' kid along for a drink. Hey?"

"Tommy doesn't drink," the old man said quietly. "You know that."

"He don't? Then what the hell did he come here for—to watch *me* drink? Here—feed it to him."

Rigler shook his head, very slowly. It was an old head, with dirty white hair, but the eyes in it were bitter.

"I reckon I won't, Waller. Tommy can do without it."

The big captain's grin died out. He stepped forward, snarling, and gripped the boy's shoulder. Deliberately he thrust the glass under Tommy's mouth.

"Drink it, you white livered—"

Old Rigler's hand fell suddenly on his arm. The mate's face was close—very close—to Waller's leering lips.

"Let the boy alone, Waller."

"Let him—" But the bad whiskey brought Waller's savage temper to the top. He swung around. His fist, holding the glass, crunched into Rigler's face like a ram. Old Rigler stumbled backwards into a table and slid to the floor. His mouth—unconscious—was filled with bloody foam.

At the counter, Waller reached down and drew his revolver. Deliberately he pointed it at young Tommy's chest.

"Don't want you to drink, hey? You yellow skinned slum rat. Thinks you're too damned good for me—does he! He'll sing another line when he sees—"

He jerked the trigger, with a hellish laugh. The revolver spit straight into young Tommy's throat, as the boy shrank back.

The boy moaned, just once, and fell.

THAT WAS the first round. When it was over, and the *Martin Jornsen* pulled out of Makassar harbor, old man Rigler was lonely. More than that, his face —still scarred by the big renegade's fist—was full of slow, cruel hate. He had a score to settle. But he was an ancient, with thin shoulders and weak hands—and he knew it. He would have to wait.

He waited patiently. The *Martin Jornsen's* clumsy hulk wallowed slowly west, through the Java Sea south of Borneo. Up toward the equator, with blistering decks and sullen tempers.

Kirk Waller stayed drunk. He had brought with him, from Makassar, a brace of wooden cases, filled with Makassar whiskey. It was good protection against the heat but it came to a head, and foamed over, before the schooner reached the line.

Old Arn Rigler was at the wheel, alone on deck, except for a knot of half naked Malays who slouched near the rail. The sun was hot, and Rigler's hand went up at regular intervals to wipe the sweat from his face. The deck was bubbling in the seams.

There was no noise. The sea, slapping against the bow of the schooner, made the only sound. Even the Malays were quiet. And when the door of the companionway clattered open, with a splintering whack, it broke a hundred mad echoes.

Old man Rigler turned casually, and turned back again. He made no move to get out of the way; he was used to seeing Kirk Waller three-quarters drunk.

But this time Waller was more than drunk; he was frothing. Like an overgrown baboon he swayed there, staring at the old man. In his hand lay an empty bottle.

Rigler's back was toward him. Rigler was indifferent; he didn't care. But when two minutes had passed, and the deck had become strangely quiet, the old man turned slowly.

His lips tightened a little. The deck was deserted, except for the giant who stood there glaring at him. The Malays had crept fearfully out of range, where it was safe.

The old man, like a damned fool, turned his back again and stayed at the wheel. He should have known better.

Big Waller lurched forward. Rigler's indifference urged him on. He was drooling at the lips.

Half way to the wheel he jerked to a stop.

"You shrivelin' little pig you. *Turn around!*" The words ended in snarling curse.

Rigler turned quietly. Looked straight into the ape's face.

"Go to hell," he said.

Then he turned back again, and took hold of the wheel.

Waller gaped for a moment, while the old man's reply sunk in. Then, with an ugly growl, he swung the empty bottle back over his head. Rigler didn't see it. Rigler wasn't even looking.

The big man's arm came down. It was a powerful arm, and Waller's aim was good. The bottle whined across the deck like a shell. Struck the wheel, directly under old man Rigler's face. Crashed into a hundred stabbing splinters of glass.

Rigler stumbled back, let go the wheel suddenly and groped up with both hands to his face. Then, with a little sob, he fell to the deck.

And Kirk Waller, with a triumphant laugh, lurched away.

THE OLD MAN was blind after that, for a long time. His eyes were wrapped in dirty bandages. He had picked the slivers of glass out of his face, out of his eyes, with the blade of a jack-knife. Picked them out himself. But he never smiled now. The only thing that kept him alive was the thought of young Tommy, and the bits of glass.

The *Martin Jornsen* was north of the line when Rigler finally removed the bandages. He couldn't see much, even then. His eyes were streaked with crimson, and his face was full of little scars.

But three days later, Kirk Waller called him to the wheel and gripped his arm.

"Know where we're comin' to, you creepin' little mummy?" Waller growled.

Rigler shook his head. No, he didn't know.

"We're almost in Kuching," Waller told him. "An' down in the native quarter of Kuching are the lousiest, rottenest gamblin' dives in the East. Great place to clean up a lot of thick niggers—only you want to be damned sure they don't find out you got a lot of money. Any guy who totes money down there is likely to lose it, with a nigger knife in his back. Get me?"

The old man nodded. He looked up, thoughtfully.

"You like to gamble, eh?" he said casually.

"Me? I know enough tricks with a deck o' cards to clean out the whole of the South Seas. You're damned right I like to gamble—and when I get to Kuching—"

Old man Rigler didn't hear the rest of it. He was thinking to himself. When he went to his cabin, half an hour later, he pulled open his seaman's chest and took out a little green thing—and set it on the table.

It was a heathen god, made out of green glass. An ugly, squatting thing, no more than six inches high, with a face like an evil dream. And the eyes, glaring from deep sockets, were little globules of red glass. A long time ago, in a Pekin curio shop, Rigler had paid a man fifty cents for it.

He bent over it now, with his jack-knife, and dug out one of the red eyes. For a while he held it in his hand, studying it. Then he rubbed it on his shirt, to make it shine. After that he dropped it into his pocket and put the idol back in the chest.

TWO DAYS later, the *Martin Jornsen* dropped anchor among the Chinese junks and native sampans in Kuching Harbor, off the Sarawak Coast.

It was late that night when the old man went ashore. He took the smallest dory, and made very sure that Kirk Waller and the half-caste crew did not hear him. He went alone.

When he left the dory at the waterfront, he shuffled across the docks with quick steps and went straight to the native quarter. He was no stranger in those twisted, unlighted streets. He had been in Kuching before, many times, and knew every filthy doorway, every sinister hang-out, of the evil sector. He also knew precisely where to find the little curio shop of Huang Lee.

He went there, as quickly as his ancient legs would carry him. Half way down a particularly narrow street, he pushed open the door of the shop and entered. A moment later he was leaning over the counter in the musty interior, talking straight into the old Chinaman's face. A little red thing lay on the counter in front of him.

"How much is it worth?" the old man said quietly.

"How much?" The Chinaman

picked it up and looked at it—and smiled. "It is worth nothing, Rigler. It is made of glass."

Rigler's hand groped into his pocket. Came out again holding a number of silver coins. Very quietly he dropped the coins into Huang Lee's fingers.

"Tomorrow," Rigler said, "I will bring this stone to you, and there will be another man with me. You will look at the stone carefully, and tell me it is worth a lot of money. Understand?"

The Chinaman glanced down at his handful of coins, then looked into Rigler's face and smiled again.

"I understand," he said. "The bit of glass is worth much money—very much money. It is a ruby such as I have never seen before."

Rigler nodded, and went out. The red stone was once more nestling in his pocket; and when he crept into his cabin, aboard the *Martin Jornsen* half an hour later, he was grinning.

THE HEATHEN gods of the South Seas must have frowned again next morning. The *Martin Jornsen* swung at anchor, deserted except for the single half-breed who was on watch. Through the streets of Kuching's native quarter prowled the rest of the unlovely crew.

On deck, just before going ashore, Kirk Waller had swung around and gripped old man Rigler's shoulder.

"You're comin' with me, you green livered water snake," he growled. "I'm goin' to take you to the filthiest gamblin' dive in town an' show you how to clean up. Get movin'!"

"I was goin' to tag along anyway," Rigler answered quietly. "Wanted to see you show the niggers how to play poker."

And now, shuffling along beside the big captain, Rigler was smiling. Waller had led the way straight to the heart of the evil sector, and the route lay through the certain street that Rigler wanted. The street was still murky, even in daylight. The clumsy buildings on either side hung over the sidewalk like spiders, holding black doorways underneath. And one of those doorways, half way down the street, was the entrance to Huang Lee's curio shop. Yes, it was the same street.

Rigler's steps became slower, almost imperceptibly. Waller did not notice, nor did he notice that the old man's hand had slid suddenly into a ragged pocket and come out again. Rigler dropped something. Then, stooping abruptly, he bent down to pick it up.

"Wait a minute, Waller," he muttered. "Looks like I found something here. Maybe—good God!"

The old man was on his feet again, holding a little red stone between his fingers. The same little red stone. But he was gaping down at it now, with wide eyes, and his mouth was open.

"A ruby, Waller! An honest to God ruby! Look at it!"

Waller was standing over him, staring. The big man's eyes were narrowed. He took the stone doubtfully.

"May be nothin' but a chunk of glass," he muttered. "If it was worth anythin', you wouldn't 've found it lyin' on the street. Just a chunk of red glass."

"It's a ruby I tell you. Don't I know a stone when I see it?" Rigler's words were full of excitement.

The big man reached out and dropped the stone into Rigler's hand.

"Maybe," he growled. "You got to show me first."

Rigler said nothing. Very quietly he shuffled forward again, at the captain's side. But he was mumbling to himself a little, and he gripped the stone securely in his hand.

And then, an instant later, Rigler gripped the big man's arm. They had reached the musty doorway of Huang Lee's curio shop.

"Look here," Rigler whispered. "Maybe this guy—"

"Maybe he can tell you if your hunk of glass is worth anything, eh? Well, bring it in then, an' let's find out. You're a damned fool, Rigler."

Rigler grinned. He was still grinning when he dropped the stone on the counter, inside the Chinaman's shop. Waller, standing behind him, was watching the Oriental intently.

Huang Lee looked at the stone carefully. His face was impassive, almost—but his eyes glittered strangely. And Waller, watching him, noticed the eyes.

"What's it worth?" Waller said suddenly.

"I will give you—one hundred pounds."

"A hundred pounds!" Waller leaned forward abruptly. "Five hundred dollars—for that?"

Old Rigler was grinning; but the Chinaman evidently misunderstood the meaning of Waller's excitement. He clutched the stone with eager fingers.

"A thousand pounds," he said quickly. "The stone is a ruby. Never have I seen a ruby like it."

"A thousand pounds—" The words came thickly from Waller's lips. Then, turning sharply to old man Rigler, he seized the old man's wrist.

"Sell it, you damn fool!" he whispered.

Rigler shook his head, and took the stone out of Huang Lee's hand. He drew Waller back, where the Chinaman could not hear what he said. Then he said, very quietly:

"I'd be a fool to sell it, Waller. A damn fool. If it's worth five thousand dollars to this dirty Chink, I can get double that much from a white man. Let's get out of here!"

Waller hesitated. He was thick witted, but he saw the wisdom in the old man's words. He pulled Rigler to the door.

Huang Lee bent over the counter with one hand out-stretched.

"I will give you twelve hundred pounds!" he said shrilly.

Rigler grinned—and dropped the bit of red glass into his pocket.

"Sorry," he said. "It ain't for sale."

Then, with Waller close behind him, he went out.

FOR A long time Waller led the way through the gloomy streets of the native quarter. The big man's lips were tight pressed. He did not mention the ruby again—not once. But the thing was going over and over in his mind, and a scheme was taking form.

The scheme was complete, half an hour later, when Waller drew the old man into a certain saloon in the heart of the native quarter. There, dragging Rigler to the bar, the big renegade called for drinks.

For the next ten minutes Rigler remained at the bar, drinking the whiskey that Waller set before him. It was a lot of whiskey, and the old man drank it straight. The more he drank, the more he talked—and his voice was loud.

"Lucky guy I am, Waller. Pickin' up a ruby like that right out o' the gutter. Just imagine it—twelve hun'red pounds. Six thousan' dollars in American money!"

Waller grinned. His clever little scheme was beginning to work. The old man was already half drunk.

But the grin would have faded if Waller had turned around. Behind him, in the shadows of the saloon, four faces had turned stolidly to look at old man Rigler. Cunning faces, with crawling hair and thin, Singhalese lips. Any time a white man mentions six thousand dollars in the evil dens of Kuching, native hands linger very close to native knives. And the gods frown murder.

"'S a lot of money, Waller, six thousan' dollars is." Rigler was drinking more bad whiskey and talking in a louder voice than ever. "All I got to do is find some guy that wants to buy the ruby from me, and take 'is money. An' if I can't do that, I can go back to Huang Lee's place an' sell it to him for the six thousan' he offered me. Can't I, hey?"

Waller moved away, very softly. Deliberately he went across the room to a table in the corner, where three of his half breed crew were handling a deck of cards. On the table stood more whiskey.

Waller pulled back a chair and sat down.

"Count me in," he said curtly. "An' play poker. Never mind your lousy fan-tan. I want a white man's game."

One of the half-breeds dealt him a hand. They continued to play, in silence. And at the counter, ten yards away, old man Rigler continued to talk in a thick voice.

"Six thousan' dollars for a little bit of a ruby. Right here in my belt, Waller, an—"

The old man turned around, sheepishly. For the first time, seemingly, he noticed that the big renegade was not beside him. He stared drunkenly across the room. His eyes rested for an instant on the four silent yellow faces in the shadows near the door—and then he stumbled forward to the table where Waller was playing cards.

Waller looked up and shoved back a chair for him.

"Sit down and play a while, Rigler," he said. "You got plenty of money. There's whiskey here, too."

Rigler sat down. On the other side of the musty room, near the door, four pairs of cunning eyes—Singhalese eyes — were watching every move he made.

FOR AN HOUR, old man Rigler drank whiskey and played poker. At first he won, because Waller wanted him to win. The more he won, the more careless he got.

Then, slowly, the game changed. The cards in Waller's hand began to get better and better. Most of those cards came up from under the table; but the big man was clever, and no one—no one but old man Rigler—knew that he was cheating.

Rigler knew, but kept his mouth closed. He was drunk. He played listlessly. Each time he lost, he pulled more money out of his pockets, and grinned. And finally, after an hour of steady losing, he pulled out the little red piece of glass.

Ten minutes later he got up from the table. The grin was gone from his face: He was very, very dejected —but he was still drunk, and he still talked in a loud voice.

"Ain't it hell," he grumbled. "Here I goes an' picks up six thousand dollars all at once, and' then I lose it. You got the damndes' luck, Waller. I never see nothin' like it. Six thousan' dollars—all gone in an hour."

Waller grinned, and pushed back his chair. For a moment he looked at the ruby triumphantly; then he shoved it into his pocket and went to the bar. He drank one glass of whiskey. Then he went out, still grinning.

Old man Rigler, standing by the table lifted up a bottle and drained it. As he held it to his lips, he glanced over the top of it, and smiled. The four Singhalese shadows who had been sitting near the door were gone.

Rigler sat down again. From his pocket he took a handful of coins and dropped them on the table. When he spoke, his voice was not quite as thick as it had been, and it was no longer loud.

"I've got a little more money," he said. "Want to play some more, you fellows?"

The half-breeds were willing. The cards came out again. Ten minutes later, when Rigler scraped back his chair and stood up, he had won back as much money as he had lost. In fact, he had won more. In his pocket lay enough extra income to make up for the handful of silver coins he had given to Huang Lee the night before.

Strangely enough, his steps were not the least unsteady as he went to the door. And when he strolled slowly back through the narrow streets of the native quarter, he was not drunk.

He returned the same way he had come—because he knew that Kirk Waller, too, would have chosen the same route. And his slow steps led him, eventually, into the particularly narrow street that harbored Huang Lee's curio shop. Of all the streets in Kuching's evil quarter, this was the most sinister, the most deadly.

And there, half way down it, old man Rigler came to a slow stop. In the gutter, at his feet, lay a dark shape, strangely contorted.

Rigler bent down carefully. His hands touched blood. He turned the shape over, with an effort. The dead face that stared up at him was the face of Captain Kirk Waller.

Before he moved away, old man Rigler ran his hands through the dead man's pockets. The pockets were empty. The little red piece of glass was gone.

"He should have known better," Rigler mused as he went quietly back to the waterfront. "He should have done some thinkin'. When a man gets as old as me, he don't get drunk on the first three glasses of whiskey. He don't get drunk at all, if he knows how to bluff!"

A Story of Stolen Teak in Burma

# MYSTERY TEAK

by

Warren Hastings Miller

"MOST EXTR'ORDINARY! Who in the world would want to steal a whole raft of teak?"

Bruce Romney, Inspector, Burma Secret Service, had been called into the case on the plea that the teak was Navy property, or at least would be when sawn to timber in the Rangoon Teak Mills, Ltd., and delivered on the steamer waiting for it. It was a rush order, that raft of teak, wanted on the Clyde as soon as the steamer could get there. But the entire last section of that raft had vanished the night before, right in Rangoon River, under the very eyes of Grierson's police launches.

Bruce had stretched a point to take the case, partly because Grierson's people had not yet found a trace of that raft, but mainly for friendship's sake. He cared little for Brumby, the portly manager of the saw mills, but his old friend Captain MacPherson, of the Moulmein tug that had towed the teak across the Bay, stood to be ruined by the loss of his raft section. Brumby was holding him strictly responsible for it, though he had not said so yet.

"You tell the Inspector just what happened last night, so far as you know, Captain. We've got to recover that raft. Quite! Rush order, y' know. Someone will suffer for it otherwise," he hinted ominously.

The rubicund and pickled Scottish tug captain rubbed his hairy nose dubiously and rumbled, "Aye. We lost the last section of the r-raft, Inspector. A wee bit o' squall hit us comin' up the Estuary; nothing that a mon could ca' weather. But thunder an' lightnin', wi' fierce rain an' wind. Syne I notice that she steers like an Ayreshire cow, an' I says to Gaygle MacGonigal, oor deck-gillie, says I: 'Roon aft, Gaygle, an' see what's wrang wi' them imps o' Beelzebub at the steerin' sweeps. Hae the black heathen drooned in th' down-pour, I dunno?'

"Syne Gayle's back on me bridge, the eyes of him poppin' like a crab's: 'Wurra-wurra! The aft section's gone adrift, Captain!' crees th' gillie, fair deementit wi' fright. 'Adrift, Genhenna!' says I, 'Not wi' chains that'll hold against a Bengal typhoon!' We are towin' six sections, ye'll understand, Inspector, secured wi' chains an' pelican hooks—"

"Two hundred thousand rupees worth of teak in each section!" cut in Brumby savagely, "The firm will not take the loss of that last section, Captain! *You* will. You're responsible for it. We'll attach your tug, my word!"

"*Mister!*" gasped old MacPherson, all taken aback, "Ye don't mean that!" he protested brokenly, "She's all I have in th' warld! 'Tis me livin', my tug; me an' th' wife an' th' bairns! I ask ye, Inspector," he appealed to Bruce, "what could a mon do? I couldna stop th' tow to look for that section. Ye ken the Irrawaddy current, four knots the hour. Tow I must! 'Tis black night an' thick. I hailed a police launch an' bade them s'arch for me missin' section, the whiles Gaygle steers wi' spare sweeps. An' I conteenue the tow up here. Could a mon do more?"

"Unfortunate," said Brumby bitingly. "But I cawn't see that the mill is under any obligations to stand the loss, Captain. We'll receipt for your five sections. You can settle for the sixth with the lumber company. It was not delivered *here*, that's certain!"

"Losh, I'm ruint!" wailed Captain MacPherson. " 'Tis no fair, Mister! I take the reesks across the Bay. I charge ye fair for th' tug's time an' coal. And now to be ruint in th' doing of it—"

Bruce took hold with vigor about then! He had had but a languid interest in Brumby's teak. It concerned him, somewhat, as a Navy job and it was an interesting Secret Service problem why anyone in Rangoon should want to steal a whole raft of teak. But now there was human sympathy involved. Poor old MacPherson! The honest Scottish tug captain hadn't a chance in the courts, he knew. The towing chain *might* have loosened of itself—the ring working off its pelican-hook, for instance. He could not prove any theft; would have to collect his damages from the thieves in any event. Before the sawmill company he stood as merely a tug boat captain who had failed to deliver his entire consignment of teak. The lumber company in Moulmein would demand the value of the missing raft from him or else attach his tug. Between those two heartless corporations poor old MacPherson stood doomed.

BRUCE THEREFORE threw himself into the case with enthusiasm. He ruminated silently over it a moment while MacPherson went on protesting his poverty to the obdurate Brumby. "Who in the world would have a motive for stealing a whole raft of teak in Rangoon Harbor?" he mused. The Navy used nearly all the teak lumbered in Burma. A part went aboard ship for San Francisco, to be used on American yachts. All of it for ship use was sawed into great beams in this very yard. Here also the native furniture and curio men came to buy small lots for carving.

From where the three men stood talking Bruce could see a dozen mighty elephants at work carrying the logs to the saw-cradle; two more of them were unloading one of the rafts at the river bank. Like a well-drilled team they were lifting off each log by a thrust of their tusks under it and a grip over it with their trunks. And everywhere sounded the shouts of their mahouts, talking to their elephants in an unknown language, *the* elephant language in fact, words of command that were neither Hindustani nor Malay but dated back to the misty antiquities of China. Each word meant a whole order—like the command, "Fetch!" to a bird dog. The great and supremely intelligent brutes obeyed these shouts with complicated manoevers. They not only answered perfectly but had a system of grunts and squeals in response understood by the mahouts. And all around them, in the early sunrise before eight, rose the great mill sheds, sounded the whining hum of saws, the puff of steam engines, the clank of carrier-cradles reversed. The mill was running full time on that Navy order.

Bruce brushed back reflectively the scanty iron-gray hair over his bony and weatherbeaten temples. This matter required thought, and he did not agree with Brumby's theories as to the theft. "Of course the thieves must have had a powerful sea-going tug," Brumby was saying to Bruce. "Are you sure, Captain, you saw no vessel? That missing section is way' down the coast toward Mergui by now, I'm thinking! Pirates!"

"Noo. There was no vessel," said MacPherson, "I was keepin' a bright lookout ahead, ye'll ken, for the night was thick and a mon couldna see the buoy-lights well. 'Twas when she'd no mind her hellum that I looked back. Then I ca'ed Gaygle MacGonigal—"

"Which way was the wind, Captain?" asked Bruce.

"My dear man! An extr'ordinary question!" protested Brumby at such irrelevancy, "It was blowing the regular northeast monsoon last night, of course!"

"Noo. Not during the bit squall, Mister," Captain MacPherson corrected him, "It came out of the east, that thunder-bully."

Bruce nodded. The affair *might* be native. They could do wonders with anything that floated. And of course they would use no tug. Such a vessel was too easily traced. Within an hour Major Grierson, Chief of Police, could account to him for the movements of every tug harboring in Rangoon. But really this affair was rather astonishing. The Moulmein tug comes into Rangoon Estuary towing her usual quota of teak rafts; a whole section of it vanishes, right here in the lower harbor, and diligent search all night by the police launch fails to discover any trace of it! One thing, it was a ten good miles down the Estuary from Rangoon to the open sea. That meant twenty miles of water-front to search, most of it jungle scrub and mangroves bordering the immense rice tracts of the Lower Delta. That scrub border was continuous. It formed a good weather-break dividing the sea from the rice. In some places the jungle was a quarter of a mile thick.

Bruce mulled it over as he took his leave of the sawmill, having got from Brumby and Captain MacPherson all the data so far. He went to the river front at first and stood watching two elephants landing teak from the raft. Sure-footed they strode out until waist deep, then pushed their tusks under a log weighing two tons, curled their trunks over it, and lifted together, carrying the log sidewise to shore. And always those strange piping commands from their mahouts, that were no human language under the sun but meant whole sentences of command packed into single words. Bruce nodded; he knew what to look for now—Elephants had landed that raft somewhere last night.

He next visited Major Grierson to get his report on the night's findings. The big, raw-boned, and beetroot-complexioned Chief of Police had a theory of his own which he was quite sure about. He expounded it with conviction: "We have found no landing-place where they could have come ashore with that raft, old skin," he told Bruce, "Therefore it is obvious that the pirate tug went on out to sea. Even a launch would answer, helped by the strong Irrawaddy current. As every launch has been accounted for it is plain that this tug came from foreign parts. I've notified both Mergui and the Andamans to send out patrol boats looking for her. The case seems closed for the present so far as we are concerned, doesn't it?"

"Perhaps," said Bruce, mildly, "I'll borrow a police launch, Grierson, if you don't mind, and have a look myself. Take Dayong along."

"You don't imagine this theft is native, do you?" jeered Grierson, "Man, the teak in that raft would last them a hundred years! And where could they land it in the harbor? And how tow it, without a steam vessel of some kind? And, can you hide a raft two hundred feet long all night, so that my patrol launches could not see it? I tell you, nothing was abroad on the river last night save a few belated rice-cargo luggers. Those were all our people saw. Of the raft, not a trace along either short."

"I'll go over it again, if you like," said Bruce stubbornly, and was shouted at for his pains. He got the launch, however, and went to Dayong Vila's small-animal shop in China Street. Dayong was S.1041 on the Secret Service books and an invaluable native ally to the Inspector. He was a Malay and a wanderer, who had seen much of jungle and piracy during his lurid past, was Dayong. He wore always his own native costume of sarong and jacket with a kris in the girdle. His hard-bitten and almond eyed features were topped by a shouting turban of violent colors embroidered in gold and silver as he salaamed to the Inspector entering his shop.

"CAN YOU talk elephant, Dayong?" asked Bruce as a first preliminary after greetings.

"Any mortal thing can do, Tuan!" Dayong grinned, with his usual Malay boastfulness, "Malay-boy plenty-much sabe elephant. How talk-talk, must be."

"Will they obey you?"

"If not listening, soak *gajah* on him toes," Dayong explained the intricacies of mastering three tons of animal with that delicate implement, the ankus.

"We'll need that lingo, I'm thinking!" said Bruce, "I have a case on for you, S.1041." And he told him of the theft of a whole raft of teak the night before.

Dayong's eyes narrowed as he nodded agreement to Bruce's theory that the affair was native. "Burmaman, Tuan!" he confirmed his chief, "No tug. Capman-feller, him see; police launch, he find . . . Po Ngkha, him do Act of Merit, man-man say in bazaars," he related his latest bit of gossip, casually enough.

It was Bruce's turn to narrow his eyes. Po Ngkha was a retired dacoit, who with his band of thieves was ageing mellowly somewhere down in the Delta. The money from his ill-gotten gains was out at interest everywhere, at the outrageous usury of fifteen per cent, but the police had let him alone during the last six or seven years—since he had escaped hanging by turning state's evidence. He had been good, as dacoits go, those famous robbers of the Tenasserim Hills. Bruce conceived that he would be thinking of Nirvana about now, and, being black as Satan with sin, what more natural than to square accounts with the Lord Buddha by an Act of Merit in his old age? Building a pagoda, say. . . The police trusted him, on good behavior; the Secret Service never.

"Topping bit of news, Dayong!" exclaimed Bruce, "Repentance, eh? —You have no idea of what this Act of Merit may be?"

"No, Tuan. Make poojah with Buddha-god. Old pongyi down at Tawku say so."

"Tawku?" cried Bruce, his nostrils expanding in that peculiar way he had when scenting war, "That's down near Elephant Point. This thing's beginning to fit up, Dayong! They make a descent on the tow, in a sampan. They capture the two steersmen and unchain that last raft section. Down below a rice-lugger is waiting. The current would take that drifting raft section down to it. . . And then, with that east wind last night, the lugger sets her big sail and would hit the west bank of the estuary just *about* at Elephant Point.—Come on with us, Dayong!"

They hastened down to the Strand and boarded the launch Grierson had put at Bruce's disposal. It was a long trip down to Hastings. The wide Estuary broiled under the high sun, glared flat and shining as a mirror. The usual cargo boats were about, clumsy rice-luggers with huge dark red sails. There were steamers coming and going, launches, sampans. The Estuary was two miles wide here. Not until they reached Hastings did Bruce put in close to shore and begin examining the scrubby banks. Calculations of the probable drift of that raft, the course and drift of the lugger towing it, enabled him to estimate about where those enterprising raft-thieves had landed it. Somewhere between Hastings and Elephant Point. Steamers took on passengers by steam packet during low tides at the former place; the lighthouse occupied a government reservation at Elephant Point; therefore it was obvious that the thieves would steer to land their raft somewhere in the long stretch of scrub between. And, as elephants could not lift the logs ashore without leaving tracks in the mud, broken bushes, trails, finding the landing place would be easy; indeed it seemed marvellous how it had escaped the police launch the night before.

But alas! Not a sign of any such disturbance appeared along the bank! Bruce felt his whole theory crumbling under him. He had based it on the supposition that what Po Ngkha proposed to build for his Act of Merit was not a pagoda but a *kyaung*, a Buddhist monastery. These required quantities of teak, for columns, beams, finials, spires, all in the ornamental carving covered with red lacquer and gold leaf so dear to the Buddhist heart. A raft of it would be none too much. And stealing it from the English would be yet another Act of Merit in Po Ngkha's philosophy! It all fitted in with his native theory; only, *where* had they landed that teak?

It looked as if Grierson was on the right track after all, reflected Bruce as the launch stood on down, slowly, past Elephant Point, and out to sea. Somebody from outside Burma had made the descent on that teak. They could have cut it adrift by a sampan raid; then picked it up lower down with a powerful sea-going tug. The weak point in that was, who would want it? The Dutch had plenty of teak of their own, and they were the nearest and only neighbors of the English in this part of the world. Mystery teak, Bruce was beginning to call it!

No; Bruce held fast to his native theory as the only strong probability. He was about turning the launch back, to search the further shore, from Elephant Point to the China Basir outlet of the Delta, when Dayong raised a cry:—

"Bush, Tuan! Over there!" he said, pointing.

It was eloquent, that floating bush; when they came up to it and raised it aboard! Its leaves were fresh and green; its stem had been cut to a sharp point and was covered a foot deep with mud. The river had betrayed the teak thieves. It had floated this bit of camouflage away and was carrying it out to sea.

"Bush screen, that's what! We got jolly well fooled," Bruce declared. "Turn her alongshore again, Ramasawmy," he ordered the Hindoo mechanic of the steam launch.

Once again they searched the shores above Elephant Point. This time Dayong in the bow pulled vigorously at every bush in the fringe of them. Back behind were rice lands or else patches of low and scrubby jungle characteristic of the Delta. And then a yelp came from Dayong as a bush came free and its pointed and muddy stem bobbed to the surface.

"*Gajah, Tuan!* Was put teak ashore here!"

The salty depths cleared of silt and Bruce saw tracks, the great five-toed spoor of elephants. Two of them at least had worked here last night, landing the whole of that teak raft, in all haste. And then all trace of their work had been cleverly camouflaged by driving in a screen of fresh cut bushes.

"Looks like Po Ngkha's Act of Merit—quite!" Bruce grinned sardonically. "The teak is not far inland. Being sawn and sarved into *kyaung* posts, most likely! Poor old MacPherson! We shall have to get it back for him, Dayong. Ramasawmy, you take the launch back to Rangoon and bring Grierson Sahib and the police. Ashore with us, Dayong!"

THE MALAY'S almond eyes narrowed as he shook his head. It was not going to be too easy to recapture this teak, even now that they had found where it had been landed! The hinterland was all jungle here, no rice lands for several miles either way. That meant that they had a retired dacoit chieftan, a number of his followers, and at least two elephants to deal with. The rash Inspector would simply vanish into oblivion, sunk without a trace, if they went at this in high-handed police fashion!

*Djaga,* (beware) *Tuan!* White man smell like sheep. Elephant wind you, he chase. Dacoit take you' head, with *dah*. Inspector-*Tuan* he come dead finish, all-same one pig."

Bruce laughed at that picture of his demise if he barged in on Po Ngkha off hand. The obvious thing to do was to wait here until Grierson came down in the launch, but that would take three hours, and meanwhile they might be moving the whole raft, log by log, to parts unknown, for all he knew. Two elephants could carry off all thirty logs of it in an astonishingly short time. "What would *you* do, Dayong?" he asked quizzically.

"Me-feller good mahout," Dayong grinned. "Sabby elephant talk. Sabby plenty trick. Me get job with Po Ngkha! Inspector Tuan him lay low. When I raising bad hell with elephant, *Tuan* is arresting Po Ngkha."

"Topping!" Bruce laughed some more. What species of "bad hell" his invaluable Dayong proposed to raise he could not imagine, but the scheme was sound. He, in his police topee and khaki Norfolk jacket and shorts, would be pounced on at sight in this jungle. Dayong, in his sarong and jacket and kris, *might* pass for a wandering Malay mahout. The Burmese always yielded them the palm in handling elephants, there were so many more of them used in Ceylon and Malaya.

"Right-o. Let's get on with it. Be back as soon as you can, Ramasawmy," said Bruce, and he and Dayong jumped ashore as the launch left.

They had let themselves in for adventures with that step. How almost foolhardy it was Bruce realized as they came upon nearly all the raft lying in the jungle not three rods inland. The sounds of saws and mallets could be heard a short distance further on in the trees. Bruce ducked for cover and was soon worming his way through the underbrush, keeping a sharp eye out for cobras. He left Dayong leisurely moving toward the dacoit camp. Bruce approached it himself by a wide detour through the forest. An outcry, yells, angry voices, sounded in Dayong's direction as Bruce neared the rear of a great thatch hut of bamboo and attap thrown up temporarily for Po Ngkha's headquarters. They had discovered Dayong, that row meant, were bringing him before the chieftan.

Bruce crept nearer till he could peer through a chink in the rattan basketry of the hut. That vast and elderly dacoit, Po Ngkha, sat in a chair with his back to him, superintending his Act of Merit in the shade of the hut's open side. Beyond him could be seen all the paraphernalia of this pious enterprise, a primitive saw pit with a teak log in it at a slant and two men hauling on the saw, several squared logs being carved in intricate Buddhist designs by more men with mallets and gouges. The stunt was evidently to stage a miracle. Having snitched the tail end of MacPherson's raft, Po Ngkha had landed it here and was fashioning it into a complete temple. The two elephants Bruce could see, carrying in more logs and moving those worked on at command, would be loaded with the finished job and all of it appear mysteriously some night on the temple site at Tawku, five miles away. The priests would be on hand to bless this material for a *kyaung,* obviously put there by Buddha during the night, most miraculously, and the erection of it would proceed amid chants and ceremonies. Po Ngkha the central figure—

"The poisonous blighter!" Bruce thought with inward amusement and looked fondly upon Po Ngkha's unconscious back. The old fellow was ending a life of sin by a supreme act of repentance—according to his lights—presenting the Lord Buddha with an entire *kyaung.* That it was also his supreme act of thievery, involving poor old MacPherson in ruin, was the principal thing the matter with it. The Navy could well spare this teak, otherwise—

Just then Dayong was haled before the chief. He had one hand on his kris with dignified reserve, so that Po Ngkha's dacoits dared not lay violent hands on him, but they were shoving him before the presence nevertheless. Dayong salaamed with civility and inquired in English:

"You got mahout job for Malay-boy, O chief? I hear was elephant work and come."

"*Where* did you hear, Malay?" Po Ngkha asked with suspicious uneasiness.

"Man-man say, in Rangoon bazaar, Po Ngkha do Act of Merit," said Dayong cheerfully. "I good mahout, chief."

Po Ngkha ignored that. He asked, still more pressingly: "How did you find this place, Malay? Is that, too, known in the bazaars?"

"In truth, O Presence. Who can keep a secret from the bazaar girls? Also the police are searching."

That was of interest, this latest news from the outside world brought by a man direct from the bazaars! Po Ngkha's eyes searched each of his men angrily for the one indiscreet enough to tell his girl about this camp of theirs for the Act of Merit. You might as well publish it in the *Rangoon Times!*

"The police are fools!" Po Ngkha declared resonantly. "But I fear Romney Sahib. If it is known in the bazaars, *he* knows."

He clapped his hands energetically. "Ba Pe, go look at the river bank," he told one of his men. "See that the bushes are not disturbed. . . They hide where we landed the teak last night, Malay," he added. "The police would pass them by, but Romney Sahib might not—curse him!"

BRUCE GRINNED over that growling tribute to himself. He saw Dayong's eyes gleam as Ba Pe left camp for a look at their camouflage screen. Bruce and Dayong had about five minutes left in which to do something, and then things would begin to happen around this camp! The least they could expect was a hasty flight of Po Ngkha and all his dacoits, taking all the teak with them. There would be nothing left here but chips and sawdust by the time Grierson got down with his police Sikhs! Dayong said:

"Is a way for load two elephants in my country, O chief, so make-carry ten tons of logs. Can do."

Bruce exploded, with wrist stuffed into his mouth, at that outrageous statement, made with guileless almond eyes upon Po Ngkha. Ten tons—my God! His shoulders shook with suppressed merriment as he forced himself to silence behind the rattan wall. O monumental liar! But Dayong was capable of anything. He heard Po Ngkha growl, "Verily thou art a mighty liar, Malay! No two elephants have carried ten tons since the world began!"

Dayong shrugged his shoulders. "Is a special hitch, with chains. Malay-boy, him savvy. Can do, O Presence," he insisted without emotion.

Bruce stopped the suppressed explosions within him, was listening intently. He began to see through Dayong, that king of whoppers, now. All Dayong really wanted was to get charge of one or both of those work elephants for a brief while. Artfully he was laying the trap for it. The messenger would come back, presently, from the estuary bank, bringing the alarming news that some of the bushes were pulled out and the mark of a police launch bow was printed in the mud bank. That would mean to decamp in all haste—and here was a Malay mahout who knew how to load two elephants with ten tons of logs. Important, if true!

Bruce drew his automatic as a hurried cry came sounding through the jungle. That messenger was coming back, yelling alarmed imprecations. Fly! The police knew their landing place! Two launches were coming down from Rangoon!—Hasten, O Presence!

Po Ngkha gave immediate orders for packing up. Baskets appeared, were filled with tools, utensils, food, vanished into the forest on the shoulders of struggling men. He looked longingly at his teak, those straight gray-barked trunks already cut in half to column length that were not to be abandoned to the police if he could help it. He turned to Dayong with appeal: "If thou hast a better way, Malay?" he suggested and pointing at his two mahouts busy arranging the usual harness for packing teak logs on the backs of their two animals. Bruce had often seen them moving along the jungle trails in the Salween country, totally submerged under squared teak, enough to cover a lumber locomotive. The enormous load was held by a diamond hitch of chains. He wondered how Dayong was going to better that harness for his mythical ten tons.

Dayong snorted. "Thou offal of a monkey!" he addressed the nearest of the mahouts with sarcasm. "Thinkest thou a camel's-weight is all he can carry? Verily I could load more on my yellow dog, in Trengganu!"

The mahout thus challenged yipped back with spirit. "*Gulo gajah!*" he retorted. "Thy mother was an ape and thy father a maggot, Malay! Talk thou to Gajah Sabar, here!" he dared Dayong and patted his elephant's trunk. "*He* knoweth the answer to lying boasters!"

Bruce, behind the rattan, doubled up with paroxysms of mirth. If you could talk the elephant language to them you might get somewhere; if ordinary human speech, you'd get about a bucket of saliva spewed all over your head out of a contemptuous trunk. He had lost a good topee himself, once, when presuming to order a strange elephant to do anything!

Dayong stepped up to Gajah Sabar and tickled his great hairy nether lip. Purring as of a bass drum being rubbed came from the great beast. They saw eye to eye, the little, red and choleric pig-eye of Gajah Sabar, the understanding brown ones of Dayong.

"*Terhum!*" he ordered in the high-pitched squeak used by the mahouts. Obediently Gajah Sabar raised a ponderous knee. Dayong stepped up on it, slid astride the elephant's neck. "*Peha klung!*" he shouted.

The elephant wheeled to the left. His mahout was looking up at Dayong with misgivings over another man in command of his beast. He turned questioningly to Po Ngkha, but the dacoit chieftan was impressed and wanted to see more of this.

"Lo, there is a length of chain with a stout hook, Malay," he said. "Show us, now, how one loads the teak in your country so that much may be carried."

"*Aiwa*!—May Allah wither your liver!" said Dayong in Arabic. Bruce tensed for action at those words. Dayong's eyes were roving the jungle for signs of him. He knew that the Inspector understood Arabic, and it was a hint for him to be ready for the "bad hell," if within hearing.

The crisis of their adventure had come, Bruce felt as he braced his legs for a spring upon Po Ngkha from behind.

*"Tehoh!"* barked Dayong to his elephant. Gajah Sabar backed, rolled his fierce little pig eyes, curled up his trunk. On the ground in front of him lay now that length of chain. Its bright links were heavy enough to moor a schooner, and it had a steel timber hook on one end; in fact, it was the very piece of chain that had tied the last section of the raft to MacPherson's tow.

And then Dayong gave an order in the elephant language that Bruce had never heard before, and possibly none of the dacoits either. At sound of it Gajah Sabar rumbled with displeasure, pranced ponderously, was looking around with ire in his red eyes. Down swooped the trunk, grasped the chain, flung it aloft like a giant flail.

*"Djalang!"* yelled Dayong and dug his toes into Gajah Sabar's ears till he squealed.

*Swishhh-Crack!*

In a giant swing that chain swept everything before him like the flail of a titanic whip! Men, posts, baskets, everything crashed down in the swath of it. Curses, cries, scamperings, a mad rush to get clear, the whole camp in a turmoil as the chain sang again in a giant backward sweep. Dayong shouted vindictively as he urged on his beast with barbaric cries. A shot rang out, the bellow of a great horse pistol that Po Ngkha had fired at him as the roof of his hut came sagging down. It missed Dayong, but it had pierced one of Gajah Sabar's flapping ears and the elephant trumpetted his ire.

Bruce had dashed around the hut the instant the vast crackle of its bamboo had warned him the edifice was coming down all over him. He sprang for Po Ngkha while yet that smoking pistol was being jerked back for a hasty reloading. The elderly dacoit grappled with him as the chair went over. He was lean, tough, unbelievably strong, and greasy to hold. Outside, squeals like a factory whistle and the ponderous thumps of huge feet told him that Gajah Sabar had gone wild with that shot through his ear. He was under no man's control now! Dayong came diving under the thatch and tackled Po Ngkha from his side.

*"Itu gajah jehat, Tuan!"* he gasped, telling Bruce that the elephant had gone rogue. "Go quick! Must be!"

Bedlam had broken lose.

IT WAS a vile place for a fight. Po Ngkha squirmed and bit and kicked, for all their efforts to secure him. A gray trunk thrust through the thatch overhead and pulled like a steam winch on the rafters, dragging the hut further down over the three of them. Splinters, sharp sticks of broken bamboo, the remains of the chain, all hindered any effective hold on Po Ngkha. Bruce felt the greasy arm of his dacoit slipping from his tightest grip, got a fresh hold on his collar bone, bore his weight on the leg kicking fiercely under him. The nickle hand-cuffs now clicked from one wrist, but get the other near them Dayong could not, though wrestling with all his strength at the arm and leg on his side. Outside, blasts of elephantine fury, human cries off in the forest, the crash of things being picked up and flung told them that Gajah Sabar had everything his own way out there. Moreover his nostrils told him that there were more humans near by to be destroyed—the three struggling under the hut roof.

Came a monstrous tug and the whole hut fell over bodily. They were unearthed like mice discovered under a tuft of hay. The three fell over in a heap in the disconcerting flood of daylight. Bruce, seizing his chance, snapped the cuff ring on the arm shoved up at him by Dayong.

They did not wait! Over the roof rose an immense triangular head with flapping ears and insane red eyes, the gleam of white ivory tusks. They grabbed Po Ngkha between them and rushed him off into the underbrush, bending low. It would take Gajah Sabar about ten seconds to run around that hut and charge them, but it was their respite. The wind, thank God, was in their favor!

They were sitting on the teak when Grierson and his Sikhs arrived. Back there in the forest Gajah Sabar was dining peacefully on the roof of the hut, having given them up after a futile search. They had no wish to go near him just yet. Albeit he seemed to have calmed down somewhat.

"My word, Romney!" That was all the Chief of Police could say to the Chief of the Burma Secret Service, who sat nonchalantly on a teak log forty feet long with a handcuffed prisoner between himself and Dayong. "It's the missing teak, isn't it? Ramasawmy came in with a wild talk about some bushes, but I brought down two boat-loads of Sikhs anyhow—"

"Quite," said Bruce succinctly. "Poor old MacPherson, we couldn't let *him* down, y'know."

The Chief of Police frowned. "Granted," he said, stiffly. "But—kindly explain what Po Ngkha, there, has to do with this. He's been on our good behavior books for years. Was it necessary to disturb *him*, at this late date, may I ask?" Grierson inquired huffily.

Bruce grinned. "Oh, him? Act of Merit, y'see. No one would want a whole raft of teak, Grierson, unless he proposed to build something with it. And no one but a dacoit would have the enterprise to steal one—right on your own river. I heard that Po Ngkha was building a *kyaung* down at Tawku, so put two and two together. . . The rest was Dayong, here. He got command of one of their work elephants and raised hell about their camp with him. We wangled your culprit out of it." Bruce indicated the handcuffed chieftan and eyed Grierson aggravatingly, for he loved to tease the good but obtuse police chief.

The latter snorted. "Deuced lucid! Am I to understand that you had a row—that there were some of his dacoits mixed up in this and yet to be taken?" he asked and turned to his Sikhs as if to give them the order to pursue.

"Rather!" said Bruce. "They landed your teak—cleverly enough—last night, Grierson. Camouflaged it with a screen of bushes and set up shop back in the jungle yonder. You'll find the makings of a fine *kyaung* there—but I wouldn't *go* there just yet! They've all skipped out long ago. But there's an elephant in charge—"

Grierson blew up with all these incomprehensibilities. "*What* elephant? I'm afraid I don't understand, Romney."

Bruce was about to tease him further, but the commercial instinct was now uppermost in Dayong. Herr Dubbs, the elephant dealer at Insei, would give him ten thousand rupees for a trained animal delivered peacefully at his gates.

"Dat elephant b'long me if can catch, *Tuan?*" Dayong asked at this juncture, his eyes alight with daring.

Bruce laughed. Dayong always combined the pleasures of a Secret Service case with his own business if he could manage to do so. He was invaluable far beyond the pay on the Secret Service books and deserved anything extra he could get out of it.

"I don't see why not, Dayong.

Spoils of war, what?" Bruce said. "Come on, Grierson. Let's see the show. You'll get the drift as we go along."

The party followed Dayong at a safe distance back into the jungle. In there could be heard swishing, the crackle of attap roof leaves being pulled out, an occasional rumble of satisfaction. Dayong looked about the wrecked camp, with its hut a ruin, the saw mill uprooted into its component logs, tools, utensils, and human belongings scattered all about. He picked up a yard of sugar cane where lying half buried in the duff under the tread of a ponderous foot. With it he approached Gajah Sabar and started a cooing conversation with him that sounded like no human tongue under the sun. Gajar Sabar rumbled, made queer answering noises that seemed to have a meaning of their own. He left off pulling thatch. His great head swung, and the little fierce eyes looked on Dayong for a long minute. Then his trunk went out for the proferred cane.

Dayong stepped in fearlessly, tickled the vast and pendant lower lip, wrapped one arm around his trunk. "*Salaamek!*" he ordered sharply, the one Hindoo-Arabic word ever used with them. For answer Gajah Sabar wrapped his trunk around Dayong's waist, lifted him high in the air, and set him down on his immense bony head. Then he rose up on his hind legs like a great dog, wheeled on the party of whites watching at some distance, and elevated his trunk for Dayong to grasp. It was a pretty picture.

For a full minute they stood there. Grierson gasped: "My word! Not for me, thank you! You say he went rogue not an hour ago, Romney?"

Dayong eyed him with a slight grin on his brown features. He had a dig of his own for police who gave up a case too easily and let the Secret Service finish it for them. "*Tuan Polis-Sahib,*" he said, "it is simple. S'pose is something you no can do? Then you do him till you could," he told the Chief of Police sententiously.

Bruce guffawed. Perseverence! It was the way his Service solved its most baffling cases when you came right down to it!

# The Great Joke of Lope Da Gamma

Story of the Hungry Country

WE WHITES have a convenient habit of terming barbarous all cultures that are not our own, and we have but little toleration for barbarism. Consider the philosophy of the natives of Ticao in Portuguese West Africa. It is so profoundly pessimistic, and so pessimistically profound, that only an inherently cheerful race could endure to accept it. In Ticao, for example, all the world knows that but for witchcraft and the spirits of the dead, mankind would be immortal, and because of this belief there has grown up an elaborate system of propitiation of the spirits of the dead, and a similarly elaborate sys-

by

**MURRAY LEINSTER**

tem of witchcraft and anti-witchcraft. The whites in Ticao view this theology and magic either as a source of amusement or as an evil to be eradicated. Lope da Gama, I think, shared both views.

He owned a big plantation about sixty miles from Ticao proper. He had about two hundred slaves, all of them from the Hungry Country or further inland. They worked in the fields, of course, tending the sugar cane raised to make rum for the traders going inland, and cultivating the minor crops da Gama cared to plant. Coffee and sugar cane were raised in great quantities, but, except for plantains and yams to help feed the slaves, little else was grown on da Gama's plantation. He was quite an advanced man in many ways. He made the rum from his sugar cane in a little mill of his own, and he had installed a dynamo and electric lights in his house. In his methods he was perhaps the most modern planter in Ticao. On the islands of San Felipe and Gomé nearly every *roça* has its electric light plant, but there are not many in Ticao. Even the streets of the city of Ticao are dimly lighted with flickering oil wicks set in street-lamps originally designed for gas.

I remember once seeing a slave being flogged on da Gama's plantation. He was not really a slave, of course, but a *servaçal*, or contract laborer, but it would be quibbling with words to make the distinction every time. The estate of the *servaçal* differs from that of the slave in exactly one particular—no, two. The first is that he has with his master a contract the provisions of which the master ignores without exception, and the other is that he is supposed to be returned to his home when the contract expires. He never is. Once on the plantation of a Portuguese, he is there until he dies or, perhaps, escapes—to die in the attempt to reach his home again.

But all that is by the way. I was saying that I once saw a slave flogged on da Gama's plantation. The slave was held fast in a clumsy wooden manacle such as has been used in Ticao these past two hundred and fifty years, and the dingy-brown overseer wielded a hippo whip such as slave-drivers have used from time immemorial. But there were two touches of modernity. As the overseer plied the whip in silence, except for his heavy breathing from the exertion, between the pain-racked yells of the slave I heard a graphophone going up at the great house of the plantation. It was playing a popular song that was then a favorite in Lisbon. The other touch of modernity was the fact that though the cane-shed in which the flogging was taking place was clumsily built by native labor, along the roof ran two insulated wires, and the incandescent filament of an electric-light bulb shed its pale, unwavering light on the pulped, striped flesh of the slave's back.

DA GAMA was indeed modern. The financial system he had instituted is a case in point. Some plantation owners simply ignore the article in their contract with the native by which they are obligated to pay him one *milreis*—approximately a dollar—a month as wages. Da Gama, however, paid that with scrupulous care. Each slave received tokens to the value of one *milreis* every month. They might be used as cash at the store on the plantation, but nowhere else. Da Gama's store charged eight prices for every article the slave might want to buy, and he served out rations which were so meagre that the slave had to supplement them at the store. The result was precisely the same as if da Gama had entirely ignored the payment question, but he was able to speak virtuously of the exceeding good care he took of his slaves, and of their delight in spending their money. I have noticed that the Portuguese is like the rest of mankind in taking great pride in those virtues he does not possess.

When I had to make a trip into the interior, my first stopping-place out of Ticao was likely to be Venghela; the second, the Padre Silvestre's mission; and the next, da Gama's plantation. They were just about twenty miles apart, and it made a fair day's journey to go from one to the other. In each case my native boys could be accommodated, and I could sleep in a more or less civilized habitation. It was in this way, stopping at da Gama's overnight every trip I made to the Hungry Country, that I learned something about his modern ideas. He had a smattering of knowledge of the native superstitions, gained, I understood, from one or another of his brown-skinned mistresses; but they seemed to him only matters to be laughed at. They do take ridiculous forms, those native superstitions, but there are many useful points about them. A native, for example, because of his fear of witchcraft, will not throw carelessly to one side anything that has touched his body. An enemy might find it and bewitch him with its aid. He buries or burns all foul matter, and for this reason his villages as a rule are free from evil smells, or trash-piles, with their attendant flies and contagion. Where the white man has taught him to despise his fetishes, he revels in an orgy of unsanitary conditions that breeds disease with deadly rapidity and carries him off by the hundred in plagues and epidemics. Da Gama never considered this aspect of the matter, but laughed and grew contemptuous by turns.

Most of the natives in the immediate neighborhood of Ticao have long since become *servaçaes*, but "immediate neighborhoods" are matters of relative distance, after all. Ten or fifteen miles from da Gama's plantation there still remained two or three squalid, huddled villages where the natives were either too sickly to be valuable as slaves, or where, from some obscure quirk in the policy of the Governor, it had been decided that they were to be left unmolested. In the largest of them Btuvo held sway. In sanctity I can liken him only to an archbishop, because he was the high priest of high priests of ju-ju, black and white magic, witchcraft, divination, second sight, and the control of the spirit of wind, water, fire, and all the dead generations back to the hinterland of time. In venerability, he might be likened to the Pyramids, were not the dates of those structures so accurately known. Btuvo's age was unknown, even to himself. He was very, very old, however, so old that he had long lost the corpulence one associates with an old and long-respected ju-ju man. He was quite toothless, and his jaws protruded before his gums in that peculiarly shrewd and calculating expression one finds on the faces of the aged. I think he was a little mad.

It is difficult for a white man to understand how an old, old black man, sitting, in ascetic state, on a raised platform of dirt in the centre of a squalid village, could arouse the reverence Btuvo aroused. He sat upon a low stool cut from a block of wood, and a monkey-skin cloak lay unnoticed on the earth behind him. He wore a necklace of unpolished stones about his neck, a breechclout about his middle, and nothing else. His only concession to civilization was a pipe, which he carried with the stem stuck through an enlarged hole in the lobe of his right ear.

And the natives practically worshiped him. Believing, as they did —and perhaps as he did, for, as I said, I think he was a little mad— believing that he controlled the spirits of the dead and all the malignant, unearthly beings of the air, and believing that there is no natural death, all death being caused by witchcraft or malignant spirits, it was only natural that they should revere this ancient wreck of a man. To their minds, he held the keys of life and death. To their minds, it was the power of his juju that kept their squalid little villages from the blight of the Portuguese slave-trade. They feared and revered him with an intensity we find it hard to understand. Someone or other has pointed out that reverence for the unseen is a sign of the childhood of a race, and irreverence, of its decay. The natives in Ticao are essentially a childlike people. Their chiefs are reverenced beyond the reverence we whites pay to our rulers, and their priests are regarded with an awe we cannot understand. Of all priests, Btuvo was most revered. He had a granddaughter—or she may have been a great-granddaughter— who was his sole attendant.

To those of you who know the African attitude toward women, it will be enough to say that because of the reverence in which her grandfather was held she was not expected to do any work, she was never sought in marriage, and that no warrior of any of the villages attempted to make love to her—the sort of love of which every native man makes his greatest boast. I learned later that one man, the young chief of another of the three villages, did love her, but from awe of her grandfather dared not seek her hand. Btuvo was invested with a sanctity that is almost incredible. A paring of his nail was considered to make its wearer invulnerable in battle. A hair from his head made the lucky possessor irresistible to women. The ordinary native would not dare part with a hair from his head or a paring of his nail for fear it would be used in bewitching him, but Btuvo was overlord of all spirits, supreme witch-doctor of all juju men, and feared no witchcraft or evil spirit.

HIS GRANDDAUGHTER walked about the village with a proud step. For her alone among the women, warriors stepped from their path to make way. She prepared the food her grandfather deigned to eat, and made known those persons to whom he granted speech. She did no other work, for the offerings from those who came to consult him were ample and more than ample for their needs. Not only the people of the villages came to him. Sometimes the slaves from the *roças* of the Portuguese dared send a pitifully small offering and beg for a charm to ease their lot or aid in their escape. These requests Btuvo discreetly temporized with or denied. He could not afford to attract the attention of the Portuguese. Not only had he himself to consider, but his granddaughter, and she possessed the strangely regular features and deep brown eyes that the Portuguese have learned to accept as beauty in default of the more normal charms of white women who cannot stand the Ticaoan climate. Btuvo played a wary game, maintaining his prestige among the natives, but being careful not to anger the Portuguese.

I HAD come from the islands, spent about a month in Ticao, and then started for the interior. There was some difficulty getting across a normally small but then swollen water-course between the Padre's and da Gama's, and I reached the latter place some time after dark. I would not have traveled after sunset but for the obvious advantages of stopping at the plantation instead of on the trail. Da Gama came out to meet me when I came in with my long string of carriers behind me.

"Welcome, senhor!" he began with elaborate gestures, and I saw that he was already drunk. I learned later that he had been in that condition for nearly a week, which is very unwise for a white man in that climate.

His effusive and confused greeting over, he snapped an order to one of his overseers as to the housing of my native boys, and grasped me firmly by the arm. He led me exuberantly indoors and mixed me a drink of limes and gin, and another, much stronger, for himself. All the time he was alternately promising me a great sight, a great joke, and scowling darkly to himself over something that seemed to make him very indignant. I caught one or two muttered phrases like "dark superstition." and "unholy practices," but could not make head or tail of them. Left to myself, I should have eaten something and rested, because the day had been very tiring, but da Gama insisted on my accompanying him and seeing his great joke.

As I had approached the house I had seen the reflections of two or three huge fires blazing in the compound, and when da Gama led me out on a porch overlooking the enclosure I saw at once the cause of his promises of a great joke. Three big wood fires blazed up, lighting the yard to its farthest corner. Along the opposite side were gathered in a huddled mass the slaves of the *roça*, with the dingy brown overseers standing guard over them.

The slaves were staring apprehensively about, the whites of their eyes showing wide in their fear. They did not know what to expect. There was another knot of natives apart from them, and in one of the figures I recognized the portly, dignified chief of one of the three villages only a few miles away. I recognized the insignia of chiefhood on two other men of the group, and saw Btuvo sitting impassively on his ceremonial stool, his monkey-skin cloak about his shoulders. His granddaughter stood proudly behind him. She was the only one who looked quite unafraid.

Btuvo dissembled his real emotions skilfully, but I saw that he was not comfortable in his mind. His granddaughter, however, was so obviously confident in the power of her grandfather's prestige to protect her that her only emotion seemed to be curiosity. She looked inquisitively at everything about the compound, at the huddled mass of slaves, the menacing figures of the overseers, each armed with a vicious hippo whip, at the great fires, and when da Gama and myself appeared, at our curiously clad forms and white faces.

In the little knot of strange natives I saw one or two men with native flutes and one of the great wooden drums that come from immense distances far back in the still unknown fastnesses of Central Africa. When da Gama stepped out of the great house an overseer went over and curtly ordered those men forward. They came, trembling. At another order they began to wail out one of the primitive and strangely melancholy melodies to which the natives dance. Their musical scale is much like ours, only one of their notes is always sung slightly flatted. Da Gama listened a moment in drunken approval. Then he yelled an order to one of his overseers.

It is quite hopeless to try to convey to you an idea of the reverence with which an African regards his chief. He may be chief of only a single squalid village, but in that village he is supreme. He does no work, does not hunt or fish, and in times of peace his sole real duty is the judging of disputes. To appeal from his decision is regarded as a crime. The lives, liberty, and property of his subjects are absolutely at his disposal. He is the repository of tradition. For his sanctity I can find no simile, but his dignity is that of a bishop and a scholar of international reputation rolled into one. The native is as conservative as a child, and the whites will always seem to him intruders, and as such, in the last analysis, barbarians.

DA GAMA had given orders that the chiefs should dance to the music of the native orchestra, for his amusement. The three chiefs stood aghast. Imagine the sensations of a Justice of the Supreme Court on being ordered to dance a jig for a water-front bartender. Imagine the sensations of . . . There is no parallel. The three chiefs stood dazedly still. The native musicians, when they grasped the enormity of the profanation that was to be done, gasped and the music wavered, then stopped. In a flash da Gama was in a drunken fury. He darted down from his place beside me.

With a whip from one of the overseers, he lashed the musicians mercilessly, cursing them in Portuguese. The music began again in panic-stricken tempo. Da Gama strode over to the three chiefs. He struck them across the face with the hippo lash—and if there is any blow on earth that is more painful than the lash of a hippo whip, I have yet to learn its nature. The rough hide tears the skin and rasps the flesh beneath at every stroke. Drunken, purple-faced in his silly rage, da Gama lashed at the unresisting chiefs. Had they lifted a hand to defend themselves they would have been shot like dogs by the overseers. Sixty miles from Ticao one is quite safe in killing any native. There will be no inquiry or punishment.

The portly chief gave in first. With his back a bleeding mass of bloody stripes, he began to yell, and a second later to dance. Da Gama followed him about the compound, curling the rasping lash of the hippo whip about the fat legs of the yelling chief. Two overseers went over to the other two chiefs. One soon gave in, but the other, the youngest of the three stood sullenly still. He was the one who loved Btuvo's granddaughter.

The exertion soon tired out da Gama, and he came back to where I stood, and signaled one of the house-slaves to bring him a drink. The slave brought it, trembling in an agony of fear. Da Gama drank it down and watched the dancing figures of the two chiefs, leaping and running about the great fires, each one with a vengeful overseer following him to urge him on with a blow from a whip should his steps lag. Da Gama beat time to the melancholy music, and poured out a volley of drunken Portuguese curses at the musicians. The one young chief still stood sullenly while a rain of blows fell upon him. Btuvo's granddaughter was watching him with a strange expression in her eyes.

Da Gama suddenly remembered me and began to laugh excitedly, while he signaled for another drink. Still beating time to the music, he gave me to understand that he was going to civilize those natives if he had to kill them to do it. They refused to buy rum from his mill; they persisted in unholy and superstitious practices. He had sent for the chiefs to come over, and, by the Mother of God! they should learn that the white man was master in Ticao, and they must do as the white man directed. He suddenly thought of Btuvo, still sitting impassively on his ceremonial stool, with his granddaughter standing proudly behind him. One of the dancing chiefs stumbled and fell, and lay in sobbing exhaustion on the ground unable to rise in spite of the blows the overseer rained on him. The young chief who had not danced quietly dropped to the ground, knocked unconscious by a blow from the butt of the overseer's whip.

When da Gama ordered Btuvo to dance, I rose. I had been sickened by what I had seen, but I could not stop it. Da Gama was in a drunken frenzy, and there was no reasoning with him.

THERE IS a stage in which a man seems to go quite insane from drink, especially when he drinks the vile stuff they have in Ticao. A white man, alone on a great plantation, with absolute authority over his slaves, even to life and death, is liable to have the loneliness and the horror of the heat and humidity turn him mad; but when he drinks on top of that there is no limit to the things he may do. In Ticao it is hard enough for a man to keep his sanity in any case. The Portuguese go there to make a fortune quickly, because if they do not make it quickly they are liable to stay there underground. Little by little they slough off the habits of civilization and become what the white man always becomes if he is left alone long enough in Africa. There are practically no white women. In all Ticao I doubt if there are a hundred, and, save for the missionaries' wives, they are all women who know the country and are accustomed to all they find there, so they exercise no influence in preventing the continuation of the present state of affairs.

Da Gama was no more than a fair sample of a Portuguese. Had I been longer in Ticao I dare say I should have looked upon the evening's entertainment as he did—as a great joke. As it was, I could not stand it. The habit of civilization was just a little too strong for me. I was powerless to stop da Gama's proceedings. He was on his own plantation, surrounded by his own overseers and his own slaves, and, in any event, it is not wise for a foreigner to interfere between the Portuguese and the native in his power. I could do nothing to stop the affair, but I could not endure watching it. I rose and left. I called my boys together and pitched camp about half a mile away. I would move on in the morning.

The night was still, and I heard the sounds that came from the compound, but in my sick rage with the entire Portuguese nation I interpreted them incorrectly. It was not till one of the overseers came to me the next morning, shaking with fright, that I realized what had happened.

Da Gama had not noticed my leaving. He watched his overseers drag Btuvo forward. Curtly he ordered Btuvo to dance. He knew something of the extraordinary awe with which Btuvo was regarded by the natives and knew that if Btuvo danced for a white man a great deal of that revence would be destroyed. As I said a little while ago, I think he was hostile to the native superstitions, both from the contempt a white man feels for a culture that is not his own, and from a belated and curiously surviving habit of regarding non-Christian customs as evils to be eradicated. Btuvo was the high priest of high priests, the most awesome being, to native eyes, in all Ticao. If he danced to the music of a hippo whip for the amusement of a drunken Portuguese plantation-owner, his prestige would be gone forever.

Old and wrinkled, toothless and feeble from his age, his watery eyes were casting this way and that for a way to escape. He was a little made, for he undoubtedly believed in some of his own powers, and he certainly tried to maintain his dignity without prejudicing himself in da Gama's eyes. In his harsh, croaking voice he told da Gama that he was old and his joints were stiff and would not move. Da Gama replied with a curse. He signaled to one of his dingy brown overseers, and the man raised a whip. Btuvo's granddaughter grasped his hand. Da Gama laughed.

The young chief who had been beaten until he fell unconscious stirred a little. The portly chief who had danced himself into exhaustion lay beside the fire, twitching, sobbing in his shame and degradation. Honored, up to that time, by all his people, he had suffered ignominy he could never outlive. The young chief saw the tableau of Btuvo rocking on his old legs, and Btuvo's granddaughter trying to keep the blow of a hippo whip from falling on the old man's back. The blood must have curdled in the young chief's veins. Btuvo, the most sacred, most awesome being of all beings, master of all the spirits, keeper of life and death! He watched with his eyes starting from his head.

Btuvo's granddaughter sprang before da Gama in an ecstasy of rage.

"TOUCH MY grandfather if you dare!" she spat at him, in the native dialect that da Gama understood quite well. "He is the Lord of all spirits, master of all witchcraft! He will cause your bones to turn to yellow mud and your teeth to become the abode of evil spirits that shall torment you! Your cattle shall die, and your fields dry up and be barren, while all men forsake you, and great pains eat out your belly and a worm gnaw in your liver! Touch my grandfather and die!"

Da Gama fairly shrieked in his merriment. He did not see the breathless hush that had come over the slaves. Btuvo was more holy to them than any other man that breathed. If Da Gama dared. . . .

Da Gama's laughter subsided a little, and he looked at Btuvo's granddaughter. She was about eighteen, I suppose, and, as I said, her features were regular and comely, her skin a soft brown, and her eyes of that indescribable soft darkness the Portuguese has come to prize. A man fresh from civilized countries and with the memory of white-skinned girls before his eyes takes little delight in African good looks, but da Gama had been long in Ticao, and his bevy of brown-skinned mistresses pleased him. He saw the slim, supple limbs of the girl who stood before him, and her well-formed features. Slowly his eyes passed up and down her figure and at last came to rest upon her face. His lips parted in an evil grin.

"I hadn't seen you before," he remarked slowly. He rose to his feet and half staggered toward her. She glared at him defiantly. Danger to herself never entered her mind. Her grandfather had been so long revered and respected, so long feared and tremblingly petitioned, that the idea of anyone's daring to molest her was unthinkable.

Da Gama reached her. He put out his arms and seized her. After one astonished instant, she struggled furiously and called to her grandfather to blast the white rat who had put this affront upon her. She was still unafraid, but mad with outraged pride and anger. Btuvo stood still, rocking on his old feet, staring at her with his watery eyes, his sunken jaws working malevolently. Da Gama whooped in drunken joy. He had not expected such sport. With a sweep of his arms he picked up the girl and turned toward the house.

His overseers, left standing in the midst of the compound, shrugged their shoulders. Da Gama would expect nothing further from them. They began to drive the huddled slaves toward the exit of the compound, where they would be taken to their quarters. Btuvo caused a diversion. He had remained standing quite still, rocking feebly back and forth, but suddenly he uttered a shrill cry. The young chief who had loved his granddaughter crawled stealthily along the ground until his hand closed on a heavy stone. Btuvo's activities prevented this movement from being noticed.

Btuvo first cried out shrilly, and the crowd of slaves stopped in their tracks and trembled. For an instant there was silence. Then Btuvo slowly began to revolve in a circle, beating his thin old breast with his hands. His voice rose in a wild chant, and his watery eyes began to glare. A ripple of fear ran along the crowded mass of slaves. In a second, without any of the usual long-continued preliminaries of a witch-doctor, Btuvo was transformed. His eyes flashed fire. Queer grayish foam came from his toothless mouth. His voice became a shriek. Still revolving, he began to pour out a mass of curses and imprecations on Da Gama. His wildly glaring eyes would have frightened anyone, and the slaves eyed him in awe.

An overseer made for him at a run, snarling out a curse. In a second old Btuvo stopped short in his whirling and pointed one skinny claw at the half-breed. The overseer suddenly stumbled and fell flat on the ground. He did not rise. The heavy stone on which the young chief's hand had closed had taken him at the base of the brain, but the slave's attention had been so concentrated on Btuvo that they had not seen the other man make a movement. There was a shudder of deathly fear. An overseer drew his pistol and fired at Btuvo, but the shot went wide. Btuvo screamed out an imprecation, then an order. A tremor ran through the whole huddled group of slaves. Btuvo had ordered them to kill the white man, or live in torment forever more. The overseers saw the tremor, and knew the cause. The entire two hundred slaves were trembling, wavering in abject fear.

As one man, the overseers opened fire on the mob. If that mass of black inhumanity tried to rush the half-dozen overseers there could be but one result. The shooting, however, instead of starting a run for the exit, merely threw the slaves into a wild panic. Two, three, half a dozen, had dropped when the young chief gave a yell and brained an overseer from behind. Btuvo's voice shrieked. . . . In a mad mass of panic-stricken terror the slaves rushed for the overseers, beat them to the earth, and tore them in pieces. Crazy with fear, they swept on to the great house. Like a dark wave they swarmed into it. There were two explosions and a hoarse yell. . . .

I heard the screaming of Btuvo at my camp, but thought he was being tortured. I heard the shots, but thought they were da Gama's affair. It was not until a single dingy brown overseer crept to my tent in the early morning that I learned what had happened. Then I understood the sounds of festivity I had heard during the night. The slaves had sacked the great house and then begun to drink up the rum at the mill where the sugar cane was crushed and distilled. With two or three of my native boys, all armed, I went up to the house. The overseer stalked by my side, brave again in my society.

The house seemed to be deserted, save for a strange wailing that came from within. In the compound I saw half a dozen black bodies in cruiously missshapen heaps on the ground. Other objects showed what the overseers had become. All about the quarters were the slaves, some dead drunk, and others staggering about, still drinking. Sugar-cane rum is deadly stuff. The few who realized what they had done sat dazedly in the sunlight, apathetically awaiting the coming of punishment. They had had all their spirit broken by the Portuguese, and were making no attempt to escape.

After gazing about for a few moments, we made our way into the house. The interior was in ruins. The slaves had rushed about in a frenzy of destruction, smashing everything they could lay their hands upon. I do not know why they had not fired the house.

If I had remained there during the night I should inevitably have shared da Gama's fate. We found him when we followed the wailing sound to its source. In a huddled heap in one corner of his bedroom there was a battered heap that still wore the clothes da Gama had had on the night before. But for that fact it would have been unrecognizable. The wailing came from Btuvo, who was squatting, froglike, over what remained of da Gama, wailing out in a cracked, falsetto voice charms and spells to cause the spirit of the dead man to wander homeless forevermore, to be persecuted of all spirits, and to find no rest through all the ages to come. The single surviving overseer had crept by my side, desperately frightened, but with my boys to give him courage he grew brave again, and I heard a sharp report. Btuvo's wailing was stilled.

Then I had to take charge of affairs. It is the white man's burden that he must act as policeman for all the lesser races of earth, maintaining peace and order, though he long to join in the battle himself. Personally, I wished nothing better than that all the revolted slaves on da Gama's plantation should escape to their homes again, but I could not help them to go. I posted my boys to maintain order, and shut my eyes to those of the *servaçaes* who slipped off into the bush. They would probably die, anyway, but they would have a chance for freedom again. I should have liked to help them all escape, but they were black men, and I was white. They had killed a white man.

White men must always and under all circumstances coöperate in maintaining the supremacy of the white race. It was for this reason that I had to keep order among the slaves, and for this reason that I had to send runners down to Ticao with news of what had happened. I had to stay at Da Gama's plantation until proper officials came to take charge. I was thankful that my business kept me far back in the Hungry Country until they had meted out their "justice." I had forgotten how many slaves they hanged, and how many were sent to work in chains for the rest of their lives, but I remember that without exception every slave was flogged with a hippo whip until he or she fainted from the pain.

THERE WAS one thing that rather pleased me, however. I sent one of my boys secretly to the three native villages to find what had become of Btuvo's granddaughter and the young chief who loved her. He returned with the news that all three villages were deserted, but from a straggler he had learned that under the leadership of the young chief they had combined and moved off into the interior. Btuvo's granddaughter went with them, or, rather, with the young chief. As it was over two months before the Portuguese made any attempt to follow them, they got safely away, and are now no doubt safely settled somewhere far in the interior, months' march beyond the Hungry Country, where the white man will not find them for many years. That is well for them, because we whites have a convenient habit of terming barbarous all cultures that are not our own, and we have but little toleration for barbarism.

## ANNOUNCEMENT

The New Author's Monthly Feature will always be published under the department heading—New Aruthor's Corner—and we hope and expect to make it one of the most interesting features o fthis magazine.

Stories to be acceptable must conform with the editorial requirements of FAR EAST Adventure Stories and should not exceed 3,500 words in length.

All manuscripts accepted for the New Author's Corner will be paid for on acceptance at our regular rates.

Stories from new authors submitted to us for this monthly feature must be so specified. To facilitate our handling these manuscripts in the most efficient manner, the coupon below, properly filled out must be attached to the upper left hand corner of the first sheet of the manuscript.

No manuscripts will be returned unless accompanied by a self-addressed, stamped envelope.

—THE EDITOR.

**New Author's Corner,** Coupon
**FAR EAST Adventure Stories, 25 West 43rd Street, New York City.**

Name ..................................................
Address ..................................................
Title of MSS..................................................
No. of Words........................Locale ........................
What Instruction Have You Had in Story Writing if Any..................
..................................................

# SCARLET IVORY

A Gripping Yarn of Strange Adventure in Pahang

By

## Leslie T. White

THE TALK was of the jungles.

"It seems mighty strange," mused the young British Agent thoughtfully, as he carefully removed the tapering Havana from his mouth, "that no one has ever found the remains of an elephant that died from natural causes!" He rested his head back against the heavy cushions of the chair and sent a thin spiral of smoke coiling and eddying towards the beamed ceiling.

The three men were seated in the Foreign Club, at Bharu, and through the open window before them drifted the warm, seductive perfume of the jungle.

The speaker traced the ring of smoke with his finger, and as it dissolved into the shadows, he sighed and went on, "I heard the legend today—the story, that somewhere in the fastness of the jungles of Pahang, there is a hidden burial-place of the elephants, a last resting place where these giants of the forest journey to when they feel life slipping away from them. Think of it! If such a spot exists—a fortune lies waiting to be plucked from the earth . . . a fortune far beyond the bounds of human conception—in IVORY." The Agent leaned forward in his chair eagerly and rested his elbows on his knees. "You've hunted in the Sakai country, Sloan, what about it?"

In the soft, semi-darkness of the long room, Sloan watched the glowing tip of his cigarette meditatively, then he slowly shook his head. "It's like the *badak api*," he answered quietly. "That fiery rhinoceros of ancient Malayan mythology. It's all part of the East—with it's magic and evil-spirits, its witchcraft and love-potions. No, my boy, a dying beast leaves a spoor, a trail that could easily be traced to your mythical sepulchre. I, too, have heard the yarn, but—" He shrugged his shoulders expressively.

The Agent, to whom all things in the East cast off a delirious mantle of mystery, clung to his point doggedly. "But what happens to them when they die? An elephant's skeleton is a pretty big thing to hide—even here on the Peninsula! Have you ever met anyone that has found one?"

The hunter looked out through the open window at the starry sky, with eyes that were focussed on nothing at all. "No, I haven't, but there's a lot of things one can't explain in the East," he said quietly. "And when one has been here awhile, well, you don't try."

Flushing slightly, the younger man turned to the third member of the group. "You've been here a long while, Cromwell, you know the story, of course?" he suggested hopefully.

The latter extracted the pipe from his lips and absently reached for the slender cane that never left his side. Setting the shaft between his knees, he idly tapped the floor with it, as though debating on the wisdom of speaking at all. "Yes," he said finally. "I've heard the story."

Sloan laughed a trifle sardonically as the Agent leaned forward again. "Is there any truth in it?" he asked eagerly.

The steady drumming of the cane continued, strangely reminiscent of the slow, monotonous beat-beat-beat of the tom-tom, exactly in time with the human heart. Cromwell looked unseeingly at the dragon woven into the grass rug at his feet.

"Yes—it is true!" he muttered dully.

Sloan shrugged indifferently. "Do you merely *believe* that? Or have you some *proof?*"

Cromwell shrank back into the deep cushions of his chair as if he wished he had not spoken. Returning the pipe to his mouth, he toyed with the long white cane and puffed without answering.

The young Britisher broke the spell. "What makes you believe it, sir? Do you know someone that actually found the place? Or have you just heard native rumors?"

In the dusky twilight, the grey haired man smiled wanly. "I knew two chaps that found the burial-pit of the elephants!"

A long silence followed his statement, broken only by the magic whispers of the Eastern night. Presently Cromwell knocked his pipe smartly against his hand to remove the ashes, and smiled a trifle wearily. "I suppose I'll have to explain," he said apologetically.

His companions slumped lower in their chairs without replying, and in the gathering darkness, the glowing tips of their smokes stood out like the fiery eyes of a beast from the jungles so near.

"THE BEST time to hunt on the peninsula," he began quietly, "is during the dry season, before the rains come in with the Northeastern Monsoon. At that time of the year, you know, the blasted jungles are about one degree dryer than when the rains are on, and the leeches, for one thing, are more peaceful.

"Gerald Davis had come out from England to do a bit of hunting. He was young, adventuresome, and with a fair allowance from the old country; enough to put on a decent hunt, within reason.

"Landing in Singapore, he was introduced to Meyers—who was rated a good, though somewhat tough, leader, or foreman of the hunting train. Davis engaged Meyers, on the spot, to take full charge of the hunt.

"Meyers was the incarnation of all that was brutal—a swarthy Dutchman that had lived too long in the tropics. His skin was the color of burnt hide, and his great muscles covered his body like knotted thongs of leather. But the brute was supposed to know his business, and—well, Davis was new to the Peninsula.

"The young Englishman explored Singapore. And Meyers hired the little brown men . . . or 'boys' for the hunt. Everything ready, they took a tramp up as far as she would go with her draught, then they took to the dug-outs and paddled up the Pahang for nearly two hundred miles, to a spot where it fades into a dirty little ditch, with another stream, the Jelai, joining it on the left as you go up. Winding up this murky creek, past Kuala Lipis, you finally reach, after many weary miles, the wild country of the Sakai.

"As soon as Meyers passed the tiny Malay villages farther up the Pahang, and only the treacherous jungles were ahead, he dropped the final thin veneer of civilization that cloaked him and drove the natives with whip and boot.

"Perchance it's the spell of the jungle country—intuition develops very highly out beyond the last lines of our civilization—or maybe it's just common horsesense, but, nevertheless, Davis had a premonition of trouble, serious trouble, and often, when the big red moon swung low in a starry sky, like a flaming ball of fire, he would wake with a start, to press his hand against the firm, hard butt of his heavy service revolver.

"Finally they left the dug-outs and strung out through the dense underbrush in a long, twisting thread of brown and white humanity. Davis tramped in silence, always watching the broad, naked back of the Dutchman—and wondering how it was all going to end. Immediately in front of the Englishman, his native 'boy,' Abas, glided soundlessly, ever watchful for the crawling, poisonous life of the jungle that crowded them on both sides.

"Soon after they had started, Meyers' lust for seeing things suffer clearly showed itself. Davis withheld himself, not wanting to quarrel with his foreman before the natives. It was this lust of cruelty, coupled with the little brown man's reverence for the sacred white elephant, that brought things to a head. And what an ending it had—!

"Even Davis, new to the East, had quickly learned that the white elephant—that eerie phantom that, once in a life time in the jungles, flits across your trail as though it were a shadow, instead of many tons of lumbering flesh—was a sacred thing to be left alone, a creature reverenced by the jungle folk.

"It was a breathless day, hot and sultry, and they had been tramping through the forest all day, and in the soft, yielding earth, they had found the slot of the deer; the hoof-prints of that strangest of all beasts, the wild buffalo; the pitted trail of the wild swine; and even the dainty little foot-prints of the kanchil. There were the markings of the black panther, of packs of wild dogs. In fact the whole valley was alive with game.

"The trail twisted suddenly and the marchers came abruptly on a salt-lick. The lead boy held up his hand for a quick halt, and Davis looking ahead thrilled as he saw the massive form of a great white elephant as it swayed dreamily against the rough bark of a tree. As the sacred animal scratched itself, its eyes were closed, all unconscious of its audience.

"Perhaps it wasn't unconsciousness, but indifference, for even in the jungle fastness, the beasts soon learn whether they are immune from the weapons of the two-legged hunter, or not.

"Davis was watching Abas—the wide-eyed reverence of the little brown boy gripped him—and so he didn't see Meyers unsling his heavy gun and stealthily raise it to his shoulder.

Not until it was too late—until the weapon roared with a blast that echoed and vibrated through the stillness of the forest, sending myriads of bright plumed birds screaming into the heavens in terror—did anyone know what had happened.

The soft nosed slug tore its way into the stomach of the unsuspecting beast and it staggered dazedly, its eyes sweeping the silent group of men. Davis felt sure that the tortured elephant knew who fired the shot, for the small eyes blazed, and with a frenzied trumpeting of pain, it wheeled and disappeared into the forest, squealing shrilly.

"FOR A moment there was silence, then Meyers dropped his gun to his side with a laugh. It was that bestial laugh that started things. Davis felt the blood surge to his temples and his fists clenched as he fought to control himself.

"But it was Abas—son of a Sakai Chief—who acted first. With a low guttural snarl he leaped for the knotted throat of the Dutchman, his small brown hands groping for something to squeeze the life blood from this fiend that had desecrated their gods.

"With a hoarse bellow of surprise and rage intermingled, Meyers sprang backwards, clubbing his gun as he moved. But Abas slipped in his spring, and falling short for an instant left himself exposed. Before he could regain his balance the Dutchman brought the butt of the gun down on his bare head, and the skull popped like a ripe mellon.

As the boy twitched on the ground, blindly seeking to struggle to his knees, the swarthy white man again raised the bloody club, and with a savage oath, jumped forward to finish the slaughter.

"If Davis was slow in getting into action, he made up for it when he started. A thin veil of red fury seemed to blur his vision until only that bestial, sweating face stood before him. Without stopping to draw his own weapon, he lunged at his foreman, taking him by surprise and tearing the bloody gun from his grip with one hand, he sent him staggering backward with a stinging smash on the jaw with the other.

"Soberly the natives formed a dark circle around these two white men that fought with their bare hands in the stifling center of a Sakai forest.

"Screaming like an angry cat, Meyers staggered backward and lashed at the drawn, white face of the other with the black bull-whip that ever encircled his brawny wrist. Davis stepped in close and the blow lost some of its force, but the cruel thong branded a livid welt across his bare neck.

"Now Davis was losing some of his hereditary calmness. With a snarl he clutched for the whip and caught it, to jerk it forward, thereby pulling the other with it. Momentarily off his balance, the cursing Dutchman couldn't avoid the solid swing that the Englishman brought up to his jaw.

"Even as he tottered uncertainly, Davis stepped in, and grunting delightedly, rained blow after blow on that drooling, unshaven chin until the big man seemed to lengthen slightly—rock forward—then as the smaller man jumped backward—he toppled downward, like a fallen tree, to bury his bruised face in the moist grass underfoot.

"Davis wiped the blood from his injured knuckles as he stood glaring at the inert figure on the ground. Then suddenly he spun on his heel and walked over to where the still brown form of Abas lay stretched in his own blood. At first he thought the lad was dead, but a fluttering of the eyelids and a spasmodic twitch of the shoulder muscles told him that Abas lived.

"Hour after hour, the young Englishman fought the inevitable march of death—fought a losing fight for Abas. It was the little brown boy himself who first spoke of the end.

"'*Tûan,*' he whispered falteringly. 'I go soon to my father who was Chief of all the Senoi'—his eyes closed for a moment, 'but there is something the eldest son of the Chief must pass on at his death to the next of kin. I have no son, *tûan,* but the secret must not die with me. The white man comes. Soon my people will be gone. You, *tûan,* have fought for me, son of Hada, Chief of all the Senoi. Come close to me, for my words are few. I tell you of the Cavern of Ivory—the secret of the Senoi!'

"So, as Davis knelt on the cool, damp ground and cradled the bloody head of the dying boy in his arms, the latter weakly drew a crude, faltering map on the soft earth. And in short, broken sentences, each that threatened to be his last, passed on the secret of the Senoi. The paths to follow, the rivers to ford, and finally the secret tunnel that would lead to the legendary grave-yard of the elephants, with its vast, fabulous treasure-house of age-old ivory.

"But during the time that the young Englishman comforted the stricken native, the Dutchman recovered from his beating and crawled sullenly into the shadows to lie, licking his wounds and panting like a creature of the jungles. His sharp ears caught the last words of the dying boy and his piggy little eyes glistened cruelly, his crooked mouth twisting into a snarl that bared his stained yellow teeth. Meyers of the jungles was now shedding his last slim covering of humanity, as a snake sheds a skin that no longer serves it.

"But in spite of the ministering of his white friend, Abas died in his arms.

"AT THE request of Davis, the natives took charge of the body and as he stood silently by watching them, they fitted the slim, broken body into a jacket of bark and laid it into a deep hole they dug by the side of the trail. Into this pitiful grave, they each flung a treasured trinket as a gift to the departed; a bit of flint, a rusty pocket knife, once just a handful of glass beads. Then, when they had all made their contribution, they looked to Davis with a certain shy expectancy. For just an instant did he hesitate, then he gently laid a small prayer-book on the still form, and turned away as the soft earth pattered on the green bark. An old man, broken and withered, spoke a few guttural sentences over the little mound.

"Then silence!

"To Davis, sleep was impossible, so he strolled through the woods to the river, where he sat on the grassy bank and smoked his pipe. The moon had risen and the river ran white between the black walls of the forest that seemed to shut it in on every side. The night was deathly still, yet the heavy, scented air was cool and refreshing after the fierce heat of the day.

"His thoughts were on the strange story that Abas had told, and now, as he reviewed the tale in the peace and calm of the jungle night, it seemed but another mythical legend of Sakai folk-lore.

"Sitting by the sluggish waters of the stream, and bathed in the soft glow of an Eastern moon, the Englishman never had a chance to see the sinister figure that watched him from the haunting shadows. The sudden snapping of a twig startled him, but even as he moved to turn, something crashed on his head. Little colored lights seemed to blind him. Then, a grateful chasm of darkness relieved the pain in his head.

"He was a long time out. And returning consciousness didn't catch up with him until the cool mists of a ruddy Malayan dawn found him to life again. When he weakly touched his fingers to his blood-matted hair, he knew that at least one dawn had come and gone since he had lost his senses. For a long time he lay still, wondering what had happened to him, and how the predatory beasts had missed him in their nocturnal wanderings. Slowly, the events preceding the attack unfolded themselves before his mind. Dazedly, and with a growing fear clutching at his heart, he staggered to the place where camp had been.

"Before he reached the charred spot left by the fire, he realized that he had been left behind. And as he stooped over the patch of earth where Abas had weakly drawn the map, and saw where the heavy boots of Meyers had carefully obliterated each mark, the reason became all too plain.

"The Dutchman had over-heard the story told by Abas—and believed it!

"Leaning against a tree, Davis sparingly filled his pipe from the small pouch of tobacco he had remaining and surveyed the hostile forest that rose sheer on every hand. Even the trees seemed to lean inward, as though to crush him into the damp earth. In the lurking shadows, he could sense the unseen eyes that hungrily watched his every move.

"A sudden thought sent his right hand darting to his side. But his gun was gone! But worst of all, Davis felt himself burning, and although the dawn was cool, the blood seemed to boil in his veins.

"FEVER!

"Sorry as his plight was, however, the white man realized that standing over the deserted camp-ground could avail him nothing. Perhaps, before the ravages of the fever overtook him, he might be able to catch up with his train. He reasoned, that, as the Dutchman had probably left him for dead, he might not hurry unduly.

"His mouth drawn into a thin, determined line, Davis singled out a small stick to use as a cane, and with his dew-drenched clothing plastered to his fever-ridden body, he struck out along the trail left by the natives.

"How many tortured miles he followed the winding trail, he knew not, but suddenly the forest thinned out into a small clearing where the ground looked as though it had been ploughed. The soil was a brilliant red, but not so much as a blade of grass graced its rough surface—an uncanny sight in a land where everything is green and rich.

"The white man knew that he had stumbled on to one of those somewhat rare saline deposits of the Malayan jungles. To this spot would flock all the living creatures of the forest, from the elephant and the wild buffao, to the tiny mouse-deer that grows no larger than a rabbit, and to the little stoats—to lick the salt and trample the earth with their countless feet.

"But at his approach, there was a scattering and the shy beasts of the jungle fled into hiding. Weakly the Englishman circled the clearing, searching for the lost trail.

"Finally he ran across a place where the thick brush was broken and beaten. And on the hard ground, he found a clot of dried blood—then another. Racked with fever, Davis unhesitatingly plunged into the forest again on the new trail he had found. Coming to a small dirty stream that flowed slowly on its way to the sea through the heat of the jungle, he waded into the cooling water and it seemed to steady the rising fire within him.

"Again on the trail, his ears caught the sound of something ahead of him, and certain that at last he had caught up with his boys, he ran blindly, crying hysterically at the top of his voice.

"SUDDENLY HE stopped and stared at the *thing* that rose up before him and a cold sweat permeated his tortured body. Vainly he brushed his withered hand over his bleary eyes as though to clear his vision, for instead of the long, weaving line of brown natives, with a swaggering white man at their head, there loomed before him the vision of a huge white elephant—a phantom of white on whose belly there was a reddish-brown stain. Even as he watched, transfixed with horror, the *thing* moved slowly away from him and disappeared again into the forest.

"Sick at heart, fever-racked in body, and thoroughly disgusted, Davis looked at the smothering jungle around him. The crooked trail over which he had just come seemed the only path leading from the spot where he now found himself.

"Frantically he listened for some sounds of the ghost as it moved through the trees, but he heard nothing. For a moment sheer terror tore at his heart and suddenly this eerie white giant seemed as a close friend to the sick man—the only living thing in an awful silent world.

"With a hoarse cry, he flung himself into the spot where he had seen the beast disappear. Now he didn't care whether it was a phantom, or a real, living pachyderm. He could see it, and when it was near—he wasn't *alone!*

"Eventually he caught up with the *thing* and together this ill-assorted pair moved through the forest, across clearings where timid antelope watched them with wide, shy eyes; through sluggish waters whose smooth gliding surfaces hid the lurking dangers of darting fangs; under low overhanging trees with branches that were twinned with quick death masquerading in twitching, scaly bodies.

"On—always—on!

"The white elephant's pace seemed to quicken, and once Davis fell weakly behind, the thick brush closing before him like the last curtain at the theater in Piccadilly. Frantically he scurried forwards, but no longer could he see the white form. With a hoarse scream he broke into a faltering run. Ahead of him a hill rose abruptly, and although the brush here was stunted and low, the white monster was nowhere in sight.

"Rushing blindly on, Davis felt his feet suddenly collapse under him. The earth seemed to disappear and he shot downward—down—down. Then a merciful veil of darkness eased his frenzied consciousness. When his senses returned, and Davis cautiously opened one eye to gaze about him, his first thought was that is was night time. But as his swollen eyes finally caught their focus, he saw that he was in some sort of an immense cavern that was lighted by a soft, reflected glow, the source of which he was unaware.

"As he became accustomed to the dimly lit interior, he gasped with astonishment at the amazing sight that met his eyes. In the soft shadows that surrounded the place, great stacks of ivory tusks were heaped in piles, and on the hard earthen floor were scattered the bones of countless elephants.

"Still believing it was but a bad dream, the white man struggled to his feet and reached with trembling hands toward the priceless piles of ivory. Breathless with wonder he surveyed the fantastic sight. The gigantic catacomb stretched out into the darkness, branching on all sides into other crypts, where lay the smoldering bones of the forest giants, their ivory tusks gleaming in the soft eerie light of the cavern.

"Then Davis knew! He was in the burial place of the elephants! The broken story, whispered from the bleeding lips of Abas *was* true!

"He brushed a trembling hand over his aching eyes as though afraid that it was all but a haunting picture—this terrible sepulchre of death.

"Suddenly a sound behind him seemed to freeze the boiling blood in his veins! Stiff with horror, he turned and was just in time to catch a fleeting glimpse of the white elephant, as it dissolved into the shadows.

"Fear gripped the fever-racked man. Terror led strength to his waning footsteps, and he ran blindly through the lofty vaults of this ghastly mausoleum. Then his strength left him, and he stopped, sick and tired, to collapse against the cold, damp walls. Vaguely he wondered why there was no stench of death with all these dead jungle monstors strewn about in endless profusion, but the spectacle of it all dazed him. Around him lay countless fortunes of precious ivory—fabulous beyond the ken of human imagination—and yet in this midst of plenty, starvation stared him in the face, even though he should win his fight against the fever that threatened to burn him alive.

WHEN HE first heard the hoarse, guttural shouts that emanated from the darkness of the cavern, he thought it was but the approaching delirium of his fever-racked mind. Then, very slowly it dawned on his senses that the guttural voice belonged to the jungle Dutchman—Meyers!

"With the realization, his brain cleared. Meyers had followed the trail described by Abas and found the pit. Then, Davis wondered: Had the white monster he had trailed been the wounded elephant, or merely a phantom—a figment of his tortured mind?

"Crouching in the shadows like a wounded animal, the Englishman waited and the man that had tried to murder him came closer, mad with the lust for ivory. In the wide-staring eyes of the Dutchman was the look of a maniac—crazy with the thought that this vast treasure house was his, and his alone!

"Still keeping his terrified eyes on the great hulking figure as he ran forward, Davis reached a groping hand into a mass of bones nearby in search of a weapon. Just as his trembling fingers closed over a smooth, slim shaft, Meyers saw him.

"The beady little eyes of the Dutchman narrowed and in the semi-darkness they glittered like twin points of flint. The thick lips curled back in a snarl that bared the yellow teeth like the drooling grin of a jackal. With an animal cry that was half fear, half rage, Meyers flung himself at this blood-caked ghost of the man he believed he had slain back in the dew-soaked jungle.

"Calm now that the crisis had come, Davis staggered to meet the attack of the madman. From the sash that girdled his waist, Meyers drew a wavy kris and slashed at the figure before him.

"Davis succeeded in diverting the blow with the shaft of ivory he used as a sword, but the heavy handle of the kris struck him a glancing blow on the head, that hurled him reeling backwards.

"There in the semi-darkness of the lost tomb of the elephants these two white men fought a fight that could only end one way. By the death of one—or both.

"Bleeding and weak, the Englishman gave ground before the maniacal savagery of his opponent. The slender, sword-like cane of bloody ivory parried the hacking blows of the razor-edged kris, but now the blood was forming a red veil before his eyes, and Davis knew he couldn't last much longer. Abruptly the Dutchman kicked out with his heavy boot and taken unawares, the blow landed full in the Englishman's stomach, and he fell to the dust in agony.

Meyers gave a harsh, guttural roar of triumph and started forward, the short kris gripped tightly in a hairy paw and his piggy little eyes spitting venom. Hypnotized, Davis watched the advance, helpless to defend himself.

"Suddenly his eyes were drawn to a white shadow that loomed behind the approaching Dutchman— a shadow that swayed slightly, but still came forward!

"The white elephant!

"Dumb with horror, he watched as the beast folded it's trunk out of the way. Then a wild tumult of noise shattered the stillness—a terrible trumpeting like the scream of a mighty siren. The beast charged forward. Two long white tusks gleamed in the soft light, and two fierce little red eyes glistened as though they recognized the man in their path.

"The Dutchman wheeled as he

heard the wild squealing of the elephant. An agonized scream of terror broke from his twisted mouth.

"The white elephant was spent, but it dove straight at the squirming form of the Dutchman. Sick with horror, Davis saw the two sharp-pointed tusks of the elephant spear the twisting body of the Dutchman to the hard ground.

"The screams of the pinioned man clove the air like a hot knife. Frantically, Davis tried to push the dying elephant off the sufferer, but to no avail. Then, grabbing his sword-cane, the Englishman fled from this scene of awful death and ran blindly away. The fever blistering his brain, and the dying screams of the Dutchman rang in his ears.

"On he stumbled. His senses began slipping away. Finally he fell in delirium in the midst of the jungle.

"He awoke beside the cool bank of a gently flowing river, that moved like a twisted strand of silver through the green of the forest. In the air overhead, brilliant colored birds hovered and screamed at him. Slowly, he made out the forms of natives bending over him. They were putting soothing herbs on his bleeding wounds.

"Several of the little brown men gently lifted him on to an improvised hammock of bark. Now, as he looked about him, the place seemed vaguely familiar. It reminded him of the spot where he had been sitting when he had been first attacked.

"His eyes were cleared and he smiled grimly. Surely it must all have been an awful dream. These were his own boys—Intently he peered into the stoical faces and a look of surprise flashed on his own. They were all strangers, and they didn't understand his eager questions.

"Someone was trying to take something from his tightly clenched fingers. Instinctively, Davis tightened his grip and looked to see what it was that he held, and clung to so tenaciously.

"It was a slender, sword-like shaft of aged ivory, and it was stained scarlet with blood!

"THAT SHAFT never left Davis's side from that moment on. Years later, he returned to that section where the river Jelai sluggishly wends its way through the darkened jungle, and tried to find the trail where the sacred white elephant had led him, for, you remember, Abas had said that the secret must be handed from father to son. But he found nothing.

"And so the secret of the sepulchre of the elephants passed with the brown boy Abas and the Dutchman, Meyers, who died a slow death pinioned to the floor of the vast storehouse of ivory, by the very white elephant he had wounded—the one that never forgot who had fired the soft-nosed slug!"

Cromwell continued his ceaseless tapping with the cane for a moment when his tale was finished. Then he rose abruptly and strode from the room as though he wished to forestall any further questions.

For a few minutes the two men watched the door through which he had disappeared, in silence. Then the young agent sighed and relaxed into the soft folds of his chair.

"Strange yarn, that," he mused thoughtfully. "I wonder if it's true? Do you know this chap, Davis?"

Sloan puffed his pipe. "Yes—I think I know *Davis,*" he muttered slowly, gently shaking his shaggy head. "I often wondered where he picked up that cane—and why he never lets it leave his side."

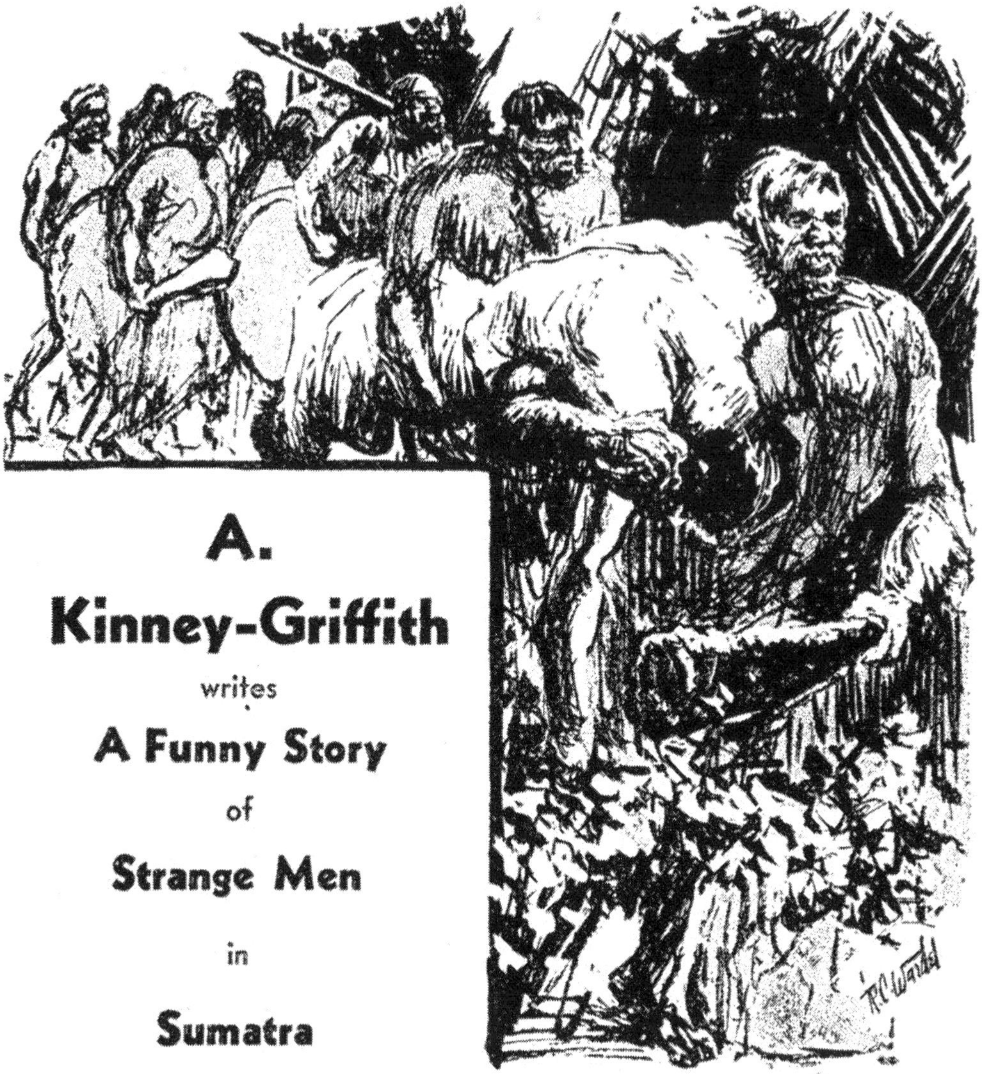

**A. Kinney-Griffith**

writes

**A Funny Story**

of

**Strange Men**

in

**Sumatra**

# SAVAGE TRICKERY

INTO THE Sumatran hinterlands, along the torturous Jamba River that flows through the wild Cheecha Ridge country—a jungle land where few white men had ever been before, and where no white man was ever meant to live—hummed the powerboat of Dick Graham and Tom Corcoran, the two adventurous field men of the American Asiatic Academy of Archeology.

Their goal lay before them. Somewhere ahead in this blaze of equatorial heat lay that which they sought. Somewhere here in the virgin jungle—a primitive land where nature runs riot, where the struggle for existence is eternal, inevitable, deadly.

As the president of the academy had said:

"Somewhere in the Cheecha Ridge country of Sumatra live the last peoples of the Neolithic Age. The Stone Age. *Gormoras.* They are savages—probably cannibals. Proof of their existence came to me accidentally. Yet the proof was incredible. I sent George Hanley to investigate. I had relied upon him to bring incontrovertible evidence of these Stone Age descendants. Such proof would convince the archeological world. Hanley cabled from Kampong. He was going into the Cheecha region. That's been two months ago. We should have heard of his success within ten days. Gentlemen, there is only one conclusion: He found the *Gormoras* and—but need I say more?" And he eyed the two men before him keenly. "Now, Mr. Graham and Mr. Corcoran, take the best of equipment, an abundance of funds, and go down there. Find George Hanley. If he is alive, bring him back. And bring me definite proof of that Neolithic people!"

And now Dick and Tom were in the Cheecha Ridge country—the last stand of the Stone Age. The Jamba River was in flood. The fiery sun was nearing the jungle rim, and with its setting, night falls with alarming suddenness in the tropics. They steered their powerboat toward the northern shore and, at a spot where the mangrove was thin and great ebony trees soared high, landed.

There the water was clean, and slim bamboo poles were convenient to support their tent. They hung their hammocks, found firewood and were ready for the night. Yet, when all was complete, Dick looked suspiciously at the dense jungle and said:

"Tom, this place gives me the shivers."

"Why?" Tom asked.

"I don't know," Dick confessed. "But I have a feeling in my bones that something is all wrong."

At that Tom too peered around. Slanting sun shafts beamed through the trees, giving good light, but revealing nothing strange. They listened. Far away a flamingo yelped in the stillness like a lost soul. No other sound came. Tom sniffed the air. It bore only the usual dank smells of the jungle.

"There's nothing wrong with this place," Tom declared. "At least no more than any other in this wild country."

Dick Graham shrugged. Saying no more, he stepped to the boat, gathered up an armful of equipment and brought it into the tent.

They ate in silence. Somehow Tom too began to feel uneasy. When darkness fell they got into their hammocks without lighting the fire and lay there with pipes going and ears open.

Only the usual sounds of the jungle night came to them. Crickets called and answered. Crocodiles splashed in the river. Somewhere a tiger screamed. Somewhere an orang-outang groaned. Soft footsteps of prowling tigers came near, then went away. Leaves rustled, became silent again. Something screamed suddenly, stopped as quickly; something being killed by something else. Finally all these sounds were smothered by heavy rain.

Then they slept. They knew the downpour would continue throughout the night, and all creatures would seek shelter.

DAYLIGHT AWOKE them. The sky was dull, the jungle steaming with heat and moisture. But the rain had ceased. Around them they saw nothing new. Tom set fire to the wood which they had been too cautious to burn before, then stepped to the river to fill the coffee pot. Dick entered the powerboat and began bailing it out. Their rifles lay in the hammocks, where they had been useless bedfellows all night.

"Well, guess we scare kind of easy, eh, Dick?" said Tom, nonchalantly lighting a cigarette. "This place is as silent as a graveyard."

Dick continued scooping water, making no answer. Tom turned back toward the fire. Then he froze.

"Hell!" he gasped. "The devils!"

Dick dropped his canvass bucket with a soggy bump. He grunted. Then they stood without sound or motion, staring at fearful figures.

Giant savages surrounded their tent, facing them with *parang* spears raised or with arrows ready on bow cords. Several held *sumpitans*—the deadly poison dart gun. Without a sound they had appeared from behind the big trees and surrounded the camp.

As the archeologists stood paralyzed, the giant of them all emerged from the tent. He carried the two rifles and pistols in one hand. He stooped low to avoid the roof of the tent. It was more than six feet from the ground, for Dick, a tall man, had that tent made special to give him plenty of room. Yet the giant savage had to bow far down in order to leave the place.

And the others were nearly as huge as he was. The shortest was at least six inches taller than Dick Graham, and twice as broad. All of them were deep chested, wide shouldered, thick limbed and mightily muscled. All were naked, except for the weapons they carried. Their heavy bows and arrows were about ten feet long, their stout spears a yard longer.

Now that their leader had captured the rifles, the giants slacked the strings of their bows, let their spears sink and grinned evilly at the white men. They were a beastly looking lot: heavy jawed, thick lipped, flat nosed, cold eyed, low foreheads; and with their sharp teeth showing, they seemed animals in human form, gloating on victims whom they meant to tear apart.

Tom dropped the coffee pot and drew a hunting knife from his boottop. At once the chief yelled at him. So sudden and so loud was that yell that Tom felt half dazed by its volume. For a moment he stood gaping.

With a sideways swing of his arm the chief dropped the rifles. Before they struck the earth he plunged at Tom, whooping as he came. His enormous paws swooped like the tearing claws of a grizzly bear. Tom dodged, slashed at the giant's face with the knife, but missed.

He thrust at the huge throat above him and felt his wrist caught in a crushing grip. The blade was torn from his grasp and he was knocked headlong. He hit the ground so hard that for a few moments he was stunned. By that time Dick too was disarmed.

He had leaped from the boat as his pal fell, his own knife drawn, a glitter in his snapping eyes. He struck like lightning. Two savages rushed him. The knife was knocked from his fist by a mighty sweep of a spear. The blow knocked the knife yards away. Then a huge creature cuffed Dick on one ear and knocked him senseless.

As Tom struggled upright a thunderous howl of laughter hit his ears. All the savages were bellowing with amusement, tickled by the sight of two white men hurt and helpless. The enormous chief grinned, swelled with pride, thumped his chest, and empty-handed, waited for Tom to attack him again.

Tom did not. Mad though he was he still had some reason. Unarmed, facing a brute far stronger, surrounded by other giants with powerful weapons, trying to think of some way to save both his pal and himself, there was nothing he could do. Nothing. So he stood still, glaring at the chief, aching to kill him, but making no move.

The giant glared back. But after a few seconds his snaky eyes wavered, just as those of an animal might do. No animal can steadily meet the gaze of a white man standing still. And this brawny brute, although strong enough to tear Tom apart, was not much more intelligent than an orang-outang. He soon proved it.

His eyes came back, furtively. He burst out roaring again and beat his chest with both fists. His tongue spoke some language unknown to white men, but his actions were clear enough. He wanted Tom and all other listeners to know that he was the mightiest man in the whole wide world.

For several minutes he bellowed, proving his greatness by his noise. Then, with a final growl, he turned to the motorboat and yanked out the iron trunk that contained the partners' exploration equipment. This he carried to the nearest tree, where, with one terrific swing, he smashed it open.

Out fell the supplies—cameras, specimen boxes, vials, cartridges, clothes, matches, tobacco, and so on. He looked at the mess, gave a greedy grunt, clawed it all over, threw it back in the wrecked trunk. He then wheeled upon his men and bawled orders.

They scattered. Two picked up the rifles and one retrieved the knives of the white men. Others tore down the tent and hammocks. The rest of them moved around, pretending to do something, but looking at the stuff in thetrunk.

THE CHIEF grabbed the guns away from his tribesmen, who gave them up gladly, seeming afraid of them. The savage who got the knives, held them in back of him. His brutal face showed selfish discontent. He was about six inches shorter than the chief, but was heavier, stouter, and unlike the others, wore a half-inch gold armlet on his left arm between the elbow and the powerful biceps. The chief snarled at Armlet and snatched away the knives. Others muttered. It was plain that they wanted shares in the plunder.

Dick Graham, fast recovering his senses, sat up and looked around.

"Steady!" said Tom Corcoran. "We're not dead yet. Take it easy."

At the sound of his voice the chief growled. Several spearmen strode forward, grinning evilly, and prodded the white men. Dick, his face a grim mask, got to his feet; then the captives were driven toward the jungle.

With the trunk under one arm and the guns and knives clutched in a big fist, the chief picked up his war club. It was an enormous thing, of ebony wood, shaped like a knobkerrie, and heavy as lead. He swung it like a toy, snarled a harsh command, and led off into the dense jungle.

Pressing along at a brisk gait, the war party soon entered a path. Along it they trod for several miles. As they went, the pals noticed a few things and thought of others.

The skins of the giants were reddish-brown; much like any white man's face who is heavily sun tanned. Their huge bodies were almost covered with short black hair and most all of them wore flamingo feathers in their long manes. None of them wore ornaments, except the stocky man with the gold armlet, and the chief who wore both feathers and streaks of white paint on his face and shoulders. Their language was a series of monosyllabic grunts; nothing like the Sumatran dialect in common use. They were of some race unknown to the archeologists; hulking creatures who seemed more like apes than like men.

But, unlike the orang-outangs, they were not accustomed to climb into trees. Nor were they river people, for they had left the powerboat lying at the shore, proving that they had no interest in water travel. They were jungle men, who relied on their stout legs for traveling.

Their weapons were of wood—black ebony and teak—hard and heavy, which, shaped into clubs and spears, could smash a man's head or pierce his vitals like metal. The arrows, though, had heads of flint. The lack of steel in this party testified that these strange folk had little or no contact with outsiders. However, they *had* been wary toward the partners' guns; possibly they had met somebody who had given them cause to fear firearms.

Suddenly the war party reached the end of the path. Tom and Dick looked sharply around. Mt. Indrapura loomed in the distance, black and forbidding. Great teak and ebony trees towered overhead, but were widely spaced, and the ground was clear of brush. In the center of the opening stood a large house. It was round, possibly fifty feet in diameter, and built of heavy bamboo cane with a palm-leaf roof. It had one high door and no windows. Beyong it were a score of smaller huts. Nearly a hundred nude people were gathered outside the large hut; men loitering, women working, children playing. One of the loafers spied the war party and yelled. Then all swarmed forward.

They surrounded the returning hunters, shouting and grinning. The women and children looked as evil as the men. Their eyes were merciless as those of beasts of prey, their teeth as menacing, their voices as harsh. All were eager to pull the white captives to pieces. Then came a yell louder than all the rest, and the mob hushed. The chief had commanded.

He himself continued bellowing, though in a different tone. He now was bragging, telling his tribe how cunningly he had caught the foreign devils.

He dropped his plunder and hammered his chest with both fists. His chest swelled mightily. He roared like a thunderbolt and reacted his story while he spoke. When his tale ended, he wheeled to Dick, gripped his neck, lifted him off the ground with one hand and tore away his clothes.

Immediately some other giant seized Tom from behind and treated him in the same way. Neither white man had been fully dressed when surprised and caught; and in no time their scanty clothes were ripped off them. Then the pair of them were dangling in air, naked and wriggling like fish.

Another roar broke from the crowd. The savages found the spectacle very amusing. Tom and Dick fought, squirmed, kicked and struck at the stout arm holding them. The watchers howled with devilish glee. At length, exhausted by the futile struggle, the pals hung limp, each nearly paralyzed by the brutal grip.

THE WORST was yet to come. The chief barked an order, and the crowd gave way. He stalked through them, still holding Dick in air. The savage carrying Tom strode after the chief. The mob trooped to the far end of the clearing. Then, surrounded by the chuckling brutes, the pals were dropped to the ground where they stared sickly at a shrine upon which were a dozen human heads.

All of these heads seemed to be very lifelike, except that they were about one-fourth the natural size. Most of them showed lines of the Sumatran bushman, several seemed to be Malays; and one was white!

"The dirty dogs!" Tom Corcoran growled, his face white with rage. "That's George Hanley's—ugh! I'm sick. Poor George!"

Utterly revolted, he turned over on his stomach and sobbed.

"Calm down, Tom," came the voice of Dick. "We mustn't let this get our goats. We're ripe for the stew pots and the head-shrinking ovens unless we can effect an escape! We must escape—these are the *Gormoras!*"

"All right, let's go now!" yelled Tom, and sprang upright like a tiger. He dived at the brawny brute who had hurt and humiliated him. Crazy with rage and despair, he smashed him in the face with both fists. Never in his past career as a pugilist had he fought with such utter ferocity. His knees drove for the groin, and the giant went down, squealing with pain. The chief dropped headlong when Dick's heel caught him in the stomach.

Taken by surprise at this furious onslaught, the *Gormoras* now rallied. Several of them rushed the white men. A war club swung a long arc. *Smack!* Then Tom was down—motionless.

His partner, in the meanwhile, hadn't had a chance. After his first kick, a spear caught him across the forehead and knocked him senseless.

An hour later Tom came back to consciousness. His body was covered with painful bruises. His head ached terribly. Dully he looked around and saw he was in a cage. Beside him was Dick, insensible. Outside were several savages looking through the bars at them. Off to the right was the shrine with its row of grisly heads.

Their cage, about twelve feet square, was built of dried bamboo poles four inches apart. Sides, ends and top were of heavy teak logs, and interwoven iron-vines held the structure together. There was one door, already laced shut, and the roof was like the sides—open enough for the next rain to beat in, but through which there was no escaping.

Tom gritted his teeth and turned to his pal. Dick was a gory sight, but his breath was coming regularly. Again Tom looked at the savages.

The chief and the man whom Tom had attacked were not in sight. Possibly they were calling upon the tribal witch-doctor to ease some painful bruises; the thought made Tom feel better. The loitering savages outside scowled and sneered, and Tom sneered back.

Then a quick thought came to him. A quiver of the old-time recklessness shot through his body. His gaze centered on one of the *Gormoras*, the one that wore the gold armlet and who had defied the chief. Tom considered: Armlet was big enough and powerful enough, to give the chief a hard fight, and possibly kill him, if he dared to try. And his eyes told Tom that he had some personal interest in him. The eyes were not friendly; merely cold and calculating. But, as a drowning man catches at a straw, so Tom caught the savage's look and held it.

Dick Graham sat up then, and the spell was broken. After he comprehended the situation, he laid back with a groan and felt his aching head. In a moment he sat upright again, then his attention too settled upon Armlet outside.

Other men and women and some children came to sneer at the captives. They sneered back at them, then lay down and shut their eyes to show that they did not think them worth looking at. There were a few growls and snarls from the men, and then quiet. After awhile they all went away, and the captives smelled the odor of meat cooking over the fire pits.

"Poor George Hanley," Tom muttered, "wonder how they got him?"

"Probably blundered right into them, same as we did," Dick replied. "God, what wouldn't I give to be free about five minutes with our 16 mm. motion picture camera! I'd get enough proof of this tribe of Neolithic brutes to satisfy all the acheologists in the world!"

"Yeah. But I'd rather have the five minutes with my rifle; or better yet—a machine gun! I'd then go back and tell the Old Man that there are no *Gormoras!*"

The pals fell silent. Fear gripped them. They knew they were being saved for a purpose which did not need discussion. They looked at everything except the row of shrunken heads.

When the savages finished their meal, the men disappeared into the large bamboo house. Soon the captives could hear angry voices; apparently a council, or a division of spoils, was being held in the chief's house, and his tribesmen were discontented with his dividing of the loot.

The captives began examining their cage more thoroughly, hoping to find a weak spot in the vines or poles. Only the vines holding the door were new, but even they were far too strong to be broken with anything short of an axe or knife. To get such weapons was a task—a hopeless one.

Soon the grumbling voices in the chief's house quieted down. A man emerged and walked across the clearing. He was Armlet. His head was bowed and his features were distorted with savage rage. Plainly he was angry at something said or done at the council.

Suddenly a desperate thought came to Dick Graham. "Get that big gorilla to come over here," he muttered.

"I'm thinking of the same thing!" responded Tom Corcoran.

THE ARCHEOLOGISTS slid their arms between the poles and beckoned. Armlet scowled at them, then turned his head, listening. The voices in the big house had turned to laughter. Armlet scowled deeper, then strode toward the cage.

He stopped at a corner where he could watch the captives and the house by quick turns of the eyes. The pals remained standing. Dick, quite expressive in the use of sign language, swung his hands and arms in a few deft movements; asking what was to be done with him and Tom.

The savage answered readily enough. He looked toward the sky, narrowed his eyes as if bothered by the sun, moved his chin westward, then hung his head as if asleep. In the same way he told of the passing of another day and the coming of another night. This time he did not act sleepy. Instead he pointed at the row of shrunken heads and made other gestures that would make an iron man shiver.

"Tomorrow night is full moon," Dick said aloud to Tom. "He says they always feast on full moons; but tomorrow will be a *special* occasion, it seems, as they consider us 'moon' warriors!"

Tom nodded grimly. Dick turned to the savage, and asked about the chief. Armlet grinned maliciously and showed that for the present the chief was suffering with severe stomach pains; he also made plain that the chief would take revenge for his bruises tomorrow night.

Tom muttered :"Hurry! Try and persuade this ape to . . ."

"Quiet," Dick rebuked. "I am coming to that point."

With that Dick began taunting Armlet for letting the chief keep all of the loot.

"You are afraid of him!" Dick pantomimed. "You could kill him in a fight. He took your share of what was ours; next he will steal your women. You are nothing but an orang-outang—big muscles and big mouth!"

The big brute growled savagely at that accusation. He opened his mouth to let out a war cry. He hit his chest with both fists. Then he hesitated, looked at the chief's house, and glowered murderously.

"If you are not afraid of him, now is your time," Dick went on. "I have hurt him. You can finish him if you work quickly."

A ferocious grin proved that Armlet enjoyed the thought. But he made no move toward the big house.

"It's working," Dick whispered to his pal.

But the big savage's mind was not so slow as they had supposed it to be. Before Dick had time to suggest that they could kill the old chief and make him the new one if they were liberated, Armlet's broad face turned crafty; and, by motions, he asked how to shoot a gun.

"Bring one and we'll show you," Dick parried.

Armlet scowled and objected: "You would kill me with it."

"No," Dick denied. "We are friends. Bring a rifle and we will show you how to use it. Then you will be chief!"

The giant *Gormoran* looked long at the white men. They looked steadily back at him, trying to appear sincere.

The plotting was halted then, as men came out of the big house. The council had broken up. At once the savage beside the cage became abusive. He bellowed at the captives, made insulting motions and gave the impression of deadly hatred. The other men came flocking around, women and children after them. Several boys poked sticks into the cage; others threw stones and filth. But this was quickly stopped. Men cuffed them away. Apparently the right time had not yet come to see the captives squirm.

Soon the savages went away, and Armlet went with them, without a backward look. Then came the afternoon rains of the tropics. The prisoners, nude and battle-worn, lay down on their backs and were glad for the deluge of water. It not only gave them rest from their captors but cured their headaches, washed them and wet their feverish tongues.

For several hours the rain battered down. Tom and Dick huddled together, drenched, stiff, miserable. Nobody came near them, nor even watched them from the big house. Finally the rain stopped, and the chief himself came out. He walked with a limp and inspected every corner of the cage. For once he made no noise; but his looks were worse than the most appalling yells. Then, with a grin as cruel as the snarl of a Bengal tiger, he went back to his house.

Night came. For a while the captives crept around in the pen. They tried every bar and vine and log, even attempting to gnaw through one of the fresh vines with their teeth. Split lips and bleeding gums were their only rewards. So they lay back down again, waiting, waiting, waiting. . . .

THE RAIN clouds cleared away and the moon poured bright beams down into the open space. An eerie quiet settled upon the jungle scene; the dark wall of wet trees sparkled with moon beams and a faint breeze increased the opalescent effect.

A movement at the far end of the clearing caused Tom and Dick to draw up tensely. A tall warrior came into view. He stopped by one of the smaller huts, and in a moment was joined by a shorter, more graceful figure. They met in close embrace, turned and moved arm in arm into the depths of the primeval jungle.

"Huh, lovers!" Dick Graham grunted.

"Quiet!" hissed Tom Corcoran, and pointed toward the other side of the clearing.

Some one else was abroad in the night. This figure moved silent as a ghost; came nearer, then the Americans recognized the giant form of Armlet, and in one huge fist, held rigidly before him, he carried a rifle!

He came forward swiftly, yet so softly that his great feet made no sound in the night. He held the rifle as far from him as he could, plainly afraid of it. When he reached the cage, Dick reached forth a hand, and he almost gave the weapon to him. He then jerked it back, distrustfully.

With the empty hand he made motions, asking how to fire the gun without harm to himself. Dick answered with other motions that meant nothing. Armlet scowled, scratched his head; then standing close to the bars and, holding the rifle in back of him, asked the same question again. Again Dick answered in movements too fast to follow, then, acting impatient, reached out as if eager to show how by actually handling the rifle.

Armlet backed away. He growled, looked sharply at the white men, then slowly brought the rifle to Dick's grasp.

"Oh, boy!" Tom released his pent-up breath. "Now, don't shoot him yet."

"Quiet," hissed Dick; then, pointing the muzzle away from the savage, pretended to try to show how to work the gun.

It did not operate. Dick tugged and yanked at it, accomplished nothing. His deft fingers flew all over the weapon from muzzle to stock, and after ascertaining that the rifle was fully loaded, he made a good show of useless work.

Finally he passed the gun to Tom, who played the same game. They muttered to each other and pointed to the rear sights. Tom acted as if trying to loosen something with his thumb nail. He shook his head, and laid the rifle down between them. Then Dick told the disappointed savage that it was stuck and that they needed a knife to loosen it. He pantomimed on, requesting the other gun, also the little black leather box with the straps—the portable motion picture Cine-Kodak—with which to charge the guns.

Armlet growled deep in his mighty chest, but did not hesitate long. He felt more trust in the white men now, as they had not once pointed the gun at him. He retreated and made a circuitous trip toward the big house.

As soon as he had disappeared Dick and Tom set to work to clean the mud out of the rifle muzzle and breech. It had become clogged some time during the scuffle down by the river. But in a few moments the pals had the weapon in perfect firing order.

"Well," said Tom, "whatever happens now, they won't torture us."

"No. One for you and one for me," Dick nodded. "And at least two for the chief. Don't lose count."

"I won't," Tom promised.

Then they sat in silence, waiting for the savage to return. An hour passed. Occasionally some wild animal screamed in the jungle. Again silence. Primordial silence. The young couple who had met and gone away for some clandestine purpose, now returned. Several hours passed. Still Armlet did not reappear.

"Treacherous savage!" Tom muttered. "He's probably thinking things over; and is trying to make the other gun work. . . ."

"He may be having trouble in stealing the other rifle," Dick said thoughtfully. "Somebody may be awake. I hope he don't fool around with those automatics and mess up things."

"Whatever the case, you see his game, don't you? He plans to kill the chief in the dark and then throw the blame on us, saying that we fired the guns by magic. Then, tomorrow night, he'll throw a big feast and our heads will join Hanley's on the shrine!"

They talked on and on, waiting, and then the dawn burst over the jungle rim.

"Quiet!" Dick admonished. "There he is—at last!"

Out of the doorway came the broad savage, carrying the other things. He ran to the cage, and shoved the objects through the bars with anxious haste: the rifle, the two pistols in their holsters, the camera, and *one* knife. The other knife he kept in his huge paw, flourishing it ferociously, his hands flying in gestures which meant:

"Hurry! Show me how to use the gun, or I'll cut your throat!"

"Try and do it," muttered Dick.

But he did not say it in the sign language. Instead he made a show of trying to work the rifle and, of course found it clogged like the other. Tom's first act was to strap a pistol around his own bare waist, the other he strapped around his pal while Dick cleaned the rifle. Thus they killed several minutes of time while the *Gormora* man fumed and fretted like a wild beast.

Manifestly the savage was worried and in mad haste to solve the problem of shooting firearms. From him broke a beastly growl, a noise of alarm and anger and hate. He crouched, facing the big house, in the doorway of which appeared the chief!

The first rays of the morning sun shone full on him, and framed in the opening he loomed more huge and terrible than ever. His great body filled the whole frame, and his painted face scowled at the cage. He stood there for several seconds.

And then Armlet went wild!

He let out a howl and thrust a thick hand between the bars, trying to seize a rifle. Though he did not yet know how to use one, he reached for it, hoping, perhaps, to kill the chief by pointing it at him. The pals jerked back. Tom, while Dick was cleaning the last rifle, had taken out the small movie camera, wound it, and now with it focused upon the giant Armlet as he snarled at the bars, the little instrument was taking close-up pictures of human savagery in the most primitive state.

Dick now had a rifle trained upon the actor. He yelled furiously, pawed uselessly toward the captives, then pulled back his hand and ceased to yell. A voice louder than his was roaring now. And at every roar it grew more powerful. Tom moved the camera and took pictures of the approaching chieftain.

His face gleamed fiendishly in the morning sunlight and his huge fingers moved with clawing gestures as he advanced. Armlet snarled, brandished the knife, then plunged at his ruler.

THEY MET halfway between the cage and the big house. The long knife flashed in the sunlight. A heavy blow sounded. The chief's bellowing stopped short. But he was not killed. His next yell was one of pain and utter ferocity. The two giants locked in deadly embrace, fell to the soggy earth, then rolled and tossed like fighting Bengal tigers.

"Got a shot of that?" Dick asked, pausing for a moment in cutting the vines at the door of their cage.

"Yep!" Tom snapped. "Wish I could record the sound. Keep on cutting. We'll be doing some *real* shooting soon. Here come the rest!"

Other giants bounded from the big house. Others came from the smaller huts. All were howling, brandishing spears and war clubs, looking around for enemies. Just aroused from sleep, they did not yet know what was going on. But they learned quickly. Swiftly they flocked around the pair of fighters who were tumbling around and growling like fiends. The little camera ground on, and Dick hacked away at the vines holding the door.

The original fighters fell again and the mob split apart. Another man darted in then, and struck at the chief. At once that man was assailed by another. And then what had been a duel became a battle royal!

All the giant savages lunged at one another. In the space of two breaths the scene became a shambles of whirling bodies and flailing weapons. Men struck and stabbed with murderous force. Others parried and swung and thrust in revenge. A few lost their weapons, but fought on, throttling, biting, kicking. There seemed to be two factions, of about equal strength, one loyal to the chief, the other rebellious; and they fought each other as bitterly as if they were of different tribes.

They now were becoming more scattered. Some were down, wounded or dead, others dodging about, several retreating. The thunderous bellowing had almost died, for the giants needed all of their breath for fighting. But there was little less noise, for now all the women and children were out of the houses and screaming in frenzy. Nobody paid the least attention to the white captives. Every savage mind was centered on the conflict.

Then came a crackling noise and the door of the cage burst open. Out came Dick Graham, the knife blade between his teeth, and a rifle at alert. Tom Corcoran, carrying the camera and the other rifle, followed.

"Let's get a few of them now!" he grunted.

*Bang!* his rifle cracked into the melee. A wild screech followed when the bullet plowed into some *Gormoran.* At once all fighting stopped. All eyes turned upon the white men. A moment of ghastly silence, then every savage still on his feet advanced upon the riflemen.

"Shoot!" hissed Dick. "Kill the brutes!"

He punctuated the command with a bullet. Tom's rifle cracked again. Then a steady volley. The savages began falling, some from the bullets, others stumbling in their haste to get out of harm's way.

Then came a bellowing roar. Through the disordered mass charged the chief, yelling, staggering as he ran, but plunging ahead, burning with rage and pain. Blood was streaming from his chest. Deep slashes on his face showed that he had been in death grips with the broad-shouldered Armlet. One of his eyes was gone and blood oozed from the ghastly hole, but he had killed the traitor, and now carried his red knife. Perhaps he was dying as he came—and knew it. He reeled headlong and swept his warriors with him.

Spears and arrows flashed through the air, missing the pals by inches. The wild yelling grew in volume, but was again checked by the steady bark and steadier aim of the Winchester rifles.

Both men shot at the chief. He bounded high in the air, uttered a groan of extreme anguish, pitched on his face and was still. Giant savages close behind him went down with dying gurgles. Men following these leaped the corpses and pressed on until stopped by a rifle or pistol bullet. In no time the clearing was dotted with huge shapes, most of them dead, the others dying.

With the frontal attack checked, they swung their guns aside and shot down savages who had attempted a flank movement. The rifles had long since clicked empty and the valiant archeologists were defending themselves with their pistols. These they reloaded from the belts.

For a few moments they stood quiet as they reloaded. So did the giants. Quite a number of them were still on their legs, but all were stopped by the downfall of so many others and the death of their chief. Their courage cooled. Their eyes darted here and there; primitive superstition was gripping them.

"Forward!" spat Dick.

And carrying the empty rifles for clubs, the pals advanced with their reloaded automatics.

The advance was just enough to break the waning courage of the savages. The women and children were screaming now with a shrill note. The shooting and the deaths of fathers and mates had turned savagery to terror; their shrieks filled the clearing with a feeling of fear. As the white men advanced, looking ready for more slaughter, the animal brains of the *Gormorans* turned weak as water.

In a body they whirled and fled toward the shelter of the jungle. They trampled on their dead and wounded comrades, knocking down women and children in their panic. In a moment the stampede was over, the clearing was deserted by the living, and became as silent as a graveyard.

TOM AND DICK stood for a moment looking around them. Not a thing moved within their range of vision. Determinedly, Tom unslung his camera, wound it, and took a last series of pictures of the battlefield.

When he looked up from his camera, he saw Dick running from the head-shrine with some grotesque object under his arm. He ran to the big house. Outside the door he halted, and fired his pistol repeatedly into the palm-thatched eaves at close range. Immediately a bright flame sprang up, as by now the palm leaves had dried since the rains.

Smoke curled upward, and when Tom arrived the whole roof was aflame. A burning fagot served to touch off a small hut on the windward side. In a few minutes the whole place would be in ashes. Again Tom paused to wield his camera, a few pictures, then:

"Come on!" Dick snapped. "Let's get going while the going is good! We've accomplished our mission."

They struck out in a brisk run along the jungle trail leading toward the river. Later, after a heart-breaking run through the steaming forest, they reached the river and found their powerboat just where they had beached it two nights before.

Dick cut the mooring rope while Tom started the engine. A push and they were off. They turned down stream. Tom found a set of greasy coveralls down in the motor compartment and donned them. Dick made himself presentable with the aid of a canvass tarpaulin. Thus they arrived in Kampong and civilization.

A month later the pals stood in the study of the President of the American Asiatic Academy of Archeology. They had finished showing the films taken during the struggle with the savages and their break for liberty in Sumatra. "Yes," said the president, "undoubtedly they are *Gormoras* every foot of this film reveals the traits of the Neolithic Age. What utter savages—giant brutes—they must be! And now, in behalf of the academy I wish to congratulate you upon your splendid achievements: your bringing the facts of George Hanley's fate: these films, the proof of a Stone Age existence that will electrify the scientific world."

# GOLD of ISHMAEL

The Further Adventures of John Solomon

by

## H. BEDFORD-JONES

Chapter Seven

THE BLACK BOX

WHILE I was making up my mind what to do, I made sure of Maillot. I took a gun from his pocket, then took off his leather helmet and used the ear-flaps as a gag, the rest of it hid his face. His wrists I tied behind his back with his own handkerchief, and that made him plenty safe. When I had crowded him over to the other side of the car—which had meantime halted by the curb—I switched off the dash light, then got under the wheel myself. He was invisible except in the full stream of lights from some passing car, and there were few cars abroad at this, the dinner hour.

Turning the car, I headed back whence we had come—one of the residency buildings. I did not know which one it was, but could find it again by the location, and sure enough, there was the entrance. I pulled up and jumped out, striding into the place. My whiskered official was at his desk with no one else about.

"Good evening again!" I said cheerfully. "M. Maillot desires that you let him have the telegram or a copy of it, dealing with one M. Keyes and a native named Bris el Benouni. I suppose you know what one he means."

He grunted and nodded, and shoved the bluish green form at me. With a salute, I took it up and departed, but dared not stop to read it.

Now I had to find my way around the whole of Rabat until I came to the street on the other side of town in which the hotel was situated. Maillot's car was a little Citroen, of no great power or speed, and I wished devoutedly that Solomon had kept his big new Renault close to hand. When I came to the hotel I drove straight on and took the car across the way under the approach to the massive walls of the Kasbah. Here no one was about and it was safe from any molestation.

When I had gone through Maillot's pockets and taken everything, I left the car and strode across to the hotel—and it was real striding, too. When I came into the office, the manager held up both hands.

"Mon dieu!" he exclaimed. "M'sieu, your friend departed not five minutes ago!"

"Who did?" I said. "Not M. Solomon?"

"But yes! When he got your message he dressed and packed, summoned his car, and departed. He had received a telegram a few moments before your message came—"

"Did he go in his new Renault?" I asked.

Even so; and he had left no message whatever. When I fully comprehended this, I realized that I was hungry, and the best dinner in Morocco was only a few feet distant. I took a chance on Maillot and went into the dining-room and ordered dinner.

Then, at the table, I opened up the telegram. It gave little information except that Tom Keyes had jumped from the train near Temara—a village about twelve kilometres out of Rabat, on the road to Casablanca. Therefore, he and Dris had left Meknez sometime during the morning by train. At Rabat, probably, men had come aboard to search for them—hard to say what had happened. This report by wire had come from Casablanca.

I looked over what I had secured from Maillot's pockets and found nothing of any importance to me except a letter which Maillot had written and placed in his pocket for posting. I tore it open and found it to be a note, like the address, in Arabic; it contained a military pass permitting one Ahmed ben Zair to travel at will through the souaffine zone—evidently one of the "closed" districts where the French exercised strict supervision over everyone. I put it into my pocket, as it might be useful in the future, and went on with my dinner.

"There's no use making a halfway job of this," I reflected. "In for a penny, in for a pound! I'll take a chance. When Maillot was talking about his little establishment, he said it was a secluded villa—and I've got his telephone number and address on this letterhead of his. Hm! Use your brains, Hank Smith, if you have any to use."

I finished the meal quickly went out to the office, and called up the telephone number on Maillot's letterhead. There was no answer—which was all I wanted to know. Five minutes later I was walking back to the car, where I found Maillot twisting and struggling. I took out his gun and tapped him over the head.

"Keep quiet, now," I told him. "You have a hard night ahead, so rest up."

I started the car and headed straight down the Street of the Consuls, where in ancient days the slave market of the corsairs was held. It was here that Robinson Crusoe had been brought by his pirate captors, for in the old days Rabat was called New Salè and was the real nest of pirates—and not the town of old Salè across the river, where tourists go. However, this is not a guide book but a story of what happened to Henry Smith, so no more digressions.

Without getting lost more than twice, I finally landed in the Avenue de la Victoire outside the walls, with the Casablanca highway ahead. Maillot's villa was in a little side street here, one of the scattered houses in a new residence subdivision, and when I drew up before it and knew I had the right number, I heaved a sigh of satisfaction. No other house was close by, and there was not a light showing in this one.

When I got Maillot out of the car, I gave him a good brisk shaking up, then started him for the front door. I had his keys ready, and when we got to the door, one of them fitted and we marched in and switched on the lights. The fact that this place was so empty showed clearly enough that he had not aimed to bring me here for dinner—probably he had intended taking me to a very different sort of place.

His drawing-room was handsomely fitted up, with huge Arab stuffed leather seats and very fine old furniture. A little room opening off it contained a flat-topped desk, filing cabinet and typewriter, and obviously served him as office; the telephone was here, too. I pulled a chair up beside the desk, jerked off his gag, and looked into his blazing black eyes.

"Now, my very kind friend," I said coolly, "there's one thing that you are going to get firmly into your thick head—who's the boss around here. But I don't intend to do the job in your style. Turn around and I'll free your wrists.

HE STOPPED spluttering oaths and turned around. I took off the knotted handkerchief—then I swung him around quickly and smashed him in the mouth. He fell into the chair, jumped up, and I knocked him back again.

For all his faults, Maillot was not only game, but he could fight. He landed a kick that staggered me, then he was up and at me.

Luckily, my first crack had left him a bit groggy, and he had not a chance in the world. I hammered him all over the waist-line until he groaned and collapsed in the chair, staring blankly at me with burning eyes of hatred. There was an extension cord to his desk-lamp, which I cut, and used it to lash each ankle to a leg of the chair. Then I put his gun on the desk, and laid the telegram in his lap.

"Now, my good friend," I said, lighting a cigaret, "you take your telephone and get busy. Find out what is being done to locate Keyes, and where he's supposed to be. Speak French and not a word of Arabic, mind! I'd be glad of an excuse to put a bullet into your belly. Be good, and maybe you'll live to fight another day. Go ahead!"

He refused, none too politely, but after he got a tap over the ear with his gun, he gave in and took up the instrument. I sat in his desk-chair and took the extension receiver usually found on French telephones, and listened in. While he talked, I pulled open his desk drawers and looked things over. The very first thing I found was a beautiful ivory-handled revolver fitted with a silencer. I laid this out and grinned at him, and saw his eyes flicker. The thing was loaded and ready for use, and he knew perfectly well that I could shoot him a dozen times over and no one could possibly hear it; with this, I had him where I wanted him.

The papers that came to light were chiefly in Arabic. There was a little steel safety-box, which one of his keys opened; this contained a good deal of cash and bank-notes, with odds and ends of jewels and trinkets. I shut it up again and put it away. Presently he laid down the instrument and sank back wearily in his chair.

"Are you satisfied?" he said.

I nodded and rose; going to a tantalus and opening it, I found a nice little stock of liquors, and mixed a whiskey-and-soda. I was entirely satisfied. With morning, searching parties would be out after Tom, but until then, nothing doing; a white man wandering around the countryside had no more chance of hiding out or escaping than would the proverbial snowball in hell. Also, I found that he had jumped from the train when it slowed for the first suspension bridge beyond Temara. So I knew about where Tom was located.

Sitting down at the desk, I enjoyed my drink and looked at Maillot. He was very pale.

"You will suffer for this outrage, you know," he muttered.

"Forget that nonsense," I said. "You didn't find me waiting for you at Fez, eh? Thought Keyes was in the trap, did you? Well, I took his place, and walked out again. Then you went to Meknez and pulled this dirty work on El Biskri. Just why did you have Keyes and Si Dris attacked on the train?"

Maillot wet his lips. "They were not attacked," he said. "They got into a fight with some soldiers and—"

"Try something new," I cut in scornfully. "And the birds you had all planted and ready, cut loose with guns, eh? No wonder Tom jumped for it! I suppose he saw Dris murdered and took the only way out. And tonight you thought you'd pull my leg, eh? Just what information did you expect to get out of me? I might give it to you free, you know."

His eyes darted viciously at me.

"Where is Mlle. Pontois?" he demanded. At this, I laughed.

"She's where you won't find her. And we thought you had a spy system? This is pretty good, Maillot. Now, where's that little box your man took away from Solomon this morning at Chella? Oh, don't look surprised! You had the place watched, and your men jumped us as soon as we'd located the box. Where is it?"

He was, of course, genuinely surprised, for he probably did not yet know that his men had presumably succeeded in their mission at Chella. He said as much; he had just come in from Meknez and the men had not reported to him. The news, however, bucked him up amazingly.

"Let me tell you something, Smith," he said, when I gave him a cigaret and a drink. "You don't know what you're getting into. You and that little old fool of an Englishman! It's a bigger thing than you imagine. You mentioned El Biskri; do you know anything about his son, young Hassan?"

"Never heard of him," I said promptly. "I heard at Meknez this morning about El Biskri."

"You'd better accept my warning, then," he said. "You and your friends are lined up with criminals, with the worst element in Morocco—with disaffected rascals who are rousing all the radical element and trying to effect a revolution."

"Is that so?" I responded easily. "What of it?"

"Prison," he said curtly. "Or a firing squad."

"I'll chance it," I told him. "What about Ishmael's treasure?"

He shrugged at this, but his eyes narrowed on me. And then, in this moment of silence, the front door bell rang. A flash showed in his eyes; he knew who is was, then!

I reached out, pocketed his automatic, and took up the silenced revolver as I rose.

"Be careful, Maillot," I said quietly, looking at him. "Don't make one little mistake, my dear good friend, or you'll be where treasure won't do you a bit of good. That's a promise, and I keep my promises."

He believed me.

I left him there—he was safe enough, even with his hands free—and went to the door. I opened it, and saw two Arabs.

"Enter," I said, and stepped back, the revolver held down at my side, out of their sight. "M. Maillot is in the library."

They walked in and on into the drawing-room. I closed the door and followed. When they came to the study, they saw Maillot sitting there staring at them, and halted.

Just how it happened, I cannot say. To this day I have never been able to understand it, for I can swear that Maillot said not a word, and made no gesture. He knew, indeed, that I was there behind those two Arabs with a gun in my hand. Perhaps they noticed his position, or the one lashed foot which they could see; more likely, they had recognized me straight off; because they were two of the four men who had been at the Chella that same morning.

I came up behind them and was just about to speak when they swung around suddenly, with an outward swing, one on either side of me. Quick? It was done in a flash, without the least warning, and I had only a glimpse of the hooked Moroccan knives, with a razor-edge on the inside of the curve, darting at me.

Only a sideways leap saved me from the first plunging blade; and as I jumped, I fired, and fired again. The Arab on my righ sprawled on the floor and rolled over, hitting against the other chap and bringing him down. He was up like a streak, and I covered him.

"Drop your knife," I ordered. "Quick!"

Instead of dropping it, he took the chance that a brave man will sometimes take—of thinking that his opponent will not shoot him down. He lowered his weapon as though obeying me; then it flicked from his hand, straight for me, and he followed it. I warded off the knife with my left arm, getting a nasty cut for my pains, and pulled the trigger. The bullet took him squarely between the eyes, and his hands clawed out for me as he fell, then he lay quiet.

"NICE LITTLE gun you have here, Maillot," I said, covering my excitement with an assumption of coolness which I was far from feeling.

Maillot looked up at me, his hands clenched, and hatred blazed in his face.

"You devil!" he exclaimed.

"You flatter me, my dear good friend," I said, and laughed slightly. "Now you'll have some explaining to do to the authorities; but you can probably wangle it all right. These look like two of the chaps who jumped us at Chella this morning. Let's see if they have the box—eh?"

Anxiety leaped into his battered features, and he leaned forward tensely as I stoped to explore the coarse, filthy garments of the two men. Sure enough, I found it—the same little black box. I held it up.

"Kind of them to bring it back to me, eh?" I said. "If anything's in it—"

I opened it before Maillot's bulging eyes and found the folded piece of vellum wadded into it—the same upon which Solomon had written. I knew that he wanted Maillot to get this, and for a moment I was stumped; then Maillot himself gave me the clue.

"Listen!" he exclaimed hoarsely. "I want that box, Smith. It will do you no good, nor your friends. I'll buy it from you."

I looked at him and laughed. "Buy it—with the money in your desk, which I could take if I were a thief?"

"There's ten thousand francs in that box," he said. "And I have a hundred pounds in Bank of England notes—I'll tell you where they are. Nobody will know. Are you fool enough to pass up such a chance?"

I hesitated, weighing the little black wooden box in my hand. Then I brought the whiskey from the tantalus and poured another drink, thoughtfully, while he watched me intently. This just suited me, but I did not want him to realize it immediately. If he thought that I could be bribed, of course, he would be well fooled as to the real character of Henry Smith—another advantage and perhaps a useful one.

"Hm!" I said, sipping my drink. "There's a distinction between robbing you and taking your money as a free gift, certainly. And, as you say, no one will know. To tell you the truth, Maillot, I think this treasure talk is all rank nonsense. Solomon's a fool about it."

"Anyone can look at him and see that he's a fool," spat out Maillot. "But you're not. What do you say?"

"I'll make a bargain with you," I said slowly. "You write out a statement that I'm using your car with your permission; then I'll run down to Casablanca tonight and leave the car for you at the Societé Auto Hall, that garage on the Boulevard Maréchal Pétain—or I'll have it sent back, if you like."

"Fair enough," he said eagerly. "Tell them to send it back here—they'll know me. Give me the pen over there—"

I got out a sheet of his notepaper and gave him the fountain pen, and he scribbled the statement I pretended to want. Then he told me where the banknotes were hidden, and I got them from a little drawer of the tantalus. I put the wooden box on the desk.

"With your permission," I said ironically, "I'll now fix your hands so you can't take any direct action immediately—put 'em behind you! That's right—"

He cursed viciously at this, but had to do it, and with another bit of the electric cord I fastened his wrists behind the chair-back. Ultimately he could get clear, but not very soon. Then I reloaded the revolver from the box of cartridges in the drawer, pocketed them, and took the bottle of whiskey as well. It was excellent liquor.

"Au revoir, my dear good friend," I said. "Next time you think up a better scheme, when you want to pull one of our gang out of jail. Some of these American tourists are really a pretty tough lot. Pleasant dreams!"

I went out, locking his front door and throwing his keys into the street, then climbed into the two-seater. Not a soul was in sight—the two Arabs had come alone. It was only a little after nine—things had moved pretty rapidly—when I headed past the outer railroad station and came into the Casablanca road.

What with one thing and another, I was feeling pretty good, because by nature I do not like to sit down and let somebody slap my face. Maillot had suffered considerably, both in his pride, his pocketbook, and his person, and the lesson would do him good. And in a way I had taken a bit of payment for the murder of poor old Dris. Of course, Maillot thought he had the whole bag of tricks in that little black box—but I knew better. Solomon had fooled him there.

Solomon was a pretty clever rascal after all. He had received my telephone message and had read it aright; he had quietly flapped his wings and flown away. A sick man, alone there in the hotel, he would have fallen an easy victim to any trick Maillot pulled on him. With money and a big car and probably a chauffeur as well, John Solomon could take care of himself.

When I reached Temara, I took the wrong fork in the road, but soon discovered it, and got back in the highway; then I slowed up and crawled along at five miles an hour. Tom Keyes had jumped from the train when it slowed for the first suspension bridge—he might have worked back this way after dark, or he might not. There was only a slim chance of my locating him at all, and it all depended on him. However, I figured that after dark he would take a chance of getting somewhere if he saw the lights of a car crawling slowly along or halted. He would be somewhere on the hillsides, or so I hoped.

And sure enough, twenty minutes later appeared a tattered figure holding out its hand—a white man, certainly. I halted the car.

"Pardon, m'sieu," came Tom's voice. "I have missed the autobus—can you give me a lift toward Casablanca?"

"Who is it that it is?" I growled in a deep bass voice. "Me, I do not like *indigènes!*"

"I am no native, m'sieu, but a tourist—an American!" said Tom, showing himself clearly in the headlight glare. And he was a sight—torn, scratched, his clothes in rags. "I have a very sick wife in Casablanca, you comprehend—"

"The hell you say!" and I threw open the door. "Climb in, you big stiff!"

## Chapter Eight

### Preparations

THERE WAS not a happier man in all Africa than Tom Keyes, when he realized who I was, and got down a good drink of Maillot's whiskey. He needed it, for he was about done up. So we both washed the dust out from around our teeth, and then Tom began to curse Maillot.

It was just as the Frenchman had told me. He and Dris had embarked for Marrakesh by train, and when they left Rabat some soldiers had come into their compartment raising merry cain generally and had picked a fuss. Dris had not wanted to go by train at all, foreseeing some such thing as this, and he had warned Tom to be careful; Maillot was not in the army now, but he had pull enough to do anything he wanted, and get anything done. However, the soldiers got pretty raw and Tom lit into them, and a couple of officers showed up and joined the scrap, and by all accounts that train must have been a wreck—when the officers pulled their guns and let fly. They drilled Si Dris and tried to get Tom, but he jerked open the compartment door and jumped.

"Si Dris was a good scout and a good sport, Hank," he said. "And damn it all, I'm going to pay out some of those birds somehow!"

"Account squared," I said, and

showed him the silenced revolver.

"Eh? What's happened?"

"Plenty. There's a hot-dog joint ahead—I'll bet you're starved."

He was, and we halted at a roadside canteen, got him some sandwiches and a bottle of wine, and found two police officers, hands on guns, looking us over very hard.

"This car belongs to m'sieu?" said one. "He has a permit to drive, also?"

"It doesn't, and I have none," I said cheerfully. "The car belongs to Captain Maillot and we are friends of his, taking it to Casablanca for him. Here is an authorization."

Maillot's note was nothing of the sort, in an official sense, but it got us a salute and an au revoir, and we drove on. Tom gulped at his sandwiches and stared at me.

"What's all this?" he demanded. "Maillot's car, and his letter? Real or fake?"

I chuckled and told him everything that had happened at Rabat, which took considerable time. The curiosity of those two police officers showed clearly enough that the roads were being watched already for Tom Keyes, and only Maillot's letter had saved us from questioning. I did not intend to give anyone else a chance at us, if I could help it.

"Well, things look pretty dark, Hank," said Tom gravely, when he had heard my yarn. He was not hurt, except for bruises and scratches, but his clothes were a mess. "What's your next move?"

"Haven't a ghost of an idea," I admitted cheerfully.

"Know where Solomon went?"

"No more than you do. I suppose he went on to Marrakesh."

"A sick man! Not likely. Where's Jeanne?"

"Search me. At Marrakesh or on the way, most likely. She was right cut up over leaving you without a word."

"Oh, was she?" Tom brightened. "Things were messed up at Meknez, and no mistake. Say, Hank, isn't that girl a wonder?"

"No," I said. "She's like all the rest—after somebody's coin. Look what that wife of mine did to me? Trimmed me cold, got all my insurance, her alimony, everything else I had, and has been hollering for more ever since. It was cheap at the price to be rid of her, but good gosh, Tom! They're all alike."

"See here, Hank," he cut in. "You know good and well Jeanne is no gold-digger—"

"Is that so? Well, isn't she after old Ishmael's treasure? Yeah. Be yourself, feller, and if you want to go praising up any skirt, pick another audience. Where do we go from here!"

"Casablanca, I suppose," said Tom. "I'll pick up my grip there and get into another suit of clothes. Are you going to leave this car at that garage like you told Maillot?"

"Do I look as big a simp as that?" I said. "Not much! He'll have cops waiting for me at that garage, you bet."

"Well, step on it, boy! We want to get there and get out." Tom looked worried. "Let me tell you, feller, Maroc is no place to start gunplay, and this game has got well into the killing stage, and it has me sort of anxious. If Maillot is playing a game that's all open and aboveboard, as he seems to be, then we're done for. Our best bet is to crawl into the U.S. consulate at Casablanca and pull the hole in after us. He'll have every French and Arab cop in the country out after us, and they'll land us in the jug."

"Sure," I said. "But take the chance—suppose his game isn't all open? Then my killing those two Arabs will call his bluff. He won't report it to the police and there won't be any trouble about squaring your case—a thousand francs or so will fix it. Right?"

"Dead right," said Tom. "But it's a hell of a gamble to take, as you'd know if you'd been through Moroccan jails. Personally, I think Maillot told you the truth—that we're all tangled up with a crowd of would-be rebels; this affair of El Biskri seems to prove it. I never heard of your friend Hajj Muhammad, but he's probably some wild hillman who hates the French. Now, if all this is so, and Maillot actually puts the government after us—"

"Do your weeping when the time comes," I said. "The trouble with you is that you've got mixed up with a pretty girl, and you're selling short on everything else—another good sport turned into a pessimist! Get back to normal, Tom. What we want to do is to find Solomon and get down to bed rock—learn what it's all about and why. I'll bet a dollar that with Ishmael's treasure on his brain, Maillot will go mighty slow about setting the police on us."

"All right." Tom clapped me on the shoulder. "Head for my hotel in Casablanca, where I left my extra grip and things. We'll get a room—"

"We will not," I said. "Remember, you're wanted just at present! Get your stuff, then we'll go get us a room somewhere else. I've got a mean gash in my left arm that needs attention, too."

THE LITTLE Citroen, which had plenty of gas and oil, hummed along like a bird, and it was barely eleven o'clock when the lights of Casablanca whitened ahead of us. Tom knew the sprawling French town like a book, and guided me to his little hotel in the Rue d'Alger, which had a café underneath. While he went upstairs I dropped in at the café and got a coffee and picked up an evening paper.

I was still sitting there, my coffee untasted, when Tom showed up ten minutes later. He had on a decent suit and hat, and had put his grip in the car.

"Hey, Hank! Wake up!" he exclaimed. "What's the matter?"

I gulped down my coffee and followed him outside.

"Where's the Hotel Majestic?" I asked.

"Near the Transat, in the Rue de Marseille. Want to go there?"

"Sure," I said. "Jeanne's there."

"Eh? How do you know that?"

"Saw it in the paper just now. Early this afternoon that blasted cub Hassan smashed up the Hispano just outside town—probably they stopped for lunch here. Wrecked the car; they had to ram a bus to avoid hitting some fool Arab woman. Nothing said about Hassan. Jeanne was cut by flying glass and badly shaken up, but insisted upon being taken to an hotel room. They put her in the Majestic."

"Good lord!" ejaculated Keyes. "Here, I'll drive. What about that arm of yours?"

"It can wait."

"We'll have to ditch this car first off. I see it has a special license. What we need to do is to drop out of sight, and drop fast."

"I don't believe it," I said. "But suit yourself. I've plenty of money for us both."

"One thing's dead sure—you won't see the paper Solomon got out of that wooden box in a hurry!"

"Why not? I saw him register the letter."

"Sure, addressed to Jeanne at the Dar ben Daoud in Marrakesh, eh? Well, feller, if you ever tried getting a registered letter from a French postman—boy! If she's not there to get it, then it won't be got until she is, and then she'll have to show everything from her birth certificate to her income tax receipt."

When we were a couple of blocks from the hotel, Tom turned the car in at the curb, shut off the lights, and we piled out with his grip, into which I had put the whiskey and silenced revolver. The street was deserted, and five minutes later we walked into the hotel and gave the grip to an Arab doorman.

"We're friends of Mlle. Pontois," I said to the desk clerk. "I understand she is here?"

"But yes, m'sieu!" he responded, beaming. "Thanks to the good God that someone has come! She is not badly hurt but she has not been able to talk—the doctor made her sleep. There is a nurse with her. We did not know who were her friends, you comprehend?"

"Well, give us a double room," I said, "and we'll go talk with the nurse. I'll fill out the police card, Tom, while you take up your grip. Then we'll see about Jeanne."

He nodded and departed to the room assigned us, while I filled out the necessary police form in the usual negligent manner — putting down my friend as Tom Jones. If nobody got after us it would not matter, and if they did, we were sunk anyway.

Then Tom was back, and we went to find Jeanne.

We did not see her, but we did see a very efficient "garde-malade"—a trim French nurse who sat down with us, had a smoke, and assured us cheerfully that mademoiselle would be out of bed in the morning. Her injuries were by no means so severe as alleged in the newspaper. Her hands and arms were badly cut by glass and she had received a rather bad shaking-up, but nothing more serious; she was sound asleep and was not to be disturbed. The nurse knew nothing about Hassan. She put a bandage on my cut arm and never asked for any explanation, either.

We arranged with her to have Jeanne ready to travel at nine in the morning, and departed.

"NINE IN the morning, huh?" said Keyes, as we made ready for bed. "You're an optimist, Hank. At nine a.m. we'll be talking to the judge."

"Forget it," I told him. "You know the ropes in this town, so you pop out early and get hold of a car. I'm dead sure we'll find Solomon at Marrakesh."

Keyes grunted skeptically, but I was asleep before he turned in.

He wakened me at eight and was gone with the comment that we were still alive. I think he had expected the police to walk in on us at any time, but I was confident of the contrary. Now that I had definitely found Maillot to be as bad as Keyes had made him out, he loomed up before me as a crafty rascal who was out to feather his own nest at all costs; and I felt certain that as long as he had any hopes of landing Ishmael's treasure, he would keep under cover so far as was possible. Perhaps this, too, had been Solomon's idea. I had gathered that the pudgy little cockney was desperately sparring for time—as he admitted to me, he had been pitched into this thing unawares. Well, I had certainly gained a little time for all concerned by my encounter with Maillot. The handsome Frenchman would be in no shape for active business in the next day or so.

I got breakfast in the dining-room, for the Majestic was accustomed to eccentric foreigners who needed a whole meal in the morning instead of the usual coffee and rolls, and in the middle of it Tom Keyes came in and joined me. He looked more cheerful.

"All set, Hank. A good comfortable Delage will be here at nine, with a driver. It's two hundred and forty kilos to Marrakesh; we'll get in sometime this afternoon, with luck. But this outfit costs money."

"I'll split my winnings with you," I said, and got out what I had looted from Maillot, and we divided it.

We went up to Jeanne's room, found her dressed and packed, and had a joyful reunion—at least, she and Keyes did. I could see right off that Tom Keyes was done for, and no wonder either; Jeanne was a pretty fine girl. However, she did not interest me. So I paid off the nurse and settled the doctor's bill, squared up with the hotel, and in ten minutes we were off for Marrakesh. Keyes and Jeanne, who was pale and had her arms bandaged, occupied the rear of the car, which was a large brougham, and I sat in front with Emile, the chauffeur. We were three tourists seeing Morocco, and out for a grand time. The Hispano was wrecked and in a garage, Hassan had vanished, and we had nothing to worry us. So far as Maillot was concerned, I was obviously correct—we had won the gamble, and Tom Keyes need not lose any sleep over the police searching for him.

We got an early lunch at El Kemisset and whirled on through vast plains and into the hills, following the railroad most of the way; and early in the afternoon burst upon us the glorious view of Marrakesh ahead and below, with the showy peaks of the Atlas in the background. There were the thousand-year-old walls, the vast date-palm groves outside, the long huddle of white houses and palaces, and rising over all the enormous minaret of the Koutoubia mosque, topped by the three huge silver balls, part of El Mansur's spoil when he conquered Spain.

"The Koutoubia yonder, m'sieu," said Emile, jogging my elbow as he started the car down the hill, "was built by the same architect who built the Giralda of Seville."

"Thank you," I said solemnly. "Do you know where the Dar ben Daoud is?"

He shrugged. "There are plenty of palaces in Marrakesh, m'sieu; you go to the hotel?"

"No. To the Dar ben Daoud. At least, we'll go there first, so you'd better locate it."

We ran through the wide avenues of the French town, and so on to the vast circuit of ominous reddish walls, which we entered at the Dukala gate, passing on down the street by the Transat hotel. Here Emile halted to get directions, then took us on into the heart of the ancient city, where the railroad meets all the commerce of western Africa and the Sahara. He came to rest before an inconspicuous doorway where an Arab stood loafing. I leaned out and asked if this were the Dar ben Daoud, and it was.

"Do you know whether a M. Solomon is here?" I demanded. The Arab looked me over.

"I do not know, m'sieu," he said. "I will inquire."

He disappeared, calling someone else. Presently he returned, and two other Arabs were with him. All three were wild-looking fellows, and one of them was red-haired.

"You and your friends are expected, m'sieu," he said, with a grin. "M. Solomon is here."

We unloaded and paid off Emile, and followed the red-haired Arab inside. There was the usual right-angled entrance, then we came abruptly upon a square courtyard with a pool in the center and flowers everywhere; this was surrounded by a colonnade of delicate marble arches. We turned to the left, entered by a door at the corner, and found ourselves in a large, high-ceiled room, magnificently decorated with tiles and the cut-and-colored plaster work of a past generation. Rugs and cushions strewed the floor. At one end of the room was a large table where an Arab secretary was waiting; and seated on a large divan, greeting us with a cheery wave of his clay pipe as he rose, was our friend Solomon.

He dismissed the Arab and came to meet us.

"Werry sorry I am to see as you're 'urt, Miss Pontois!" he exclaimed wheezily. "I only 'eard about it last night when I got word from Hassan, and I called up the Majestic and found as Mr. Smith was there; so it was all right. Make yourself to 'ome, miss—no great 'arm done, I 'opes?"

"Nothing but some cuts and a bad case of nerves, thanks," and the girl laughed as she sank down on the divan. "Hassan is all right, then?"

"Yes, miss; we'll see 'im 'ere this werry afternoon," said Solomon.

"You got here last night?" I asked him. He gave me a look and chuckled.

"Yes, sir. I got me new car and come right along, and 'ere I be, all shipshape and ready to 'ave a good sharp talk. Would you like to rest up a bit, miss, before we get down to business?"

"Mercy, no!" Jeanne took a cigaret from the tabouret at her elbow. "I'm quite all right, I can use my fingers and my tongue, and these pillows are perfectly delicious to sink into! So go right ahead."

"Werry good, ma'am." Solomon resumed his seat and held a match to his pipe. "There's a mortal lot to go into."

"I'm glad you read the implied warning in my message and skipped out," I said.

"I ain't often mistook in such things, sir, as the old gent said when 'e kissed the pretty 'ousemaid. I thought as 'ow you could 'andle that 'ere Maillot. Now, suppose we get things cleared up; 'cause why, I 'ave some werry important wisitors a-coming 'ere this afternoon. You take the floor, Mr. Smith—we'll 'ave some drinks fetched in right off."

AN ARAB fetched in a tray, and we set in to have the clearing-up that was so sadly needed by us all. Solomon assured us that we could speak perfectly freely; he had four native men and two women on the place, arrived only this morning—and all were Berbers, sent to him by the wild saint, Hajj Muhammed. What was more, Muhammad himself was coming this afternoon, and with him several other gentlemen from the hill-country.

"And what's more," added Solomon, his blue eyes twinkling, "they all 'ave a price on their 'eads, too! Werry interesting session, it will be. But you move ahead, Mr. Smith."

I moved ahead, and Tom chipped in at the right moment, telling all that had happened the previous day. Solomon sat puffing at his clay pipe, and very ridiculous he looked, with his Basque beret cocked over one ear and wisps of gray hair sticking out around the edge. His round features remained absolutely blank, even at mention of Dris, and his placid blue eyes were devoid of all expression. I had come to realize, however, that behind this odd exterior were some startling brains.

"Werry good," said Solomon, when we had told all our story. "Mr.

Smith, you look out for yourself; that 'ere Maillot will be after you proper. You took 'im by surprise last night, and werry lucky you did—but 'e ain't nobody's fool, sir. Now, Miss Pontois, I expect as 'ow you want to know what was in that 'ere wooden box. Well, 'ere it is, let's get this 'ere treasure business settled and then go on to more important things."

He handed Jeanne a bit of old and tattered vellum upon which the English writing was black and perfectly readable; and I smiled to myself as I remembered what I had thought about this writing. Jeanne passed it on to Keyes and me. The message was curt and explicit.

> "Wee have hidde Semain's monies in ye grot yt is under ye French sun dile in ye palace garden 2 wains of coin Wm Hearne."

I looked up at Solomon. "What did you write on the bit of vellum Maillot has now?"

"The werry same thing, sir, two wagon-loads and all—only I put it in a corner of the women's palace, just like that. Let 'im find it if 'e can!"

"Well," spoke up Tom Keyes, "is there any chance that slaves would have been so employed?"

"It's the werry thing as proves itself true, sir," answered Solomon. "I've been a-looking into this 'ere business; we know o' two just such occasions in Moroccan 'istory, one under Ishmael's brother, one under 'is son Zidan, when slaves up and saved their lives by telling where they 'ad 'id treasure for their masters. And Semain was the name them 'ere slaves used for Ishmael. Yes, sir, this 'ere paper proves itself, it does that, and I expect the treasure is right there; but we can't go and look, so to speak. It 'as to be 'andled proper, all shipshape and Bristol fashion."

"All right," I said. "Grotto or cave under the sun dial in Ishmael's palace—that means Meknez. And that means authority to dig. Let's burn that vellum, first."

"Right you are, sir," said Solomon.

I struck a match. The vellum curled up like a tortured snake and finally turned into a twisted black char. It made a frightful stink, too.

"Clever of old Ishmael!" observed Keyes. "That riddle—remember? 'My shade is in my treasure and my treasure in my shade', with the treasure down below the sun dial all the while!"

Solomon waved his pipe and looked at Jeanne.

"Miss, this 'ere will take time. Now, what share o' that 'ere treasure will satisfy you?"

"What do you think?" she demanded, smiling. "You mean you'll have to pull wires and promise a few bribes and so forth, before you can get permission?"

Solomon nodded. "All o' that, miss. The sultan 'as to be fixed, and so do the French."

"I'm in your hands, John," said Jeanne. "I'll agree to anything you do."

"Werry good; I'll 'old you to that 'ere bargain, miss. If we—"

"Hold on," said Keyes, leaning forward on his cushions. "If this game is to be played out in Meknez, why are we down here in Marrakesh?"

"I'm a-coming to that, sir," said Solomon, "and a werry ticklish business it is. This 'ere treasure is mixed up with something a mortal lot bigger, just like that. Now, miss, werry sorry I am to say it, but these 'ere Arabs don't want no women a-mixing in their business, and if I was you, I'd go to me room and rest up a bit until dinner time. Then we can tell you all about it. I'll 'ave one o' the women take care of you."

Jeanne nodded understanding, and at Solomon's call an Arab entered, then departed. A moment later a woman appeared—a tall, unveiled, fine-looking woman with blue tribal marks tattooed on brow and cheeks and chin. Solomon spoke to her, and she smiled and beckoned Jeanne.

"Now, gents," said John to me and Keyes, "this 'ere situation is getting serious, as the old gent said when the 'ousemaid sued 'im for breach o' promise. Let's 'ave it straight afore them Arabs come. Mr. Keyes, you and Mr. Smith look over that map on the table and I'll do me best to show you what's up."

We got the map spread out—a large-scale map of southern Morocco—and then we heard something that brought us up all standing.

## Chapter Nine

### The Prophecy

"ME FRIENDS," said Solomon, as he scraped out his clay pipe, "there's a 'undred and seventy thousand Arabs 'ere in Marrakesh; and outside o' troops, there's five thousand Europeans. Inside o' thirty days them 'ere five thousand will be corpses, just like that."

In this calm utterance there was something incredible, something beyond comprehension; it grew upon us slowly, with gathering reality. The quiet, wheezy voice had fallen silent, yet it lingered in the room like the aftertones of a bronze bell—a hundred and seventy thousand Arabs, five thousand Europeans!

"Yes, sir," Solomon eyed his pipe critically, blew through it, then his expressionless blue eyes settled upon us. "Fez 'as a bit over four thousand Europeans, with a 'undred and twenty thousand Arabs. You think o' them 'ere figures, gents; werry interesting they be. Or look at Mazagan, what 'as two thousand Europeans and eighteen thousand Arabs. Or Safi, with fifteen 'undred Europeans and twenty-seven thousand Arabs—"

"Nonsense, John, nonsense!" Keyes wakened with a start and a laugh. "Are you talking about a possible revolt—here in Morocco? That's plain nonsense. The Arabs know better. Even if it were possible, every city has a French garrison, a camp outside the walls!"

"Well, sir," and John Solomon chuckled, "*why* 'as every Arab city a French camp outside its walls? You stop and think over that for a minute. It's me what 'as the last word this time, as the old gent said when 'e buried 'is second!"

And he was right. Keyes frowned and said nothing.

Now, for several weeks I had been poking my nose into odd places around Morocco, talking with colonists and French and Arabs, and I had uncovered a whole lot of things. Any talk about revolution seemed utterly preposterous—but was it? There was a tremendous lot of disaffection in the country. Men were crawling in from the hills to die of hunger around the tombs of their saints—this had happened in Rabat itself, the grand new capital.

"Well, Mr. Smith," said Solomon, "are you a-going to say as it's impossible, too?"

"I'm from Chillicothe, Missouri, John. Go ahead and show me; my ears are pinned back."

Solomon grunted as though pleased, and got out his plug of tobacco and his knife. Then he cut loose with some staggering information — if true.

Oddly enough, it did not surprise me as much as it did Tom Keyes, because it was no new thing to me. The country was now under civil rule, but the preceding military government had aroused much hatred even in French hearts. I had heard colonists swear that the war with Abdel Krim had been deliberately promoted by the military to keep the army occupied, and that the French had kept Krim supplied with munitions—active service pay, wound stripes, service stripes, promotion! Truth it was that the civil government had ended that war in sixty days. Solomon went over all this, and a dozen more things, chiefly the attitude of the great caids.

Then he went into religion and recent history. The whole south of the country was a zone of insecurity even now. Fifty miles from Marrakesh the guns were booming and the Atlas mountains was alive to the roar of military planes. The veneer of conquest was thin; the Gueliz hill, which overlooked Marrakesh itself, was a solid system of batteries designed to overawe the city. The fanatical Berbers and hill tribes were ripe for revolt at any moment from south to north. The caids were at each other's throats. The French backed them, and they exerted a worse oppression over the natives, in consequence, than ever before. The puppet sultan was not acknowledged by half his subjects—there were plenty of other pretenders to his throne.

The amazing thinness of the veneer was shown by the fact that up north at the holy city of Mulai Idris, in the very heart of the French power, no tourists were allowed abroad after dark.

"Now, gents, you look at that 'ere map," concluded Solomon. "The military ain't in control no more, remember; their big men ain't 'ere now. All the fighting is concentrated between Marrakesh and the Sahara. Down there in the mountains is pretty near the 'old effective French army, and the camps are stripped to keep 'em supplied. They're seventy mile deep in them 'ere mountains. And it was right there, about ten mile deep, that the Emperor Ismail took in an army o' sixty thousand trained troops—and he only got out wi' two thousand of 'em. Now, then, what would 'appen if there was a sudden uprising, if the mountain passes were blocked and the roads cut, and if the towns all over Morocco were to come to life? They'd 'ave the country in their 'ands in no time—and the army bottled up in them 'ere mountains."

"Not a bit of it," objected Tom Keyes. "From a practical standpoint —who'd do it and why?"

SOLOMON LIGHTED his pipe, sighed wheezily, and went on to paint an alarming picture of what might happen if any of the numerous pretenders to the throne started a real revolt and enlisted the fanaticism of the Arabs to his standard. All over Morocco was an endless surge of natives in movement—pilgrims by the thousand to various shrines and cities, caravans, nomad groups. Nothing would be easier than for the hill tribes to flood into the cities, ready to rise on a certain day, massacre right and left, seize the military camps and the vast dumps of munitions and supplies—some of which were almost unguarded, as I had seen for myself at Taza. And what would be the result?

"It'd be plain hell—for a while," admitted Keyes. "The Indian mutiny all over again."

"Right you are, sir. And—"

"Hold on," I cut in. "What about

arms and supplies and money for such a revolt?"

Solomon's blue eyes twinkled slightly.

"You've 'it it first crack, sir," he said calmly. "This 'ere revolt would throw out the civil administration, just like that. The military would come back into power. There'd be no end o' fighting and so forth. Now, if there was certain Frenchmen willing to back all this 'ere deviltry in a quiet way, so to speak—"

"No Frenchman would do it," snapped Keyes. Solomon cocked his head on one side and surveyed him blandly.

"Dang it, you're a werry 'ard person to conwince, Mr. Keyes! Guns can be run in all the while, and are bein' run in, just like that. Did you ever 'ear o' the Societé Agricole in Casablanca?"

"Eh?" Keyes frowned. "Sure. They're a big French importing firm —farm machinery, tractors, and so forth. American, mostly. They've got a big establishment, warehouse, parts, repairs."

"Werry good, sir. And in that 'ere warehouse at this werry blessed minute there's two 'undred machine guns, a thousand automatic rifles, and ammunition to go with 'em, waiting for shipment upcountry."

This was a bomb and no mistake. Keyes was thunderstruck.

"John, are you certain of this?" I asked. "How do you know? Do the police know?"

Solomon regarded me blankly. "Them as asks questions gets less'n they asks, says I. No, sir, the police don't know, but I do. And who owns the control o' that 'ere Societé Agricole?"

"I don't know," said Keyes. "Do you?"

"Yes, sir—"

At this instant the red-haired Berber came in and held open the door. Into the room stalked our wild-eyed friend Hajj Muhammad, and with him five other Arabs or Berbers—bearded, smiling men. The saint halted, lifted his hand, and barked out a greeting. Solomon returned it, and then beckoned to the red-headed Arab, who remained at his side.

"We will talk in French, chiefly, for your benefit," said John to us. "Ali here will interpret all that is said. Ali, say that these two men are my friends. Say that this man with the gray eyes was with Si Dris el Benouni when he was killed on the train; this tall American last night slew two men in the house of Maillot, and left Maillot tied in his chair after robbing him and beating him."

I was startled by this, but at once the eyes of the six visitors went to me, and their smiles passed into quatters of approbation; Maillot had no friends here, evidently. Solomon turned to us, the suspicious eyes of the hillmen following his every move.

"These five men," he said, so that the interpreter would miss no word, "are mountain chiefs or leaders of the tribes, and I think all of them are fugitives. Ah! There's Hassan now."

Into the room came the slim form of the boy Hassan. He smiled at us, and then greeted the six Arabs, who kissed his shoulder respectfully—he was a descendant of the prophet. Whether he had just reached Marrakesh, or had been here in the house, did not appear.

The doors were closed, after trays of refreshments were brought in, and the saint introduced his companions in a long singsong recital of titles and so forth—a regular "began" chapter. They studied Solomon, and so did I, for now I began to glimpse the little man as he really was. I say "began" advisedly, for as yet I was far from comprehending his actual position here.

If I was looking for the point of contact between Solomon and these Arabs, I soon had it; and with it a chapter from Solomon's past life, or more strictly allusions to one, into which I never probed any deeper. I had already learned that he had once been established at Port Said and was known among eastern Arabs, but now came more definite hints, as Hajj Muhammad struck into the reasons for his presence, and the red-haired interpreter kept up a running murmur at our elbows.

"We have heard of you, Sidi Suleiman," said the wild-eyed fanatic. "I have heard of you at Mecca and elsewhere; others who have made the pilgrimage have heard of you. We know that the emirs of Arabia are your friends, and that in your hands is the ancient Seal of Suleiman, on whom be blessings! We know that you have great power of magic and can foretell the future, and when I received word two weeks ago that you desired to meet me, I was glad."

Keyes gave me a glance. Two weeks ago! How long had Solomon been at work down here? Had he really been pitched unexpectedly into this business, or had he been engaged in it for some time—and suddenly found it to be of serious and immediate importance? Hard to say. There was a lot more to him than appeared on the surface. Now he made answer, talking partly in French, partly in Arabic.

"I have desired to talk with you, that is true, and meantime the son of El Biskri has placed himself under my protection. I wish to find out why he and these other chiefs are now fugitives from the law."

"For what reason?" spat out Muhammad. "Do you wish to help us against the French?"

"As Allah liveth, I desire to help you," said Solomon. "Whether against the French or not, remains to be seen. It is in my mind that your grievance is against the sultan."

"May his name be accursed!" cried the saint angrily. "May the air that he breathes be poison unto him! Allah upon him, he is no sultan, but a puppet of the French, a tool in the hands of those who surround him! It is the French Resident-General who rules Maroc!"

"And a very fine man he is, Hajj Muhammad," said Solomon.

"He is a good man, for I have talked with him," said the saint, more quietly. "But he does not know what is going on under the surface, and is helpless. Now, swear to us that you, and those friends of yours, will keep secret what passes here."

THE INTERPRETER swore us by all sorts of Koranic oaths, and then the holy man plunged into the business of his visit—explaining some of the reasons why these six Arabs were fugitives.

It was an involved affair in each case, naturally. The gist of it all was that a group of three or four men around the sultan influenced him against them, goaded them into action, brought false charges against them, or stirred them up by *agents provocateurs.* What had happened to them, had happened to a dozen more, who were scattered over the country—all of them great men. Wealth seized, lands confiscated, crimes committed — an incredible tale, but true. The pashas, or chief judges, were appointed by the sultan, and obeyed his will blindly.

"Now," went on Hajj Muhammad, "here is the meat of the nut, sidi. A conspiracy has been formed to overthrow the sultan and to set up in his place another of purer blood, on whom is the blessing of the Prophet—may his name be exalted!"

"Stop," said Solomon placidly. "Who has formed this conspiracy!"

"It is a sworn secret among some half-dozen chiefs from south to north," said the saint. "I know of it; one other of these my friends knows of it—the rest do not. When the time comes, they will be brought into it—until then, it is kept secret."

The six Arabs stirred, shot looks one at another, were obviously uneasy. Solomon chuckled.

"And you are not so sure about it yourself, Hajj Muhammad," he said. The saint scowled at him. "This conspiracy is fomented by one man. Who?"

"That I cannot tell you."

"Then I shall tell you," said Solomon, his blue eyes wide and unblinking. "This man is John Gayland, whom you call El Gezar, the Butcher. He is manager and governor of the lands owned by Captain Maillot, and lives at the castle of Helal. At this place the rifles and munitions are stored."

Hajj Muhammad stared as though petrified. The other Arabs sat blinking at Solomon in utter amazement. He held a match unconcernedly to his pipe.

"Now, then," he went on, "does Maillot know about all this or not?"

"Allah upon him, he does not!" snapped the saint, rousing himself from his spell. "How do you know these things?"

"By the power of the Seal of Suleiman," and Solomon held out his hand, upon which was the gold ring graven with the interlaced triangles. "I shall tell you more. Through you and your allied chiefs, this El Gezar can cause an uprising of fifty or sixty thousand armed men upon a certain day. He will furnish machine guns and automatic rifles, which are now in Casablanca, and more are on the way. I can go on and tell you further details; of what use are they? What I want to know is this: Is Maillot in this plot?"

"He is not!" cried Hajj Muhammad, who was excited, suspicious, alert. "And I have no liking for the plot, by Allah! Nor have these men my friends."

"Nor," added Solomon, his blue eyes twinkling at Hassan, "has the son of El Biskri—he whom you have chosen to sit upon the throne of Morocco."

Now there was sudden dread silence, and hands crept under brown jellabs as though seeking hidden weapons, until Solomon waved his pipe in the air and spoke quietly.

"Come! We have sworn an oath; let us talk frankly. You, Hajj Muhammad, are tempted by this plot. So are your friends. And yet you have misgivings; am I not right? You know that you might sweep the French into the sea, as Krim swept the Spaniards, but that more would return. And yet your friends are desperate. Am I right?"

"You are right, Sidi Solomon," said the saint in a low voice.

"Good. Now you have heard that El Gezar expects to find the vast treasures of Mulai Ismail, which he will place in the hands of the new sultan. Is that right?"

Hajj Muhammad blinked, and his jaw dropped in amazement. Solomon chuckled.

"Well, he will not find those treasures. I have found them myself; rather, my friends here have found them. Ali! Call in the scribe."

The red-headed interpreter went out and came back with the secretary. Solomon now told each of the chieftains to dictate his grievances, beginning with young Hassan. Each obeyed, and each affixed his seal to the sheet of paper handed him to read over. Hajj Muhammad had no grievance; he was simply the most holy saint in a country of saints, and more men obeyed him than the sultan. Solomon took the papers and held them up.

"I am here to help you, in the name of Allah," he said quietly, and looked at his watch. "Now tell me; if these wrongs were to be redressed, if those who caused this injustice were to be punished, would you still seek to rebel against the power of France and bring ruin on Maroc?"

One by one the six answered, beginning with Hassan. Their answers were the same, "No!"

"Then," said Solomon, "when you leave here go away quietly, say nothing of what has passed, and hold aloof from this revolt. If you do this, your wrongs will be redressed inside of thirty days."

"What?" exclaimed Hajj Muhammad. "How do we know this?"

"Because I say it," said Solomon. "And in exactly seven minutes I shall give you proof of my ability to keep my word, if I am alive. Ali, a French gentleman is coming here in seven minutes, more or less. Be at the door to admit him properly."

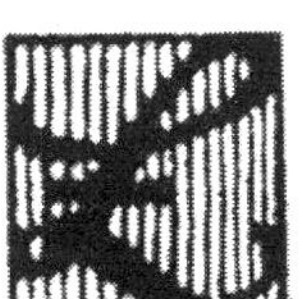

ALI WENT OUT. Keyes lighted a cigaret and drew a long breath.

"John, you've got me beat!" he exclaimed in English. "I can see now how the treasure is mixed up in it, and I can understand—"

"You don't understand a thing, sir," cut in John, with a trace of irritation. "Beggin' your pardon, sir, it ain't what it seems—and will you 'ave the goodness to speak French or else keep your mouth shut? These 'ere gents are mortal suspicious."

The Arabs were talking excitedly among themselves. Then Hajj Muhammad spoke harshly.

"Sidi Suleiman, how can we tell that you are not a spy of the Resident-General? He is here in Marrakesh, and it may be that when you report to him he will guard the gates and seize these men."

"In the name of Allah, have a care!" said Solomon, and now his voice was suddenly edged with steel. "Have your friends draw the hoods of their jellabs over their faces—quick! This man must not recognize them."

The six moved their ungainly garments, drawing up the hoods. A moment later the door was thrown open and into the room came a Frenchman all in white from sun-helmet to shoes, a stick in his hand. He was alone; a handsome man, elderly, who glanced around and then strode forward to Solomon, removing his topee and extending his hand.

"This is M. Solomon?" he said, smiling. "I expected to find you alone—no matter. I know Hajj Muhammad, and shall be glad of a word with him also."

"Good lord!" muttered Keyes, and dug his elbow into me. "The Resident-General—alone with this gang! Get your gun ready."

(Be sure and get your copy of the May Issue for the Fourth Instalment of this intriguing novel.)

This is the fifth story of what we hope will be a long series of yarns by new authors who have never before appeared in print. We would appreciate our readers' opinions and comments regarding this department.—THE EDITOR.

# The Leopard of Azzur

A gripping story of Arabia

by

DELL H. PATE

THEY HAD caught him. True, they had slipped upon him when he carelessly rode away from his men to spy upon the walled city of Sheik Ibrahim. Even then, he had slain three of his captors before they could secure him. But he was theirs. No more would the Leopard of Azzur ride, like a hooded ghost, at the head of his Touareg thieves.

Somewhere, outside the wall, his men were waiting. He could picture their stoic faces, hear their lamentations. They waited merely to rob the jackals of his broken body when it would be hurled from the city. They could attempt no rescue. Even if they gained entrance to the city their hundred swords would be silenced beneath the blows of a thousand. They would bury him and, some day, they would avenge him. It was the will of Allah.

The prisoner stood, straight and tall, his inscrutable eyes fixed upon Sheik Ibrahim whose dark frown held no promise of mercy. A group of warriors stood about the sheik whose supple body rested on silken cushions. In the background stood the black eunuchs, blending with the shadows that covered them. The sheik eyed him keenly, spoke finally.

"You, whom they call the Leopard of Azzur, have plundered traders going to and from my city. You have stolen from my flocks. It is written that you shall die." The sheik's voice was low and even. The black slaves trembled and stirred in their shadowy corner. "It is written," he repeated somberly, "that you shall die."

The Leopard laughed. His laughter was a braver challenge than these warriors expected. They glanced at each other then at the insolent captive.

"O Sheik," said The Leopard, "you but repeat the sentence of Allah. All my life I have known that I shall die. Death and I are comrades. Together we have ridden and fought, on river and dune and mountainside. I, The Leopard of Azzur, have no fear."

Sheik Ibrahim's dark eyes flashed.

"So," he hissed, "you would laugh at me? By Allah, I believe you. Death would be merely another adventure for you. I must find a more fitting atonement."

The room was seeped in silence while the sheik thought. At last he smiled. And his smile seemed more cruel, more terrifying, than his frown.

"The Leopard," he said, "shall be a lamb. You shall be the slave of a slave-woman. She shall brand you with a hot iron and her lash shall stripe your back. What sayest thou now, O Leopard?"

The Leopard of Azzur straightened very erect.

"Truly, you are cruel, O Sheik. I but stole from your flocks to feed my men when they were hungry."

"Why did you plunder caravans of camels, cloth, and slaves?"

The Leopard's voice was unchanged when he answered.

"To buy sweets and jewels for girls in the cities we visit."

"Very well. Your claws shall be sheathed and your fangs shall gnash in vain. Your tasks will be humble. It will amuse us to see a slave-woman tame a leopard." He turned to the eunuchs.

"Bring Maisa," he commanded, and the eunuchs left the room.

Presently the slave woman was ushered before him and bowed low. She was fat and her hair was disheveled about her expressionless face. Her coarse garments were soiled. Still, about face and body, there was hint of former beauty.

"Maisa," said the sheik, "I am giving to you a slave. He is yours, to do with as you will. Slavery has filled your heart with resentment. It should awaken your pride to have, as your slave, the Leopard of Azzur."

The warriors laughed at the bewilderment in her eyes. She turned and looked at the prisoner who stood there, impassive, in his bright silken aba—a statue in golden bronze.

It was he who spoiled their jest. He was an actor as well as a fighter and a thief. The renegade Touareg dropped to one knee before the woman.

"I am thine, O queen of the world," he said. "Take me to your palace."

He followed her from the room, pausing in the doorway to glance back at the sheik and laugh.

"What sort of man is he?" asked one of the warriors.

Sheik Ibrahim settled back upon his cushions. "He is a fool who smiles at fate," he said. "But he shall suffer unendurable agony and humiliation. He has forgotten that it was he who sold Maisa into slavery."

THE OIL lamp in Maisa's room flared and sputtered, revealing a pile of burlap which was the bed and the rugs which were skins of sheep. There was nothing else.

"Sit down," Maisa said, and her slave sat upon one of the skins and leaned his back against the wall. She sank down upon the burlap.

"Do you remember me?" she asked.

The Leopard lifted his brows.

"Where, in Allah's great world did we meet?"

The woman laughed mirthlessly. "Sheik Ibrahim had good reason to present you to me. Time and again, when my misery overwhelmed me, I have cursed you. At first, I was a favorite and surrounded with luxury. Now, I do menial tasks. Yes, I have cursed you, O Leopard! You are the one who doomed me to a life of slavery."

"I?" exclaimed The Leopard. "Well, it is possible. Go on."

"The caravan of my tribe was returning from Mektoubi when you swept down upon us. There was the flash of guns, the screams of camels and the curses of men. Yes, and the screams of women while swords rang. Suddenly it was over and I was riding a camel, my hands and feet bound. You were there when they put me on the slave-block and one of Sheik Ibrahim's men bought me. When he tired of me he turned me over to the women who put me to work.

"Yes, I cursed you. I had remembered your name and I called upon Allah to destroy you when I was branded and each time I was whipped."

"And now," said The Leopard, "your revenge shall be sweet. Fate has delivered me into your hands."

"But it could not undo what the years have done. I could shame you and you would laugh at me. Beneath my lash you would smile and taunt me as you taunted the sheik. You are The Leopard, intended by Allah to live and die by the sword. It has dawned upon me that revenge is an empty victory."

There was a moment of silence. Through a little window cut high in the wall trickled the dancing light of the shining stars. From afar came the sound of music, the laughter of women. Out in the narrow street a dog howled.

"Where are your followers?" asked Maisa.

"A short distance away, behind the dunes, waiting. One of them signalled to me as my captors brought me in the gate. Tomorrow they will give up. They merely wait now, thinking that my body will be thrown out for the jackals, in which case they would carry it away for burial."

"Then they are near. Listen, O Leopard, you are tall. From my shoulders you might spring to the wall and drop down to freedom."

"Why torture me," he asked, "with such subtle cruelty? Why not heat your irons and bring your whip?"

She smiled and got to her feet. "Come," she said softly, "I shall untie your bonds." And, as he rose to his feet, she freed his wrists. Her soft hands rubbed the chafed marks they bore.

"By Allah!" whispered The Leopard. "Do you mean it? But, what will they do to you?"

"They will devise a most shameful and excruciating death. But that will not matter. You shall be riding safely at the head of your men. I am only a slave woman whom the years can cheat of nothing. You are The Leopard of Azzur.

"Do you remember, O Leopard, the night after you took my tribe's caravan? It was just before we reached the slave-market. You came to my tent. Do you remember?"

The Leopard smiled and looked into her eyes.

"Yes," he said. "I remember. I told you that if I were anything but a desert thief, hunted by Arab and Franzawi alike, I would make you my first wife."

Her eyes were shining with the memory. "And I have never forgotten. You said that you loved me. Come with me, silently. I think they do not know that your men linger."

He stood and stared at her queerly, for her words seemed as strange to him as the stories of snow and ice that the Franzawi told.

"But, Maisa," he warned her—as though she did not already know, "this means death for you!"

"And it means life for you," she replied. "Follow me."

They slipped out the door into the garden. There was the musical splash of a fountain and its lashing spray was cool against their faces. The shadows of trees reached to the very wall, only a narrow street being between it and the garden.

"I am strong," said Maisa. "Can you get to my shoulders as I stand against the wall?"

"That should be easy, but—"

"Then, farewell," said Maisa, "and Allah go with you."

"Farewell," said The Leopard, and raised her hand to his lips.

With agile strength he vaulted to her shoulders, leaped high and drew himself to the crest of the wall where he crouched for an instant like the beast he was named for. Then he dropped into the darkness and the freedom which lay beyond —and was gone.

AT FIRST he ran. Ran from the accursed menace of that walled city. It seemed as a hideous dream to him, this swift succession of events which had ended in a miracle. They have given him to Maisa, thinking it would mean torture and shame. He had seen the Arab women punish their slaves and knew what was expected of Maisa.

Instead, she had freed him. Freed him, because he had given her an hour of love in some half-forgotten episode of his plundering career. An hour of love before he had sold her as a slave.

"Strange," he muttered to himself, "are the ways of women—and of men."

A figure rose up from the shadow of a dune and halted him. It was Hamed, his staunchest friend, the able lieutenant of his roving band.

"Allah is merciful," he cried. "By his hand you have escaped!"

The warriors thronged about him with cries of exultation. They brought him food and water and, as he ate and drank, they offered their profuse Moslem prayers of gratitude.

"Let us hasten," said The Leopard, "from this accursed city. Some day, when we have gathered sufficient numbers, we shall return and scale its wall. Our swords shall paint their streets crimson. But, alas! that day will be slow in coming."

Hamed rode at his side and all the men were strangely silent. The Leopard was busy with his thoughts. Things that the years had erased came back to his mind. He heard again the cracking of rifles, the ring of swords. Heard the screams of camels and of women, the hoarse shouts and curses of men, followed by the pagan roar of triumph.

In his fancy, he stole through the darkness to a little tent and crept within. There was a frightened, beautiful girl peering up at him. Then the slave-block, the rude auctioneer calling for bids while this same girl looked about her with hopeless defeat in her eyes. He remembered, too, the silent plea as she saw him, The Leopard, standing idly by. She did not know that a bandit Touareg who made and sold slaves had no desire to buy them. They were for rich merchants in the lazy cities.

Now, after these years, fate had given him into her hands. And she had given him freedom, knowing that the dawn would bring her a reward of torture and death.

"Strange," he muttered again, "are the ways of women."

"What do you say, O Leopard?" asked Hamed.

The Leopard drew rein. "You must ride on without me. I have a debt to pay back there in the city of Ibrahim."

"They have your horse, and you would try to obtain him? But, that is foolish," said Hamed. "We have extra horses and camels as well."

"It is something you would not understand. By Allah, I understand it not, myself. But I must go."

They were grouped about him with hoarse cries of protest. Stern, brave, old warriors and reckless youths who would have followed him through a thousand hells.

"And I must go alone. Farewell, brothers and warriors!"

"But," pleaded Hamed, "it means death to go back!"

"It means worse than death," said The Leopard. He wheeled his horse and started back toward the city which was, by this time, far away.

The men sat and watched him until the darkness swallowed him up. Even then, they could hear the sand stirring under the hoofs of his mount as he rode back to doom. The old warriors shook their heads and muttered in their beards.

"The devils have stolen his mind," said Hamed. "He is seized with madness. We can do nothing but leave him."

They rode on. It was not long until the sudden dawn streaked the desert horizon with flame and the punctual sun glinted on the sand as it had always done and would always do. Allah is changeless.

The riders halted and dismounted for their morning prayers. From the gilded minarets of Moslem cities, the muezzins were calling. These thieves needed no call. With bowed heads and outstretched arms, they called, "Allahu Akbar! God is great!" And Hamed added, "Rest the soul of The Leopard."

THE GATE was open. Men and camels passed in and out. A small caravan, guarded by warriors on prancing horses, sallied forth. Slaves were going to the grazing lands to tend the flocks.

The Leopard was weary but he rode jauntily through the gate. No one noticed him as he found the street between the wall and the sheik's garden. Hastily he dismounted and went to the door through which Maisa had led him a few hours before. He recognized the window, cut high in the wall and, when he stepped quietly within, he saw the strip of leather by which his wrists had been bound still lying on floor. But Maisa was gone.

He went out into the corridor. At the far end stood a black eunuch with a huge sword. Calmly, The Leopard approached him. The murmur of voices came from the sheik's room.

The eunuch stared at him in the dim light, then turned to block his way, the sword raised to strike. This one had been in the room when sentence was passed on The Leopard. In his eyes was recognition—and fear. As he stood there, indecisive, The Leopard charged.

Like lightning playing about a stolid rock, the Arab dodged the futile sweep of the slave's weapon and closed in. He found the black throat with his strong fingers. There was a gasp of pain and the massive body crashed against the wall, then slumped to the floor.

"The Leopard has his moment of glory before he becomes a lamb," said The Leopard and pushed his way through the heavy curtains.

There were drawn swords and cries of surprise in the room of Sheik Ibrahim as he entered. He smiled and raised his hands. His eyes found Maisa, cringing upon the floor, her hands bound behind her.

"What were you going to do to her, O Sheik?" asked The Leopard.

Ibrahim smiled darkly. "I was trying to decide," he said, "between impalement and flaying alive." Maisa's body trembled as the terrible words came to her.

"I have spared you the trouble of deciding," said The Leopard. "I have returned. I, though a thief, could not forget my debt of honor. May the slave release his mistress?"

There was silence in the room. The warriors grouped about the sheik, glanced at each other and stroked their beards. Would the wonders of Allah never cease?

But there was clamor outside. One of the sheik's children had run forth and spread the news. The court-yard and the street was a seething mass. They would witness, now, not only the death of the slave-woman but that of The Leopard as well.

"Release her," said Ibrahim, and with quick hands The Leopard freed Maisa. He smiled at her and bowed.

"I am yours," he said. "What is thy will, O Mistress?"

Sheik Ibrahim looked from one to the other. He was cruel, this Ibrahim, cruel as the noonday sun. But he was just. Somewhere, deep in his stern heart, there was a sense of humor. No man has a sense of humor without having, also, a sense of honor. Then, there was something about acts of bravery that stirred his soul.

"Why, O Leopard," he asked, "did you return when freedom was yours? What made your freedom, your life, seem less than the life of a slave?"

"Because, O Sheik, even a warrior and a thief wants one decent act for Allah and himself to remember against the day when he lies on his back, staring up at the sky, waiting for the vultures to come."

"Then, perhaps, you can remember other decent acts by letting my flocks and my caravans alone. My one weakness is in sparing those who are brave though they be cursed by Allah. Hassan!"

A slave boy came running.

"Order that mob to disperse. Saddle the horse which The Leopard rode yesterday. See that water and food are at the saddle."

The boy bowed and turned to obey.

"Hassan!" the sheik bellowed. "Prepare also a pack for the horse on which he came this morning. Two such fools as these should ride together." He laughed, and there were smiles on the faces of the warriors. Ibrahim had turned the joke upon The Leopard, after all.

"Go," he said. "Both of you are as free as the winds. Go. And Allah be with you."

The Leopard took Maisa's hand and walked jauntily to the door. A few moments they paused on the threshold—then they were gone.

## The Reader's Own Department

### Conducted by the Editor

WELL, DESPITE the rain, storm, flood and high tide, we are getting out another issue of FAR EAST Adventure Stories. This doesn't mean that as yet we are well over the hump. We aren't, but we are going to do our damndest to keep the book on the stands both for your sake and ours.

For the past two issues we have imposed considerably on your kindness and generosity in asking you to do everything possible to gain increased newsstand circulation for us. I am asking you to do the same thing this month. It's bound to help us considerably, even if only ten percent of our established readers go out and hustle us an additional sale.

We are pretty firmly convinced that FAR EAST is a good magazine, and those persons who have read a copy of it like it. Of course, it is not perfect; it could be considerably better, we appreciate, but we are depending on our readers to let us know just what they like and what they do not like,—what their preferences are in the matter of writers, illustrations, make-up and editorial policy. For, in the final analysis, the success of FAR EAST Adventure Stories rests squarely on pleasing the reading public.

Once again, just for a few additional months, keep up the good work and boost the circulation of FAR EAST Adventure Stories on the newsstand.

AND NOW, just to give you some idea of what a few of our readers think of the book we are appending beneath a few of their letters.

### MORE POWER TO YOU, MR. WALLS

Dear Sirs:

This is just a line from a satisfied and enthusiastic reader who wishes to say that he is getting you all the new readers possible and helping in every way to keep the "good ship FAR EAST" up.

Why not sell the original cover picture, both those inside and outside the magazine. You might also sell the original manuscripts of stories. Every dollar counts.

Yours faithfully,
SCOTT WALLS,
1046 N. Warman,
Indianapolis, Ind.

### TELL IT TO A FRIEND

Gentlemen:

Please find enclosed my check for $2.50, my subscription for the year starting with the March issue of FAR EAST Adventure Stories.

I am more than pleased with this magazine, as it covers the stories and the country I have always been interested in. I am pleased to state that I have no favorites among the authors, as I am more than pleased with every one of them. The stories you give I have in the past always tried to find in the various magazines. Now, it is not necessary for me to look further, as you give me exactly the reading I desire.

Wishing you and your FAR EAST the best of success, I remain,

Sincerely yours,
F. J. L. SCHNEIDER,
Minneapolis, Minn.

## CRITICISM DULY NOTED

Gentlemen:

The writer picked up the January issue of the FAR EAST Adventure Stories at a local news stand, and being interested in the Orient was duly impressed by your novel magazine.

However, all the stories seem to be written in the same vein, as if by the same author or edited by the same person. Why don't you inject a little individuality into your magazine? I would like to subscribe to it.

Respectfully yours,
B. L. HOUCK,
1419 Grange Ave.,
Philadelphia, Pa.

## WE'LL SEE THAT FAR EAST REACHES YOUR TOWN

Gentlemen:

I have just received the February issue of FAR EAST Adventure Stories, and a previous letter of mine will tell you what I think of the magazine and its authors. But to get down to business, I read your plea for more readers and I couldn't contain myself, therefore this:

I'd hate like the deuce to see FAR EAST drop off the stands, because the darn thing's just what I've been looking and hoping for. In this town there are two stores that sell magazines, in neither of them have I found a copy of your magazine. Incidentally, I discovered FAR EAST in a neighboring city. There are a bunch of chaps here that just dote on adventure stories and such magazines as Argosy, Short Stories, and Adventure are read eagerly. Therefore I am sure that if they found FAR EAST on the stands it would be gobbled up like "nuthin'."

Very truly yours,
JACK HELLER,
Colchester, Conn.

## IT WON'T BE LONG TILL WE HAVE TALBOT MUNDY IN THE LINE UP

Dear Mr. Bamber:

This is the third letter I have written to a magazine. Once to Adventure when they sold out to Butterick's and they tried to ruin it by canning the best damn editor in any magazine, Mr. Hoffman. Once to Black Mask for calling a serial a novel.

You deserve a word of praise for starting from scratch with a good magazine. I think your story in January issue "Sing Lee—Weaver of Mats" was a lemon and probably written by a woman.

I read more magazines in a month than most people do in a year and if you have competent men to oversee your stories (before printed) you cannot fail. Don't gamble on your squawks, have first class stuff—it pays. Pay *real* talent *real* money and FAR EAST will sell itself. Don't be a piker and wreck our hopes.

Sincerely yours,
W. P. COON,
6937 Princeton Ave.,
Chicago, Ill.

P. S. Why not the cream of them all? Talbot Mundy.

## THANKS FOR THE GOOD WORK

Gentlemen:

In regards to your magazine FAR EAST Adventure Stories, I want to say that I hope it stays on the market.

Previous I bought a magazine (any one) as long as it contained a story of the Far East and I have subscribed to three magazines the past three years just to read Far East stories. It was accidental that I came in touch with your magazine. It was left on a seat in a New York Central train. Now I know I don't have to hope that a Far East story is in any of the magazines I have subscribed to. I'll just go and buy a FAR EAST Adventure Stories magazine. In a month I will subscribe to your magazine.

Respectfully,
LEO. P. J. BACKES,
288 Lenox Ave.,
New York City.

P. S. I have informed quite a number of friends who I know buy Adventure just to read an Orient story to go and get FAR EAST magazine.

## MAKE THE THREE GET AN ADDITIONAL NINE

Dear Editor:

Just a few words to let you know that I have taken your appeal to heart. I have personally taken three friends by the neck and made them buy copies of Far East from our local newsstand. They came around the next day and thanked me. In Cincinnati you now have at least four satisfied readers and boosters.

I hope you can hang on long enough until FAR EAST Adventure Stories goes over. I am sure it will if you keep on giving us the stories you have in the past. You have the best line up of authors I have seen in any magazine and I read about six of them every month.

Keep on giving us more of H. Bedford Jones' stories. That man tells a story like nobody's business. But I like stories complete in one issue rather than serials. Just the same I would read about John Solomon if it was continued for a year.

You have a new author who I think is very fine. I am referring to Jack D'Arcy. His "Fall Out the Gentlemen" in your first issue was a cracker-jack yarn. I would like to see some longer stories by Mr. D'Arcy about British Army Life in India.

Keep plugging away and keep the good ship "Far East" afloat.

Sincerely yours,
DENEM GRIMM,
3520 Michigan Ave.,
Cincinnati, Ohio.

## WE ARE GLAD TO GIVE NEW WRITERS A BREAK

Dear Mr. Bamber:

I am taking advantage of the kind offer you are making to new authors and sending you a mms. entitled, THE EASY EAST. I hope you like it. But whether you do or not I want you to know that I am pulling strong for you and your magazine. It seems impossible to me that it can fail for every one I have shown it to says it is a very attractive book. Editorially it is excellent and if you keep up its high literary content you are bound to succeed.

I liked your straight forward appeal for new readers very much and I am sure it will achieve its purpose.

Keep up the good work with Far East and continue encouraging new writers and luck will be with you.

Very truly yours,
NORMAN STERLING,
1214 DePuyster Ave.,
Marion, Kansas.

## A SUGGESTION WE ARE GOING TO CARRY OUT

Gentlemen:

I have read your magazine Far East Adventure Stories since it first appeared on the stands. That is enough to tell you that I like it very much. Consequently, I thought that every one else did and I was very surprised to read your appeal for more readers.

Being interested in your magazine I tried to analyze it and find out why your book did not meet with instantaneous success. Your stories are first rate. No kick there. It is one of the cleanest books I have ever read and the make up and typography are very attractive.

I finally decided (Though more than likely I am wrong) that the trouble lay in your covers. I am not saying that they are bad from an artistic view point. They aren't. In fact, I think they are too high class.

I notice that you alternate a native with a white man on your covers. To me it would be a much better idea to keep a white man—preferably an American Adventurer—on your covers. Make your covers carry more obvious punch and action, for after all they sell new magazines.

But whether I am right or wrong I will do all I can to secure more sales for your magazine.

Sincerely yours,
ARTHUR PAUL,
Chicago, Ill.

## INDIA STIRRED BY RENEWED RIOTS

BOMBAY, INDIA.—Renewed violence in the independence movement today created a tense situation as the results of the Mahatma Gandhi's peace negotiations at New Delhi were awaited.

Police clashed with a mob of men and women volunteers who invaded the Corporation Hall in an attempt to prevent the city fathers from meeting to vote farewell to Lord Irwin, the departing Viceroy, and welcome to the new Viceroy, Lord Willingdon. Police dispersed the rioters.

Meanwhile, Congress leaders arrested yesterday at the Esplanade Maidan were sentenced to six months rigorous imprisonment. Three hundred volunteers also were tried in groups and several were sentenced to various terms, intensifying the hostility of the demonstrators in the streets.

The situation raised a menace to the efforts of Gandhi, who summoned Congress leader to New Delhi by telegraph for a decision of major importance. The decision to be made probably will decide whether peace or continued opposition to the British will be the future policy of the Nationalists.

Lord Irwin and Gandhi will resume their conversations at New Delhi tomorrow. Most of the observers at New Delhi have been encouraged by the negotiations and hoped for a peace agreement.

Two Nationalists were killed, six were injured and one policeman was wounded when police and troops dispersed a demonstration at Utmanzai, a village near the northwest frontier, yesterday. The natives had gathered and demanded the release of Abdul Ghafarkhan, Nationalist leader. They pelted the police and native troops with a barrage of stones when the authorities sought to disperse the gathering. The police fired ten volleys in breaking up the demonstration.

In Bombay the members of the volunteer corps of the all-India Congress, including members of the Congress "War council," were arrested while attempting to hold a demonstration on the Esplanade Maidan. The volunteers had gathered to hold a monthly flag salutation ceremony and rally, against orders of the police.

The East is alive with news, color, life and action, and here, in the pages of this magazine we propose to give you the most vivid fiction stories from the pens of our best writers, laid in the most colorful, adventuresome corner of our globe. THE EDITOR.

Running Hot Water
From Your Cold Water
Faucet Instantaneously
Only $3.75 Complete
Agents! This Marvelous Invention Will Make Up to $40.00 a Day Easy
Just plug in at the nearest electric outlet and presto!—you have instantaneous, continuous running hot water from your cold water faucet. This tells you in a nutshell why the invention of the Tom Thumb automatic electric hot water heater will make it easy for you to make up to $40.00 a day.
The electric heated steaming hot water comes direct from the faucet instantaneously—yes, as quickly as you can turn on the current and the hot water runs indefinitely until you shut off the electricity. The cost is small—convenience is great. Useful wherever hot water is needed—no fuss or bother—attached to any faucet in a jiffy. Works on either AC or DC current. You and your customers will marvel and be delighted at this new discovery of electrical science. The small cost of $3.75 for the Tom Thumb, Junior (110 volts) or $5.75 for Tom Thumb, Senior (220 volts) does the work of any expensive hot water heating equipment costing several hundred dollars—the Tom Thumb absolutely eliminates the plumber or any other additional expense.
No Installation - Stick One On Faucet and Sale Is Made
Think of it! no installation, no extra expense—nothing else to do but to stick it on the faucet, turn on electricity and it is there ready for duty. Easily removed when not wanted and easily carried to any part of house where cold water is running and hot water is wanted. Has many uses—too numerous to mention here. Weighs only 1 lb., made entirely of aluminum. Cannot rust, no moving parts, nothing to get out of order.
If $40 A Day Sounds Good To You Rush Coupon
This new scientific invention offers tremendous sales possibilities. At the low price of $3.75 you should be able to sell at least 40 a day. You pocket $1.00 cash commission on every sale. If you would like to know all about this proposition, sign your name and address to coupon or, better still, get started selling at once. Attach money order for $2.75 to coupon and rush to us. We will send complete selling outfit containing 1 Tom Thumb electric hot water heater, order blanks, selling particulars and everything necessary to help you get started making up to $40.00 a day at once.
KITCHEN
SHAVING
BATH
DOCTOR
FACTORY
Terminal Products Co., Inc.
Dept. 603, 200 Hudson St.,
New York, N. Y.
The Tom Thumb electric hot water heater looks like a big money maker to me. I am sure interested in knowing how to make up to $40.00 a day with this proposition. I have checked below the proposition I am interested in at this moment.
1. Enclosed find money order for $2.75. Please send me one Tom Thumb Junior, order blanks and selling information. It is understood upon receipt of this sample outfit I will be permitted to take orders and collect $1.00 cash deposit for every Tom Thumb, Jr. I sell, or $1.50 for every Tom Thumb, Sr. I sell. It is understood I will send the orders to you and you will ship direct to my customers C.O.D. for the balance.
2. I would like to have additional information before acting as one of your agents. Please send this by return mail free of obligation.
Name
Street
City
State
If you live outside of the United States, price is $1.00 extra on each unit, cash with order.

# An Unpardonable Sin

Must every women pay the price of a moment's happiness in bitter tears and years of regret? Must millions of homes be ruined—lovers and sweethearts driven apart—marriages totter to the brink of divorce—the sacred joys of sex relations be denied? YES—just as long as men and women remain ignorant of the simple facts of life.

An Unpardonable Sin is total ignorance of the most important subject in the life of every man and woman—SEX.

## Away With False Modesty!

Let us face the facts of sex fearlessly and frankly, sincerely and scientifically. Let us tear the veil of shame and mystery from sex and build the future of the race on a new knowledge of all the facts of sex as they are laid bare in plain, daring but wholesome words, and frank pictures in this huge new library of Sex Knowledge.

## "Modern Eugenics"

**39 Chapters — Startling Illustrations**

This volume abounds in truthful illustrations and pictures of scientific interest that one seldom, if ever, finds outside of the highly technical medical books which laymen fail to understand. Every picture is true to life.

*learn the* TRUTH

# 544 *Pages of startling Secrets*

The 544 pages of personal secrets revealed in this astounding work were not put together and assembled by the authors with any thought of spreading obscenity—no, on the other hand, the authors' sincerest belief that modern eugenics is a present-day necessity—his heart-felt wish to carry the message before young and old so they may know the truth prompted them to complete this edition and offer it to those who are deserving of knowing the information therein revealed. If you wish to move onward in life without fear, knowing that you are in the right, fortified with knowledge you are entitled to know, send for your copy today.

## EVERYTHING A MARRIED WOMAN SHOULD KNOW

Experience is expensive—you do not have to pay, the price—you do not have to suffer—you can know in advance what every married woman should know.

**How to hold a husband**
**How to have perfect children**
**How to preserve youth**
**Warding off other women**
**Keeping yourself attractive**
**Why husbands tire of wives**
**Dreadful diseases due to ignorance**
**Diseases of women**
**Babies and birth control**
**Twilight sleep—easy childbirth**
**Diseases of children**
**Family health guide**
**Change of life—hygiene**
**Why children die young**
**Inherited traits and diseases**
**What will you tell your growing girl?**
**The mystery of twins**
**Hundreds of valuable remedies**
**Nursing and weaning**
**How to care for invalids**

## Girls! DON'T MARRY

**The very freedom enjoyed by the present modern girl demands that no secrets be kept from her—yes, those who intend to marry should know:**

**The dangers of petting. How to be a vamp. How to manage honeymoon. Beauty diets and baths. How to attract desirable men. How to manage men. How to know if he loves you. How to acquire bodily grace and beauty. How to beautify face, hands, hair, teeth and feet. How to acquire charm. How to dress attractively. Intimate personal hygiene. How to pick a husband.**

## Secrets for Men

Your opportunities are limited by your knowledge. Your very future—your fate and destiny are guided through the power of your own actions—Modern Eugenics arms you with sex knowledge so as to be your guiding star for future health and happiness so you will know:—

**Mistakes of early marriages. Secrets of fascination. Joys of perfect mating. How to make women love you. Bringing up healthy children. Fevers and contagious diseases. Accidents and emergencies. Hygiene in the home. Limitation of offspring. Warning to young men. Dangerous Diseases. Secrets of sex attraction. Hygienic precaution. Anatomy and physiology. The reproductive organs. What every woman wants. Education of the family. Sex health and prevention.**

## *Important*

This work will not be sold to minors. When ordering your book, state your age.

## What will you tell the ..... growing child

**Will you let your children grow up in the same dangerous ignorance in which you yourself perhaps were reared—or will you guide them safely through puberty by the aid of this truly healthful book?**

## *Over* 350,000 SOLD

This huge volume of sale enabled us to cut the cost of printing so that you may secure your copy of Modern Eugenics at $2.98 instead of the original price of $5.00. Would YOU risk your health and happiness for the sake of having $2.98 more in your pocket?—Of course not!

MODERN EUGENICS

*Rush Coupon for this precious book*

Another opportunity to secure this marvelous book at almost half regular price may never be offered to you again. Do not be guilty of an Unpardonable Sin. Order your copy today. Sign your name and address to the coupon and forward it to us. It will bring your copy in plain wrapper by return mail—SIGN NOW—do not forget.

**Preferred Publications**
**56 West 45th Street** **Dept. 904**
**New York City.**

Please send me "Modern Eugenics" SEALED, in plain wrapper. I will pay $2.98 and postage to the postman on delivery, in accordance with your special half price offer. My age is............

Name ..............................................................

Address ..............................................................

***Orders from Foreign Countries must be accompanied by express or money order of $3.45.***

# Amazingly Easy Way to get into ELECTRICITY

**Don't spend your life waiting for $5 raises, in a dull, hopeless job. Now . . . and forever . . . say good-bye to 25 and 35 dollars a week. Let me show you how to qualify for jobs leading to salaries of $50, $60 and up, a week, in Electricity—NOT by correspondence, but by an amazing way to teach, RIGHT HERE IN THE GREAT COYNE SHOPS. You become a practical expert in 90 days! Getting into Electricity is far easier than you imagine!**

## *Learn Without Lessons* in 90 DAYS

### *By Actual Work—in the Great Shops of Coyne*

Lack of experience—age, or advanced education bars no one. I don't care if you don't know an armature from an air brake—I don't expect you to! I don't care if you're 16 years old or 48—it makes no difference! Don't let lack of money stop you. Most of the men at Coyne have no more money than you have.

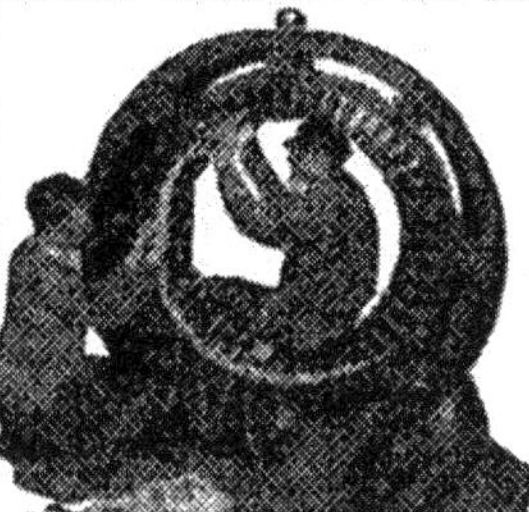

## EARN WHILE YOU LEARN

If you should need part-time work while at school to help pay expenses, I'll assist you to it. Then, in 12 brief weeks, in the great roaring shops of Coyne, I train you as you never dreamed you could be trained . . . on a gigantic outlay of electrical apparatus . . . costing hundreds of thousands of dollars . . . real dynamos, engines, power plants, autos, switchboards, transmitting stations . . . everything from doorbells to farm power and lighting . . . full-sized . . . in full operation every day!

### Prepare for Jobs Like These

Here are a few of hundreds of positions open to Coyne-trained men. Our free employment bureau gives you lifetime employment service.

Armature Expert up to $100 a Week
Substation Operator $60 a Week and up
Auto Electrician . $110 a Week
Inventor . . . . . Unlimited
Maintenance Engineer up to $150 a Week
Service Station Owner up to $200 a Week
Radio Expert up to $100 a Week

## NO BOOKS
### *No Printed Lessons*

No books, no baffling charts . . . all real actual work . . . right here in the great Coyne school . . . building real batteries . . . winding real armatures, operating real motors, dynamos and generators, wiring houses etc., etc. That's a glimpse of how we make you a master practical electrician in 90 days, teaching you far more than the average ordinary electrician ever knows and fitting you to step into jobs leading to big pay immediately after graduation. Here, in this world-famous *Parent school*—and nowhere else in the world—can you get this training!

## Jobs, Pay, Future

Don't worry about a job, Coyne training settles the job question for life. Demand for Coyne men often exceeds the supply. Our employment bureau gives you a lifetime service. Two weeks after graduation Clyde F. Hart got a position as electrician for the Great Western Railroad at over $100 a week. That's not unusual. We can point to Coyne men making up to $600 a month. $60 a week is only the beginning of your opportunity. You can go into radio, battery, or automotive electrical business for yourself and make up to $15,000 a year.

## Get the Facts

Coyne is your one great chance to get into electricity. Every obstacle is removed. This school is 30 years old—Coyne training is tested—proven beyond all doubt—endorsed by many large electrical concerns. You can find out everything absolutely free. Simply mail the coupon and let me send you the big, free Coyne book of 150 photographs . . . facts . . . jobs . . . salaries . . . opportunities. Tells you how many earn expenses while training and how we assist our graduates in the field. This does not obligate you. So act at once. Just mail coupon.

## Get This *Free* Book

## NOW IN OUR NEW HOME

This is our new fireproof, modern home wherein is installed thousands of dollars' worth of the newest and most modern Electrical equipment of all kinds. Every comfort and convenience has been arranged to make you happy and contented during your training.

# COYNE ELECTRICAL SCHOOL
**H. C. LEWIS, President**
**500 S. Paulina Street, Dept. 41-41, Chicago, Ill.**

Mr. H. C. LEWIS, President
**Coyne Electrical School, Dept. 41-41,**
500 S. Paulina Street, Chicago, Illinois

Dear Mr. Lewis:
Without obligation send me your big free catalog and all details of your Free Employment Service, Radio, Aviation Electricity, and Automotive Courses, and how I can "earn while learning."

*Name*..................................

*Address*..................................

*City*.......................*State*....................

Made in the USA
Las Vegas, NV
27 July 2022

52210324R00076